A NEW BARGAIN

"Our arrangement would need rearranging." Luke's eyes devoured her. "Don't you agree?"

Anne's breath caught in her throat. "Our arrangement?"

"The bargain we made when we married," he explained gently. "Or have you forgotten so soon?"

"The bargain we made . . ." Her voice trailed away, and she stared at him with sudden realization. "You mean the one where we split up after . . ."

"Exactly," he said wryly. "That bargain. And you realize that more than the length of our marriage must change, don't you? We can't live together for years without some kind of closeness developing between us." Something flickered in his dark eyes, something hungry, needful. "A man has needs, Anne."

"Yes. Well . . ." She cleared her throat. "I suppose you're right."

"Then you agree?"

She nodded, unable to look away from him. And then his head lowered until his mouth hovered only inches above her own. "Shall we seal our new bargain with a kiss?"

Before she could answer, his mouth covered hers, and Anne thought she had never before felt a kiss so sweet, so full of yearning. . . .

BOOK YOUR PLACE ON OUR WEBSITE AND MAKE THE READING CONNECTION!

We've created a customized website just for our very special readers, where you can get the inside scoop on everything that's going on with Zebra, Pinnacle and Kensington books.

When you come online, you'll have the exciting opportunity to:

- View covers of upcoming books
- Read sample chapters
- Learn about our future publishing schedule (listed by publication month *and author*)
- Find out when your favorite authors will be visiting a city near you
- Search for and order backlist books from our online catalog
- Check out author bios and background information
- Send e-mail to your favorite authors
- Meet the Kensington staff online
- Join us in weekly chats with authors, readers and other guests
- Get writing guidelines
- AND MUCH MORE!

**Visit our website at
http://www.zebrabooks.com**

THE WAYWARD HEART

Betty Brooks

Zebra Books
Kensington Publishing Corp.

http://www.zebrabooks.com

ZEBRA BOOKS are published by

Kensington Publishing Corp.
850 Third Avenue
New York, NY 10022

First Printing: November, 1999
10 9 8 7 6 5 4 3 2 1

Printed in the United States of America

Prologue

The Wyoming storm lashed at Anne Farraday, stinging like whips against her skin. She hunched over the bars of her Harley Davidson, willing the cycle forward, into the wall of rain.

She had to keep going forward. Behind her, the storm was even worse, the sky gray and threatening. And here, here there was no place to hide. Here, the land was flat and empty, with only the highway and a railroad track running alongside it.

Maybe somewhere ahead. Please, God, let there be something ahead.

Like lightning to a lightning rod, she felt drawn to look in the rearview mirror, to watch the clouds roil behind her.

Why hadn't she stayed at that last rest stop? It would have been some sort of refuge. But, oh, no, she'd had to go on. She, the intrepid adventurer; she, the one who could take care of herself, dammit. . . .

Again, her gaze was pulled to the mirror. In the few

seconds since she had last looked, a gray condensation funnel had dropped from the clouds, descending toward the ground behind her, a fragile, ropelike funnel.

A twister.

God almighty. Quickly, she decelerated. Flat on the ground in the ditch beside the road was a million times better than upright on a cycle.

Then, like a gift from the heavens, there was a drainage culvert ahead, a place for the runoff from the rare storms and flash floods of this country. Okay, it was small and tight and enclosed, but claustrophobia be damned, it was her only choice. She had to hide.

As she laid the cycle in the ditch, she offered a little prayer that the twister would miss it, then scrambled toward the culvert. Halfway there, a piece of windblown debris struck her shoulder, and she stumbled to her knees.

Rain thudded against her, heavier now, sheeting down the faceplate of her helmet. She could hardly see two feet in front of her.

Knowing she had to reach shelter, and quickly, she scuttled forward, crawling on hands and knees, using the ditch as a map to reach the drainpipe.

Once inside, she pulled off the helmet and pivoted toward the whirling world outside the drain. Suddenly lightning struck, a tremendous bolt so blindingly visible that it was like watching ancient Zeus cast down a jagged streak of fire.

Her hands clenched on the helmet, Anne muttered, "One, one thousand, two, one thousand, three, one thousand—"

Thunder rolled like a cannon. Anne tried to control her fear as electricity crackled in the air, followed again by the great roar of thunder. She crept farther inside the drainpipe, where she huddled, her legs folded, listening to the renewed violence of the storm.

The wind continued to howl around the opening as a

barrage of lightning flashed overhead, the sky's response shaking the culvert where Anne waited.

Then, as quickly as it had come, the storm was gone. Stillness lay over her like a heavy blanket. And in the quiet, the circular concrete walls seemed to move, closing in, rippling around her.

She squeezed her eyes shut, her heart hammering. Her claustrophobia had kicked in, she realized as she started shaking.

You're safe, she told herself. *It's only your imagination.*

Anne could hear the sound of her own breathing, quick, short, jerky breaths.

And when she looked again, she could have sworn the drainpipe was smaller—by feet, not inches—and no denial, no matter how strongly voiced, could have convinced her otherwise.

Crablike, she shot forward, scrambling toward the opening, then bursting outside, where she could breathe, could suck in the heavy air.

Eyes closed, she knelt in the mud, fighting to control her trembling. *You're all right,* she told herself. *It's over now. The storm is done.*

Confidence settled over her like a blessing. She had made it. She had tolerated the confinement long enough to survive the storm.

Exultant, she lifted her face to the sky . . . and felt her confidence shrivel to nothing. Above her, far above her, a hole of bright sunlight broke through the heavy mass that rippled and swirled around her.

The mass was nothing more than fog, surely. But the wind hit her, shrieking like a train, and hail poured from the sky, large, bruising pellets pounding at her, and the noise . . . a deep, ominous rumble, as if the world were tearing apart.

Judas priest! She hadn't made it at all. She had crawled out of the culvert into the eye of the storm.

She could go back, though. The culvert was behind her, wasn't it? Or was it to the side? She couldn't see a thing.

Then, before she could move, the storm snatched her up, swirling her off the ground, into the heavy air. Within the mass of wind and fog, debris from the storm spun around her, each piece as if caught in its own orbit, separate and yet apart.

Thunder rumbled, and lightning flashed inward, blinding her. As she instinctively squeezed her eyes shut, a sudden irony hit her. She might be dead meat already, but she would damn sure be able to see.

Then, as if she were a candy bar wrapper flicked away by God, Anne felt herself plunging downward. Down, down, down. . . .

There was no time to pray, no time to fear what fate had in store.

No time for anything.

Chapter One

Pain drove her awake, a relentless pounding at her temples, as though someone was using a hammer there to get her attention.

Anne Farraday groaned and opened her eyes.

She was facedown in the dirt, groggy, bleary-eyed, her senses dulled.

How had she survived the storm? she wondered. Had she only imagined the violence of the wind and lightning, that incredible destructive barrage that had struck her from every side? Or had it been real?

It couldn't have been as she remembered, or she would not be here now, alive, aching in every joint, every muscle in her body.

Rolling over, Anne narrowed her eyes against the startling brightness of daylight. The pain in her temples intensified, and she groaned, squeezing her eyelids together, hoping to alleviate some of the discomfort.

Veils seemed to flutter against the darkness within her eyes, creating movement that made nausea sweep over her. She remained motionless until the feeling subsided; then, shading her eyes against the glare, she opened her eyelids a mere crack.

The sun was still there, a bright ball of pain, burning hot overhead.

Oh, God! She needed some aspirin to stop the throbbing at her temples. With her hands clutching her head, she sat upright, gasping as dizziness rocked her.

Slowly, she silently chided herself. *Breathe slowly. In and out.* As the world righted itself, Anne squinted against the brightness. Where was she anyway? "Definitely not in Kansas," she muttered. Or even Oz.

She searched the area around her, looking for her motor-cycle, but it was nowhere in sight. The highway was gone, and the railroad track. Desert stretched all around her; dry, barren land, dotted here and there with a few gray tumbleweeds.

But the blacktop was out there somewhere. All she had to do was find it. And she *would* find it. Or a ranch house. Or something. *Somebody.*

According to her gold Rolex, little time had passed. It was still midmorning. The real heat of the day was ahead of her.

Taking her direction from the sun, Anne began to walk west toward, she hoped, Laramie.

The sun was relentless, beating down on her endlessly.

Anne removed her motorcycle jacket and slung it over her shoulders, leaving only the oversized pullover to cover her upper body.

The hot ball of fire overhead continued to beat down on her, and as the morning passed, Anne could actually feel her skin begin to burn.

She looked at her watch. She had been walking four hours, yet she had seen no signs of civilization. Not a plane, not a telephone. Nothing.

As she walked, she began to imagine she truly was in

Oz. A twisted country, a devil's world. She remembered the wagon train she had seen in Kansas, moving along at a snail's pace as it followed the old Oregon Trail like the pioneers more than a hundred years ago.

What she wouldn't give to see them now. She didn't care if it took a century to cross the desert if she could only have a little cover from the sun, a sip of water. Dear God, what she would trade for a sip of water.

A gold Rolex, anyone?

There were no takers. Money meant nothing to Mother Nature.

The land out here was barren, no trees, no growth of any kind large enough to offer even the tiniest bit of shade. It took all her energy to keep moving, yet she realized there was nothing else she *could* do. She had to keep going, at least until she reached the blacktop.

Then she could rest. Then someone would find her.

Rest, the desert whispered to her. *Lie down for a while. Close your eyes. Sleep. For a few minutes. An hour.*

Or eternity?

Anne remembered her father's warning. ''You'll wind up in the middle of nowhere with only yourself to depend on, Annie.''

And she had done exactly that.

She should have listened to him. But he was so determined to keep her dependent on him, had even bought a designing company when she had graduated from UTA. Of course, she could have refused to work there, but it would have been cutting off her nose to spite her face.

So she had been bought, had traded her independence for a chance to own the business, to turn the near-bankrupt designing company around in the year her father had allowed.

And she had done it. The company was in the black now, yet her father's attitude toward her had not changed one iota. It had been two weeks since he had come to her office and told her of the vacation plans he had made for her.

"No," she had replied. "I have no intention of spending my vacation in Bermuda with Rodney St. John and his parents. I already have plans."

"Then, cancel them!" he snapped. "Rodney is just the kind of husband you need, Anne. His family is—"

"The cream of society," she recited, having heard the words so many times before.

"Don't take that tone with me, missy! You should be glad he's interested in you."

"Why should I be glad?"

"He's a millionaire, girl!"

"That won't make him a good husband."

The quarrel continued, but Anne refused to be swayed, and when her father finally left, he did so in anger.

"Do what you want, then," he raged. "Buy yourself a motorcycle and join one of those gangs that ride the roads and terrorize people for all I care! But don't come crying to me if you get in trouble!"

The quarrel had been smoothed over, but the idea had been planted in her mind.

So you bought yourself a motorcycle and set off on your vacation. Way to go, Anne.

She grimaced wryly. It had been a foolish thing to do. And he had been right to worry about her, to demand that she telephone him each night so he would know her exact location. He would expect that call tonight, since today was his birthday.

"I have to find a telephone," she muttered. "Before he gets worried and calls out the National Guard." Or one of his friends at the air base in Laramie. That would be embarrassing, but even so, she wouldn't mind seeing a helicopter . . . or even a crop duster.

Sighing, she wiped beads of sweat off her forehead.

She was losing moisture fast, needed to find shade, somewhere to rest.

Narrowing her eyes, she scanned the horizon, searching for a tree, a bush, a cactus even, anything that could provide comfort.

The landscape was empty. Not even a telephone pole, or a trail from a jet plane. But wait—

"No," she muttered aloud, focusing her gaze on the horizon. "There is something."

She squinted, trying to focus on the wavy line that appeared to move along in the distance.

Hoping it wasn't a mirage, Anne broke into a run, stumbling forward with renewed energy toward the object that shimmered seemingly forever out of reach. Time passed, minutes, hours, while the relentless sun continued to spread its burning heat across the land.

Anne searched the skies again, hoping . . . praying for a helicopter. She was ready to put aside her foolish pride, was eager to see a search party. But there was nothing . . . save that long, wavy line in the distance.

She tried to ignore the heat, concentrating instead on the slow movement ahead of her, a movement that finally began to take form.

There appeared a long, white column of wagons, moving along at a snail's pace. The Pilgrimage: The one she had heard about on the news. Pseudo pioneers headed for Oregon as the pioneers had done more than a hundred and fifty years ago.

They even had livestock with them, something the news reports had not mentioned.

Anne opened her mouth and tried to shout, but her voice, coming from between cracked, dry lips, was barely distinguishable to her own ears. Surely, though, they could see her. Surely they would not pass her by.

She waved her arms above her head, but the wagons kept moving. Rolling inexorably onward.

They hadn't seen her.

Desperation gave her another burst of energy, however weak. Again she ran, lurching like a drunk, waving her jacket above her head, but nobody appeared to notice. She needed something bright to capture their attention, not the black motorcycle jacket.

Even as she was despairing, a rider broke off from the wagons, directing his horse toward her. She fell to her knees, laughing hysterically.

The nightmare was over. Done. And she had survived.

This time, she truly had survived.

Shimmering in the bright sunlight like a saint, the rider reined up beside Anne.

His torso was bare, his shoulders sun-bronzed. He wore a black hat pulled low over his forehead.

"Looks like you got some troubles, boy." In one smooth motion, he dismounted and stood over her.

Troubles? She wanted to laugh at the sheer inadequacy of the word, but feared that once started, she would never stop, that her laughter would become a shriek, a shriek of madness.

"Thirsty?"

Yes! She *was* thirsty. Even so, she was unable to tear her eyes away from his bronzed shoulders. The muscles of his upper arms rippled and gleamed as he took a canteen from his saddlebags and offered it to her.

With a quickly muttered thanks, she snatched the canteen and took two long, greedy gulps, before he withdrew it from her.

"Take it easy, now," he said. "Too much too soon won't do you any good."

She eyed the canteen longingly as he replaced it on his horse.

"You can have more later, son."

For the first time his words sank in. She wiped her mouth with the back of her hand. "I'm not a boy," she muttered.

"Takes more than years to make a man, son. Not that you've even got the years yet."

"I'm not a man either." She felt chagrined that he had taken her for a boy, but supposed that her jeans and oversized shirt were to blame.

"You will be one day, though," he replied. "Until then . . ." His gaze narrowed as Anne moistened her dry lips with her tongue. *My God! He—she's a female! A female in britches.*

How could he have known, though, with her brown hair so short that it curled around her face, and that man's shirt that covered her from shoulders to hips? There was nothing feminine in her apparel, nor in her look. But her eyes were a dead giveaway. Framed by thick, dark lashes, they were a brilliant blue. The prettiest eyes he had ever seen.

"Sorry," he said abruptly. "Should have known eyes like that wouldn't belong to a boy."

She smiled at him. "Did you just pay me a compliment?"

A frown creased his forehead. "Just stating facts," he said brusquely. "What are you doing out here?"

"Walking." Her tone was as abrupt as his. Then, suddenly realizing how totally dependent she was on his goodwill, she shut her eyes and took a deep breath, let it out slowly, and once again faced him. "I don't know where I am, or how I got here, but that's no excuse for my rudeness." She gave him an appealing smile. "When you were riding in, I was thinking how much an angel you are."

He laughed then, a harsh sound, and pushed the brim of his Stetson higher. "Angel's the last name I answer to."

Beneath his hat, his black, shoulder-length hair was fastened at his nape with a leather thong. Obviously, he had really gotten into the role of old-time cowboy.

As he bent closer, his bulky form blocked the harsh light, enabling her to see his features clearly.

His dark eyes were set beneath ebony brows that arched like a crow's wing. His nose was straight, his mouth wide and perfectly formed, his chin slightly dimpled.

"Move over, Fabio," she muttered. "You've just been dethroned."

"Fabio?" He frowned down at her, as if she were delirious. Maybe she was. "How'd you come to be out here?"

"It was the storm. The tornado." She ran a trembling hand through her tangled curls. "I thought it was over and I crawled out of the culvert. But I was wrong." Anne shuddered in remembrance. "I came out inside the tornado, yet I managed to survive."

His frown deepened. "You were in the tornado? You're damn lucky then. We saw the twister from the wagon train, but it was several miles north of us." He paused. "You say you were caught in it? Were you on a wagon train? I didn't know there was another one along this trail."

She shook her head. "Not a wagon train. It was just me and my Harley. I took cover in a culvert, until I thought the storm had passed. Except it hadn't." She hesitated, swallowed. "Do you think I could I have some more water now?"

He gave her the canteen, but as before, allowed her only a few swallows. She savored the tepid water, letting it slide down her throat. Lord, it was heavenly.

"What happened to your companion?" he asked, as he stowed the canteen away.

"I told you, there was only me."

His gaze narrowed sharply. "You mentioned someone named Harley."

"My bike." At his confused look, she went on, "My motorcycle. A Harley Davidson." She grimaced wryly. "My father didn't want me to come on this trip. Said I'd get into more trouble than I could get out of. I hate when he's right. The storm took my motorcycle and left me afoot." She laughed shakily. "I'm not really surprised, though. The tornado destroyed everything in its path."

The stranger wasn't listening. Instead, he frowned up at the sky. "We'd better get back to the wagons. It's going to get a lot hotter out here before it gets any cooler."

After he mounted his horse, he reached down and wrapped his fingers around her wrist. "Put your foot in the stirrup and I'll give you a hand up."

With his strong grip for support, she placed her booted toes in the stirrup. The movement made her dizzy, and she paused, hanging on to his hand as the world whirled around her.

Blue skies. Sand. Sagebrush. The colors rushed together causing the dizzy feeling to intensify. As a red haze formed around the outer edge of her vision, she heard a harsh exclamation.

Then the world went blank.

Chapter Two

Lucas McCord stared down at the unconscious woman he carried on his mount. It had been a long time since he had held a woman in his arms. Too long, judging by his body's reaction to this one.

How could he have mistaken her for a boy?

Although she was dressed in male attire, her features were delicate, completely feminine in appearance. He fought the urge to move his hand upward, to cup the fullness of her breast. Only a cur would take advantage of her in such a way.

He studied her closely. Her eyebrows were finely drawn, her lashes long and thick as they lay against her sunburned flesh. He must have been blind to have taken her for a boy, even with the short curls that framed her face.

Why had she cut her hair when it was the fashion to keep it long? He brushed aside a silken curl and ran his thumb over her full bottom lip. It was dry, cracked in places. She had been too long in the sun.

He spurred his horse toward the wagon train.

* * *

Anne woke slowly.

First came sound. Low voices, speaking, laughing, singing, complaining. Activity. A peculiar jingling noise. Dull thuds. Mingled with those human sounds were those of animals. Cattle lowing. Goats bleating. Horses nickering. Dogs barking. The sounds were familiar to Anne, sounds from her childhood, down on the farm.

Through a mist of sleep, Anne smiled. Gram would be waking her soon, but for now it was just the sound, the peaceful, wonderful sound of the farm. And the teasing smell of food cooking.

She was starving.

Anne forced heavy eyelids open.

"Ma!" shrieked a child. "She's awake, Ma!"

"Awake?" a female voice called. "Lawsy mercy! It's about time! See if she needs anything, Jessie. Then go fetch Doc."

Anne sat up. A young girl, maybe seven or eight, shrank away from her. "Do . . . do you n-need anything?" the child asked.

They were outside, Anne on a pallet beside a wooden-wheeled wagon. Shadows danced and twirled on the outskirts of the campfire nearby. Night.

Anne licked lips that were dry and cracked. "I sure could use a glass of water."

Lickety-split, the child ran toward a wagon, returning almost immediately with a brimming gourd dipper. Anne thanked her, then drank thirstily as she surveyed the area around her.

The wagons had apparently been formed into a circle, inside of which multiple campfires burned. It seemed a mass of confusion, with the women in long skirts tending pots that hung over those fires, and children scurrying here and there, doing chores, Anne assumed.

But the men? Where were the men?

Becoming aware again of the child who waited quietly beside her, Anne said, "Did I hear you called Jessie?" Her voice was not quite so raspy now.

The girl's lips twitched as she controlled a shy smile. She nodded and ducked her head so quickly the blond curls appeared to vibrate.

"Well, Jessie, my name is Anne."

"Pleased to meetcha, ma'am." Jessie twisted her hands in her skirt, obviously nervous of the woman who was a stranger. "Do you need anythin' else?"

Anne thought of her father. A quick glance at her watch and she realized he was probably already pacing the floor, wondering why she hadn't called him. "A phone," she said. "I need a phone."

Jessie frowned. "A fone?"

"Yes. I need to call my father. He'll be worried about me."

Jessie's expression was puzzled.

"A cellular phone, Jessie," Anne explained. "Surely someone brought along a cell phone."

The child shuffled her feet in the dirt. "I never heard nobody say they did."

"Jessie!" The voice was sharp, louder. "I told you to go fetch Doc. And get Luke, too. No! Wait! Luke's still gone. Find Zeke Masters instead."

Both Jessie's and Anne's heads swiveled to watch a large-boned blond woman, dressed in a worn, long gown, approach. "Stop dilly-dallyin', child." The woman frowned down at Jessie. "Doc said to fetch him the minute she woke up."

"You said see if she wanted anythin'," Jessie protested. "And she does, Ma."

"Please don't scold her." Anne was aware of people stopping their work and drawing near. Nowhere, though, did she see the man who had rescued her. She had felt safe with him, secure in his presence. Had he just brought her in and dumped her?

"Jessie's been known to dawdle more than once." A smile helped to take the sting out of the woman's words. "Run along now, Jess. Tell Doc his patient is awake."

"Anne," Jessie said importantly. "Her name is Anne, Ma. And she wants a *cellarfone*. But I didn't know where to find one." She paused, her forehead wrinkling. "I ain't rightly sure I ever heard of one neither."

"Jessie." The woman's mouth flattened, and her voice was suddenly tight, proof of her displeasure. "You heard what I said. Get Doc. Now."

The tone of her mother's voice accomplished what her words had not. With a backward glance at Anne, the child scurried off.

"Guess I don't have to tell you I'm Jessie's ma," the woman said. "The name's Mary Baker. And Jessie said you're Anne?"

"Anne Farraday."

"Well, Anne Farraday, you've had quite an ordeal, haven't you?" She appeared to need no answer. "I put some ointment on your face to help the sunburn. But your lips are split; they'll take longer to heal."

She hunched down next to Anne. "Doc didn't find any more injuries, but he wanted to look you over again when you woke up."

"Where'd you come from, girl?" The question came from the crowd of people gathered in the shadows. A wiry-looking man, dressed in rough clothing, stepped forward. "What happened to you?"

Mary straightened again, facing the man with squared shoulders. "Doc said no questions till he says so."

"But Doc ain't here, is he, Mary?" Colby's gaze fixed on Anne again. "Injuns get your people, girl?"

Another voice said, "Where's the rest of your party? Was it Injuns?"

As though a door had opened, allowing them through, the people crowded closer, their eyes suspicious, their voices harsh.

"What happened to your people, girl?"

"Why're you dressed like that?" another asked. "Ain't hardly decent, a woman wearing men's britches."

Questions were flung at her from left and right as eyes bored into her, demanding answers. Pain stabbed at her temples, and Anne closed her eyes momentarily, hoping to shut out the noise.

"Shame on the lot of you!" Mary's voice was sharp, her gaze sweeping the crowd. "She needs time to recover her senses. And that ain't likely to happen with the lot of you throwing questions at her."

Anne felt grateful for Mary's intervention. Her head ached so badly that she could hardly think straight. She was unaware of the approach of another man until his voice boomed out.

"All right, folks, go on about your business now."

A man of magnificent proportions pushed his way through the gathering. The bushy red beard that covered his lower face gave him the appearance of a wild man, and his green eyes did nothing to dispel that image.

"Go on, now! Break it up," he growled. "You'll have your answers soon enough."

The newcomer was obviously someone of importance because most of the crowd dispersed. Several of the men, though, continued to hover nearby.

Red Beard crossed his arms over his chest, leaned his weight against the wagon and looked down at Anne. "You're a mighty lucky young lady. But I guess you already know that, don't you? Wouldn't have lasted much longer out there with no water. Luke said you was talking nonsense when he found you. Figured you'd had too much sun. You feeling better now?"

"Yes. Much better, thank you." Her voice was a husky whisper.

"Good. Got some questions for you."

Her gaze skittered to the men who continued to hover nearby. One of them was the wiry-looking man who had been badgering her. He met her eyes with a grim expression.

"Don't worry about them folks." Red Beard shifted his huge frame slightly. "They're just naturally skittish, worrying about the Injuns."

He frowned down at her, making her feel like an insect on display, with her sitting on the ground and everybody else so tall and big. She drew her knees inward and pushed herself upright.

"Wait a minute," Red Beard said gruffly. He pressed a large hand against her shoulder, holding her down. "Don't know as you should be getting up, ma'am. You still ain't looking too good. Kinda pale under that sunburn."

Trying to shrug off his hand was like trying to shrug off a boulder. Anne couldn't do it alone. So, rather than struggle, she stayed where she was.

"Get on with it, Zeke!" a harsh voice nearby grated. "We wanta know what happened out there."

So the behemoth was Zeke, not the doctor, and he wasn't used to taking orders, obviously, because he glared into the shadows.

"You'll hear when you hear," he growled. "And not a minute sooner."

Then, returning his attention to Anne, he explained, "You see how it is, ma'am. Ever'body here is wanting to know what happened out there."

"You might start by introducing yourself, Zeke," Mary said shortly. She stood at his elbow, her calm smile soothing.

For a moment Zeke looked startled. "Guess I forgot

my manners," he said. "I'm Zeke. Zeke Masters, the wagon master. It's my job to get these folks to Oregon with all their hair still attached to their heads."

Anne's lips twitched as she met his eyes. Zeke Masters played the part of wagon master so well that he should seek a career in the theater. But then, perhaps he was already an actor.

Anne introduced herself, then said, "I'm pleased to meet you, Mr. Masters."

"Zeke." His green eyes softened slightly. "I know you've been through a lot, Miss Farraday," he added, "but Colby is right. We need to know what happened to the rest of your party."

"There was no party. I was alone."

"You were alone?" The question came from the wiry man whose sole purpose appeared to be heckling her. "That don't make no sense, Zeke. She wouldn't of been out there on her lonesome."

"Keep out of this, Colby!" Zeke snapped. His voice softened when he continued. "He's right, though, ma'am. It don't make no sense a'tall. Why would you be out in this wilderness alone?"

Slowly, carefully, as if enunciating could make them understand, Anne said, "I was on vacation. Riding alone. On my Harley. I didn't find it after the storm; the twister must have gotten it."

"Maybe not," Mary said soothingly. "No horse likes a storm, and that one was a real doozy. Maybe he just went on back home . . ."

"You don't understand." Shakily, Anne wiped her eyes. She still felt so weak, and these people refused to leave her alone until she had answered their questions. "I saw the storm coming, but I—I thought I could make it to Laramie." She stumbled over her words. "It's—it's still hard to believe I survived."

"Not many folk can lay claim to such a thing." Zeke

Masters frowned at her. "You say you were headed for Fort Laramie? What in tarnation were you doing out alone . . . with no escort? My God, girl, Laramie's another ten days from here."

"Ten days? How could that be?" Anne felt as though she were speaking a language no one understood, as if she had stepped through a mirror and come out in Alice's Wonderland. The landscape looked the same, but all the rules had changed. "Don't you have some other means of transportation? A motorbike or something? I have to let my father know where I am."

"Your father shouldn't have let you leave the fort in the first place," Zeke said grimly.

Her mouth dropped open in amazement. She snapped it closed and, with gritted teeth, said, "Just because you all decided to get dressed up and ride across the desert in some kind of make-believe melodrama doesn't change the way the real world works. My father doesn't dictate what I do. No man does."

Zeke's bushy eyebrows lifted. "I reckon that's your father's problem," he said coldly. "Ours is what to do with you now."

"They're coming, Ma!" Jessie's voice preceded her into the circle of firelight, but only barely. She was running, her long skirt clutched in her hand. "I found Doc, and Luke, too. They're both on their way."

"Jessie!" Mary said in a shocked voice. "Put your skirt down, girl! Do you want everybody here to see your underdrawers?"

Jessie blushed bright red and quickly dropped her skirt. "Sorry, Ma," she mumbled. "I was just tryin' to hurry like you told me."

"Where's she gonna stay, Zeke?" asked the man called Colby. He'd inched forward until he was standing just behind Mary. "We got no room for nobody that don't pull their own weight on this wagon train."

Zeke's gaze went cold. "Nobody's asking you to make room for her, Colby."

"She can stay with me and my family, Zeke," Mary Baker offered.

"You hear that, Colby? The Bakers are gonna take care of her." To Anne, Zeke went on, "Luke will have plenty of questions for you, Miss Farraday. And I'd be much obliged if you'd cooperate with him."

Anne recognized the man the minute he strode into the firelight. It was he who had rescued her. But he was no longer shirtless. He resembled an old-time buffalo hunter with his fringed buckskin shirt and britches. The gun belt he wore buckled around his hips appeared to be an extension of himself.

Momentarily, Anne wondered if the gun was loaded, then silently scolded herself for being foolish.

"Ma'am," Luke acknowledged. He hunkered down beside her, his ebony eyes penetrating. "Feel well enough to tell me what happened?"

She had told her story so many times, she felt as if every one of them ought to be able to repeat it verbatim, but if he wanted to hear it again, she'd tell it again. "I was on vacation . . ."

As she talked, he picked up a stone and tossed it in his hand. Then, when she was done, he said, "Why were you alone?"

"She came from Fort Laramie," Mary Baker said quickly.

Before Anne could correct the woman, Luke swore. "What in hell were you thinking about, leaving the safety of the fort like that?"

"First of all," Anne said, her anger held tightly in check, "I wasn't at the fort, and secondly, who in hell do you think you are—"

Mary's gasp stopped Anne. Luke's forehead had knotted into a frown, and there was a rustle of sound from the people gathered in the shadows.

"Well, I never . . ."

"Did you hear what she said . . . ?"

"She swore like a man! Must be . . ."

Anne drew in a ragged breath. "I apologize for my language," she said, even as she wondered why they had found it so offensive. She struggled upright. This time no one stopped her.

Luke stood, too, just in time to catch Anne's elbow when the dizziness hit her. Steeling herself, she shrugged off his hand. "But just because," she went on shortly, "you people are pretending to live in the past, does not mean that I—"

"What the blazes are you talking about?" Lucas demanded grimly. "Pretending what?"

"She said something like that before, Luke." Zeke loomed over Luke's shoulder. "I didn't pay no attention, though, figgered she was just agitated."

"Of course I'm agitated," Anne snapped. "The storm was bad enough, but you people—"

Mary curled her fingers around Anne's forearm. "Lucas saved your life, Anne," she reminded softly.

Anne swallowed hard. "I know he did, Mary. And I appreciate it. But I just don't know . . . I don't . . ." She raked her fingers through her short, nutmeg curls. "Surely you have a telephone, something to make contact with civilization?"

Luke laughed harshly. "You're the only outside world we've seen since we left Missouri."

"Don't you have a motorbike?" she pleaded. "Or a cell phone that I could borrow?"

"See, Ma," Jessie said quickly. "I told you she wanted a cellarfone."

"She ain't in her right mind," said a voice from the shadows.

"That's all we need," said another. "A crazy woman on a wagon train."

"Hush, Elijah," scolded a woman who had lingered in the shadows. "It's our Christian duty to be charitable to the unfortunate."

Anne was beginning to feel as deranged as they claimed her to be. "Are you going to take me to Laramie?" she asked tightly.

"Move along, folks!" The voice belonged to a new-comer, a man with thick, sandy-colored hair. He looked around at the crowd. "The show's over now. Let's give the little lady enough room to breathe."

With a murmur of farewell, Mary left with the rest. Anne hated to see her go. She was the only tolerant one of the bunch.

Other than the doctor, only Luke and wagon master stayed.

"Hello, there," the sandy-haired man told Anne. "I'm Robert Wilson. The only doctor hereabouts. Sorry I didn't get here sooner, but I had a bull by the tail and couldn't turn him loose."

"I don't really need a doctor."

"Probably not," he agreed. "I've already checked you over pretty thoroughly. Just to make sure you weren't going to die on us. But some things have to wait for consciousness before the examination."

Robert Wilson looked pointedly at the burly wagon master and Luke, who were still standing nearby. "Go on, you two," he said shortly. "Scat out of here. We'll let you know when we're done."

He might as well have been whistling in the wind, for all the good he had done. Neither man left.

The doctor ignored them. "Do you have any particular place causing you pain?"

She laughed wryly. "Physically, you mean? I feel

bruised all over, but one would, wouldn't one? Especially if they'd been caught in a tornado."

"Indeed they would," he agreed. "You have a large bruise on your forehead." He touched a spot that made Anne wince. "Guess that hurts. You're not having any trouble with your memory, are you?"

"Of course not!"

He leaned back on his heels and smiled widely, showing even white teeth. "What day is it?"

"Thursday."

Frowning, he shot a glance over at Luke and Zeke. "You sure?"

"Of course I am."

"Well, you're a mite off. Not surprising, though. Not with a bruise that size."

"Off?" she questioned. "What do you mean?"

"Today is Sunday."

"That's impossible!" She blanched. "Unless I've been unconscious for several days." She hesitated, then had to ask. "Have I?"

"Not unless you were lying out on the desert for three days," he replied. "And that didn't happen. If it had, you'd be in worse shape than you are now."

"Then, it can't be Sunday. You must have lost track of the days somehow. See—" She brandished her watch. "It's Thursday, the seventh."

The doctor lifted her wrist, studied the watch. "Where did you get this contraption?"

"It's not a contraption. It's a Rolex."

"Look here, Luke. It's a clock on her wrist." Dr. Wilson raised her hand in display.

Lucas McCord bent closer, then slid the watch down her wrist to get a better look.

"You say it tells the date, too?"

"Of course it does."

"So what day is it, exactly? What month?"

"July," she replied. "July, 1999."

Luke's hand tightened around her wrist, and Zeke Masters shrank away as if she had sworn again. Even Dr. Wilson looked perplexed.

"Guess that storm really knocked the stuffing out of you," he said.

"What do you mean?"

"This is the year of our Lord, 1851."

Chapter Three

The year of our Lord, 1851.
Our Lord, 1851.
1851. 1851.

The doctor's words echoed over and over again in Anne's mind long after she had bedded down beside the Baker wagon with Jessie.

The evening meal had been something of an ordeal, with Mary Baker's tall, thin husband, Henry, trying his best to be polite, yet obviously brimming over with unasked questions. The other travelers kept their distance, as though suspecting Anne might have some communicable disease.

Why were they doing this to her? Anne wondered. What possible motive could they have for trying to convince her that she had been thrown back in time?

The idea was completely ridiculous! And easily disproved . . . in time. Sooner or later they would reach civilization, and Anne would leave them and make the long-delayed call to her father.

Daddy.

Charles Alphonse Farraday, owner of Farraday Computers, a nationwide chain of computer stores that would soon go international.

He was fond of saying he had worked his way to the top. And it was true.

Raised on a farm in east Texas where generations of Farradays before him had barely made a living, Charles was determined to make a name for himself.

And he had done so.

Today, Charles Alphonse Farraday was one of the richest men in Texas. And now that he had accomplished that goal, he had set goals for his only child. And he was just as determined to accomplish those goals.

He was an opinionated, stubborn man, her father. Yet he was all she had, and she loved him dearly.

Daddy will be so worried about me.

And, if he hadn't heard anything from her by tomorrow, he would be sure to call out the National Guard and put them on her trail.

Anne smiled smugly as she thought of helicopters descending on the wagon train. The stock would scatter, and the travelers would lose time rounding them up again. It was no more than they deserved either, for trying to intimidate her.

Suddenly she felt ashamed of her thoughts.

If not for Lucas McCord, she would be wandering alone on the desert. And Mary and Henry Baker had treated her with kindness from the first moment she had wakened.

Perhaps tomorrow they could be persuaded to stop the pretense, to help her reach the nearest town, because it was a fact that if her father had to organize a search party, she would never be free from his interference.

* * *

The day had been a long one, and Lucas was looking forward to his bed.

He had consulted with Masters—as was his usual practice upon returning to the wagon train—and was now intent on stretching his tired body out on his bedroll and sleeping the whole night through.

Lucas spread his blankets beside his wagon, unbuckled his gun belt and placed it near to hand in case it was needed during the night.

He had removed his boots and prepared to settle down for the night when a mere whisper of sound—a sudden displacement of air—caught his attention.

"I thought you had already left for the fort, Hawk," Luke said, turning to face the Comanche warrior who stepped out of the darkness.

"Masters changed his mind."

"Any particular reason?"

Hawk grunted. He had always been a man of few words. "Spotted a Crow village not more than a day's ride from here."

"How big?"

"Maybe fifty lodges."

"Women and children?"

"And old people. Not more than thirty or forty warriors."

"Not enough to cause much trouble," Lucas said. "Is Masters worried?"

Hawk shrugged his shoulders. "It's his job to worry. And the Crow are unpredictable."

Lucas grinned at the man who had become his blood brother when they were only boys. Both outcasts, they had formed a lasting friendship.

Hawk was a big man for a Comanche, only an inch under Luke's own height of six feet. Like Luke, he had broad shoulders and narrow hips. But, unlike Lucas, he wore his long black hair in braids.

"I heard about the woman you found," Hawk said, his black eyes curious.

"Guess everybody's heard by now. She's been the main topic of conversation since I brought her in."

"Do you believe her?"

"That she comes from the future?" Luke's lips thinned, and his eyes glittered. "I'm surprised you even have to ask, Hawk. And if she really believes that, then it's obvious the sun did a good job of baking her brain."

Hawk refused to leave it alone. "Masters spoke of a strange clock on her wrist. A clock that tells not only the time, but the date as well."

"Yeah. But that doesn't prove a damn thing."

"Have you ever seen such a clock before?"

"No," Lucas replied. "But that doesn't mean a thing. The Europeans are coming up with some new contraption every day. And it's not called a clock when it's that small, Hawk. They call it a watch. They've been making pocket watches for years."

"But none that show the date."

"Dates can be changed. As they obviously were on that watch. I don't know what she hopes to gain by spinning such a yarn."

Hawk crossed his arms and looked up at the night sky. "There are many things in life we don't understand," he said softly. "Perhaps this is just one of them."

Luke grinned widely at the Comanche warrior. "Is this where you are going to remind me of Comanche legends, Hawk?"

"No need to do that. You've heard most of them before. Many times." He focused his dark eyes on Lucas. "From your own mother, Lucas."

"Yeah," Lucas agreed. "She taught me the legends of the Comanche people. And like you, she believed they were true."

"And you doubt."

"My father taught me, too, Hawk. I spent more time with him than my mother." And too soon they were gone, lost to the fire that destroyed their home.

"I wonder sometimes what my life would have been like had your parents not perished," Hawk said softly. "Do you, Lucas?"

"Wonder about your life?"

"No. About yours."

"No. Thoughts like that are useless," Lucas said abruptly. "They died. And my uncle, Red Wolf, found me. And that day my life took a new path."

Lucas had never spoken of the sorrow he had suffered at the death of his parents. How, barely six years old, he had struggled to survive, sleeping in trees to escape the wolves who appeared with the night, eating berries and roots when hunger was too strong to be ignored, yet staying close to the burned-out cabin where his parents had perished.

It was the only reason his uncle had found him.

Red Wolf had taken his nephew and raised him as his own son, but the others in his village had not been so charitable. Lucas had been reminded of his white blood on a daily basis, by the children, and by the old women who had lost loved ones to the white-eyes.

But Lucas had not been the only outcast in the village, as he had learned within days of arriving there. Hawk was being attacked by two boys older than himself when Lucas had first seen him. Although smaller than the others, Hawk had been a fierce fighter, bent on proving himself. When Lucas had waded in and evened things out, it was the beginning of a friendship that had lasted throughout the years.

"Where's Jules?" Hawk's voice jerked Lucas back to the present.

"Riding herd."

Jules Turner was the mule skinner Lucas had hired to

drive his wagon to Fort Laramie. He would have to make other arrangements there, since Jules had no wish to go farther.

"How'd you get him to agree to that?"

"Didn't. It was Masters' idea. He talked the folks into paying Jules four bits for every night he rides herd."

"You're already paying him two bits a day for driving your wagon," Hawk said gruffly. "By the time we reach Fort Laramie, he'll have enough money to go on a month-long binge at the local saloon."

That remark needed no reply, so the two men bedded down; but it was a long time before Lucas' thoughts allowed him to sleep.

Fort Laramie played a crucial role in the settlement of the frontier. It was a landmark and a way station for the countless trappers, traders, missionaries and emigrants who made their way west.

The fort was founded in 1834 by fur trader William Sublette, who was searching for a site for a trading post when he happened upon Laramie's Point, on the Laramie River near its confluence with the Platte. He erected Fort William on the site, then sent out runners to inform the neighboring Sioux and Cheyenne chiefs of his interest in trading for their buffalo robes.

Sublette's business was only moderately successful, so in 1836 he sold the post to the American Fur Company. The AFC had a monopoly on trading until Fort Platte was built only a mile away in 1841.

With its strategic location on the more than two-thousand-mile trek from western Missouri to the Pacific Northwest, the fort made a good stopping point for the large wagon trains following the Oregon Trail. The American Fur Company enjoyed a bustling business in the sale of supplies to travelers.

Although relations were most often friendly between the Indians and the whites, as more and more settlers flooded through the area, young warriors from both tribes began to harass the wagon trains.

It was then the army acquired Fort Laramie as a military installation.

Soon afterward, Major Cleveland was assigned as fort commander.

Darkness had long since settled over the fort when Grizzly Barnes rode in. Although he had expected the major to be in his quarters located above Post Headquarters, he could see by the lamplight that shone from the downstairs window that he had been wrong.

Pushing open the door, Grizzly stepped inside the room where Major Cleveland was bent over a map spread out on his desk.

"You're back early, Hank." Major Cleveland refused to call Hank Barnes by the outlandish nickname the other man had been dubbed after his years of bringing in the hides of grizzly bears. "I take it you didn't run into any trouble out there."

Since Grizzly had never been a man given to unnecessary words, he remained silent. He was here, and that, as far as he was concerned, spoke for itself.

But Cleveland wasn't satisfied. He leaned back in his chair, crossed his hands behind his head and studied the old man.

Grizzly Barnes was slightly stooped, and looked ancient. His wrinkled, lined face seemed to be made out of the same buckskin that clothed him, and a battered coonskin cap was pulled low over a beetled brow. Deep lines ran from the flare of his nose, disappearing into the snow-white walrus mustache. His chin was covered with a beard the same color and fullness of his mustache.

The Winchester rifle he held in the crook of his arm appeared to have taken root there. As Cleveland watched, the old man spat a stream of tobacco at the spittoon that stood a good ten feet away.

"Gotcha!" Grizzly muttered. Then he turned back to the major, and his faded blue eyes held a glint of humor.

Cleveland leaned forward again. Getting information from Hank Barnes was almost as hard as pulling teeth. "Did you see any sign of trouble out there, Hank?"

Grizzly's blue eyes held Cleveland's. Instead of answering the question, he asked one of his own. "What kind of trouble you lookin' for, Major?"

"Indian trouble," the major replied. "The kind that would require intervention."

"The Sioux ain't never caused much trouble," Grizzly reminded bluntly. "You know that, Major. They ain't no real need for your troops to stay here. Just a waste of good money that could be put to a better use."

"There's every need," the major replied. "Our presence at the fort insures safety for the settlers. The Sioux are gettin' restless. They aren't happy about the wagon trains that keep coming through here."

"If you was Sioux, Major, you'd prob'ly be a mite riled, too."

"Well . . . be that as it may," Major Cleveland replied, "our job here is to protect the settlers and insure the pioneers' safe passage."

"You got your work cut out for you, then," Grizzly growled. "You hit the nail right on the head when you said they was gettin' restless. T' other night I chanced on some of them young bucks that was out huntin' buffalo. I snuck close enough to hear their powwow, and they was talkin' about how the settlers keep comin' along, no matter the promises that had been made. Said that if them wagon trains kept on comin', and bringin' white settlers to claim Injun land, they wouldn't be nothin' left for their own people."

Cleveland frowned heavily. "They gave permission for

the wagon trains to cross their land. Why are they getting so riled about it all of a sudden?''

''I reckon they didn't expect so many of 'em, Major. And now, with Masters coming along with that train of his—must be nigh on to a hundred wagons in that group—the Injuns figger enough's enough.''

''The Masters wagon train? Would that be Zeke Masters?''

''Reckon it would.''

''I thought he wasn't due to come through for another month.''

''Guess they been makin' good time.''

''I heard Luke McCord signed on as scout.'' He leaned forward in his chair. ''You and Luke go way back, don't you, Hank?''

''Knowed him since he was a young'un . . . afore he got took by the Comanche. Knowed his folks, too. They was mighty fine people. Hated to hear they was burned out that way. Mighty hard way to go, bein' trapped in a fire. Took it hard, Luke did, mighty hard.''

''Yes,'' the major agreed. ''It would have been hard on anyone.'' He scraped back his chair and stared out the window, but his thoughts had returned to a time long past, when he had been a young officer. ''I was there the day he was rescued.''

''Rescued?'' Grizzly arched a snow-white brow. ''Rescued from what?''

''Why, from those damned Comanches. Too bad he'd been with them so long. He fought like a tiger that day. Wouldn't stop fighting either, even after he was roped and tied to a horse. Not until we'd agreed to take the Indian boy along, too.''

''Hawk?''

''Yeah. He was a fighter, too. But we'd have tamed him right enough if he'd been left in our hands.''

''Yeah,'' Grizzly grunted. '' 'Spect you would have.''

"Any sign of the Crow bucks who stole those horses?" Cleveland asked.

"Nope. Figger they've gone to ground."

"I hope to hell they stay there, then. At least until the wagon train passes through." Cleveland sighed and reached for the leather pouch. "Go on and get some sleep, Hank. I may need to send a reply to General Clark."

Grizzly didn't have to be told twice. He'd had only a few hours' sleep in the last four days, and stretching out on a bed was just what his old bones needed in the worst possible way.

Moments later the door closed behind him.

It was barely daylight when Anne woke abruptly to a buzz of activity. The sound of human voices, both male and female, mingled with the sounds of animals.

She opened her eyes and, for a moment, with rough boards only a mere foot above her, couldn't remember how she came to be in that position.

Then memory returned as abruptly as she had wakened. She was sleeping beside the Conestoga wagon that belonged to the Baker family.

Whispers sounded nearby, made indistinguishable by the louder crackle of flames eating at wood. Anne could easily identify the latter sounds since she had spent her summers in the mountains, camping with her family.

A flurry of movement nearby caught her attention, and she realized Mary must have already started the morning meal. Since Anne was determined not to be a burden to anyone, she flung back the quilt and crawled out from under the wagon.

Mary was bent over a wooden barrel that she was using for a table, kneading biscuit dough in a large wooden bowl. She greeted Anne cheerfully as she pinched off pieces of dough and placed them in a Dutch oven she had left near to hand.

"What can I do to help?" Anne asked quickly.

"You could rake some of those coals aside."

Anne quickly obeyed, spreading the coals evenly to distribute the heat across the bottom of the Dutch oven.

Mary dropped the last biscuit in the iron kettle, covered it with the lid, then set it on the coals to bake. Anne scooped up more coals and spread them over the lid so the biscuits would have all-around heat, then turned to Mary for further instructions.

"It won't take those biscuits long to cook." Mary reached for a large wooden spoon on her makeshift table and stirred the contents of a pot. "The grits are done. So's the coffee. Help yourself to a cup while I wake that lazy family of mine."

"Who're you calling lazy, Mary?" The deep voice belonged to Henry Baker, and it came from the front of their wagon. "While you been lolly-gagging over your breakfast fixins, I been out doing man's work."

"Man's work, indeed!" She snorted. "More like you been out flappin' your jaws."

Henry slid a sideways glance at Anne. "You see what I have to put up with?" he complained. "This old woman is meaner than blue blazes."

"Don't you call me an old woman!" She waved the big wooden spoon threateningly. "Not less'n you want a big knot on that swelled-up head of yours."

"Swelled-up head?" Henry's gray eyes glinted with humor. "Now, Mary . . . is that a nice thing to say about your husband?"

"I tell it like I see it," she replied smartly. "And if you don't stop insulting me in front of company, then I'm gonna feed every one of those biscuits to the mule."

"Aw, Mary . . . you wouldn't really do that." He slid

his arms around her waist and smiled down at her. "Now, would you?"

"Just keep on and watch me!"

Even though Mary's tone was hard, her eyes were dancing, and for some reason, Anne felt her presence was an intrusion on the couple. She thought about her own parents. Had they been as happy as these two appeared to be?

Anne turned away to give them a little privacy and saw Jessie crawling from her bedroll.

"What's all the racket about?"

Mary heard her daughter. "Breakfast will be ready by the time you're washed up, Jess. Hurry now."

Breakfast was over, and the adults were lingering over a second cup of coffee when a tall, wiry man with jet black hair and mustache approached them. It was hard to guess his age since his face was cured like old leather by sun and wind.

"Morning, folks." His piercing dark eyes slid from one to the other before lingering on Anne. He tipped his hat in a polite gesture. "Hope you had a good night, miss."

"Thank you," she murmured.

Mary introduced them, giving his name as Thomas Warren, then adding, "Help yourself to coffee, Thomas."

Warren poured himself a cup, then squatted down on his haunches across from Anne. "Sorry I wasn't here when you woke up yesterday," he said. "But I was taking my turn watching the horses."

"There's no need to apologize," she said, wondering why he was doing so.

"There is for a fact," he said gravely. "I heard some of the folks wasn't too friendly. Durn shame, too—pardon my language—that you had to put up with that when you'd just come through . . . uh . . . whatever you'd already come through."

Anne saw Mary hide a smile behind her hand.

Before Anne could reply, they were joined by another man. He was slim, with red, pudgy cheeks and a wild shock of brown hair. Unlike Thomas Warren, he was clean-shaven. As he greeted them, his Adam's apple rode up and down.

Mary introduced the newcomer as James Odelbert, who had been their neighbor in Missouri, and after pouring himself coffee, Odelbert stood silently, leaning against the wagon and listening to the conversation flowing around him; but his eyes strayed often to Anne, making her feel slightly uncomfortable.

"Party's over, folks!" The booming voice belonged to Zeke Masters, who strode quickly toward them. "It's past time we moved along. We got a lot of ground to cover before sunset." The rising sun caressed Masters' head, making his hair appear even redder than before. He stopped beside Anne. "How're you feeling this morning, little lady?"

"Slightly bruised, and bent out of shape," she responded. "But, other than that, I feel wonderful."

"Glad to hear it," he said gruffly. His gaze slid to Henry Baker. "You ready to move out, Henry?"

"Just need to hitch up the mules," Henry replied.

"Good." Masters looked from James Odelbert to Thomas Warren. "What about the two of you?"

"My oxen are already in the traces, Zeke," Warren replied. "All it takes is me climbing on the wagon."

"Better do it, then." Masters' gaze moved to Odelbert. "How about you, James?"

"I'm ready, too," Odelbert said quickly. "Just thought I'd stop by for a quick cuppa coffee while I was waiting . . . since Thomas was already here."

Zeke nodded. "Your wagon's a far piece from here, ain't it?"

"Yeah. Twenty wagons behind this one."

Zeke's lips twitched at the thought of Odelbert counting the wagons separating him from the Bakers' . . . and the unattached woman that would be traveling with them for several days. A nice-looking woman, too. He hoped that wouldn't cause any trouble between the single men, yet wouldn't be surprised if they were soon at each other's throats. After all, married men were allotted twice as much land as single men were.

He was frowning as he moved on to the next wagon. "Okay, folks. Time to move out!"

Chapter Four

"Move 'em out!" The call came from the front of the wagon train. It was taken up by others down the line.

"Move 'em out!"

"Set 'em rollin'."

"Eeeeehawww!"

The sounds were mingled with those of straining beasts and metal scraping on wood as the lead wagons began to roll forward.

"It's time, Mary," Henry Baker said, taking the basket his wife carried in one hand and her arm in the other to hurry her forward. "Don't want to lose our place in line."

He flung the basket behind the high seat and lifted his wife onto it, waiting as she settled her skirts around her legs and picked up the reins. "Careful as you go," he said gruffly. "We don't want to be fixin' any more broken wagon wheels."

Then, turning to his daughter, who stood beside Anne, he said, "Make sure you keep up with your ma, Jessie.

No dilly-dallying along the trail. Nor wandering off to pick flowers either.''

"I don't do that anymore," Jessie said quickly. "I was young that time I got lost."

"Yeah," he replied. "Of course you were. Four whole months younger." He chucked his daughter under the chin. "You just be sure and move right along with the wagon."

"I will, Pa."

"I'll look after her," Anne said quietly.

"Appreciate that, ma'am." Henry tipped his hat politely, then mounted his horse and rode away from the wagons.

"Where is he going?" Anne asked the child beside her.

"He helps herd the stock. Keeps 'em movin' along with the wagons." Jessie peeped at Anne from beneath her sunbonnet. "You sure don't know much, do you?"

Although Mary Baker had been watching the wagon ahead of her, she fixed her daughter with a stern look. "Jessica Lou Baker!" she scolded. "You apologize to Miss Farraday."

"No, please," Anne said quickly. "It's all right. She didn't mean anything."

Mary ignored Anne. "Jessie?" she prompted.

"Sorry, Miss Farraday," she muttered, staring at her feet. "Wasn't thinking."

As the wagon in front of Mary began to move, she snapped the reins over the mules, then yelled, "Ye-haw! Get along there, mules!"

The four mules strained against the traces; the wagon shifted and moved forward, leaving Anne and Jessie to follow along beside it.

Sensing the girl's embarrassment, Anne tried to get her mind off the scolding. "Do you always walk, Jessie?"

"Course," the girl replied. "The wagon's loaded with our furniture and other stuff . . . supplies. You know.

They ain't no room in it except for the driver. Sometimes, though, if I'm feelin' kinda poorly, Ma lets me ride up beside her.''

Jessie's calm acceptance of her circumstances was nothing short of amazing. "What about school, Jessie?"

"What about it?"

"Don't you worry about falling behind in your grades?"

"Uh-uh."

Jessie had been surreptitiously peeking at Anne's watch as they talked.

"Do you want to look at my Rolex?" Anne asked.

"Your what?"

"My watch."

"Can I?" Jessie asked eagerly.

Sliding the watch over her hand, Anne handed it to the girl, who ran a finger over it wonderingly.

Jessie smoothed her fingers across the gold band, then looked up at Anne, her eyes wide with something like awe. "Is it really gold like?"

Anne nodded, smiling down at the child. "Yes. It is real gold."

"And does it really tell the date?"

"Um hum. See." Anne pointed at the spot. "Right there."

"Humph," Jessie said, expressing her disgust. "I ain't surprised it's wrong. Something so fancy wouldn't work right nohow."

The fine hairs on Anne's neck stood on end. "The watch *is* working right, Jessie."

"No, it ain't," Jessie replied stoutly. "I know my numbers good enough. That there watch reads 1999. And it dang sure ain't that."

A chill shuddered down Anne's spine as she clutched the girl's shoulders and spun her around, holding her in place while she studied her closely. "Jessie. This is very important to me. What year do you think it is?"

Jessie's blue eyes were wide, innocent, nothing there of lies, nor of subterfuge. "Why, don't you know, Miss Farraday?" she asked.

"I need you to tell me, Jessie."

"It's the year of our Lord, 1851."

1851. No! Anne thought wildly. It couldn't be 1851. The girl was just repeating what she had heard. She was teasing. She had to be! But she was not. It took only one moment to discard that theory, because Jessie's expression was completely serious. She believed she spoke the truth.

Nevertheless, Anne could not accept that truth, no more than she had accepted the doctor's words. Time travel was only a theory, something to wonder about, yet not really consider as truth.

All day long Anne continued to remind herself of that fact. She constantly scanned the skies overhead, looking for airplanes, or helicopters, that might be searching for her. Her efforts were in vain, though, because except for a few buzzards, hawks, and an eagle in flight, the skies remained completely empty. No sign of civilization. Not even a telephone pole. Or a power line. Empty.

The western sky was awash with long ribbons of lavender and pink when Zeke Masters finally called it a day.

Despite their obvious weariness, the travelers went about their duties of settling in for the night with good cheer. Soon campfires glowed in the thickening twilight as women bustled around preparing the evening meal.

As Mary cleaned and skinned the brace of rabbits Henry had killed during the day, Anne peeled, sliced, and washed potatoes, then set them aside for later use. The coffee came to a boil, and Anne raked a few coals aside and settled the pot over them to simmer.

She was no stranger to outdoor cooking, had gone camping at Lake of the Pines every summer during her teenage years, but watched Mary closely; beginning to realize she might have to learn a few new—or old—survival skills.

"Do you want me to make biscuits, Mary?"

"No." Mary tugged at the rabbit skin, trying to separate hide from meat without leaving hair behind. "Thought we'd have johnnycakes tonight."

"I'll make them, but you'll have to give me instructions."

Moments later Anne was mixing cornmeal and flour together. She added leavening and salt, then stirred in two cups of buttermilk and two tablespoons of molasses. When the mixture was smooth enough, she poured the batter into a preheated, greased, iron skillet, set the heavy iron lid in place, then placed it over hot coals.

"That was easy enough," she muttered. "Wonder why nobody makes them now?"

Mary looked up from her work. "You say something, Anne?"

"Just wondering if there was anything else I could do."

"No," Mary said. "There's nothing left to do except fry up these two rabbits Henry brought me." She coated the pieces of meat with flour and placed them in a hot skillet. Then, wiping her hands on her apron, she turned to Anne. "We're sure to have company show up after supper, Anne." Her voice was hesitant when she spoke again. "The folks here . . . Well, we don't want them to get the wrong idea about you."

Anne arched her brow. "Wrong idea?"

"About your character and all." Mary was obviously embarrassed. "They ain't used to women wearing britches. Most of 'em don't think it's decent."

Anne's lips twisted wryly. "I don't have anything else to wear, Mary."

"I know," Mary said quickly. "That's why I laid out a shirtwaist and a skirt for you. Reckon my clothes will be a mite too big, but maybe if you tuck the shirtwaist in and use a belt, the skirt would stay up. It oughtta look respectable enough so the gossips don't have nothing to chew on."

"My jeans are perfectly respectable where I come from. Everyone wears them. Men and women."

"Is that so!" It was more a statement than a question, needing no reply. "I reckon pants is more practical, but, fact is, women don't wear 'em in our part of the country." Her mouth thinned. "Some women do, though. Women like Maisie. But you ain't Maisie's kind. That's easy enough to see."

Anne decided she would like to meet Maisie.

"The dress is on the tailgate of the wagon," Mary said. "And I shifted stuff around inside so you'd have enough room to change your clothes."

Although Anne rebelled against being told what to wear, she realized her very life depended on the goodwill of these people. And, since Mary had been especially kind to her, she didn't want the woman to be made uncomfortable.

It was for that reason alone that she went, albeit reluctantly, to change her clothing. And when she was finished, and the white shirtwaist was buttoned high under her chin, she belted the blue linen skirt tightly around her waist and returned to help Mary finish the evening meal.

As twilight covered the land with deep purple shadows, Lucas stood beyond the circle of light cast by the many campfires and watched the woman he had rescued talking and laughing with the Baker family.

It was hard to believe she was the same woman. Dressed in feminine apparel, there was no mistaking her gender. Even the short curls framing her face enhanced her beauty.

"Mighty pretty lady you found, Lucas."

Luke didn't have to look at the man to know it was Jules Turner, his driver, who spoke.

"Why don't you set about courting her?" Jules continued. "A wife would be a useful thing to have. You could file on twice the acreage and get a housekeeper and cook in the bargain. Not to mention other benefits . . . like a woman to snuggle up to on cold winter nights."

"I've got no use for a wife, Jules. No use at all."

Even so, Lucas couldn't help wondering how it would feel to hold her against him, to cup the firm, high breasts in his palm while he covered her mouth and tasted her sweetness.

As though his thoughts had touched her, she looked up and met his eyes across the distance. Moving gracefully, she came toward him, her skirts swirling softly around her ankles.

"Look!" Jules gripped Luke's forearm. "She's coming over here."

Lucas turned cold eyes on his mule skinner, and taking the hint, Jules Turner disappeared into the surrounding shadows.

It took only moments for Anne to cross the distance that separated them. And when she stood before him, his hooded eyes ran up and down her length before lifting to meet hers again.

A jolt of awareness flashed through Anne, as though she had stuck her finger into a light socket, and her breath quickened, her pulse pounding rapidly.

She was close enough to feel the heat of his body, to smell the mingled scents wafting from him and surrounding her. Horseflesh, leather and the musky scent of man.

Feeling almost intimidated by his nearness, Anne took a backward step to put distance between them. But somehow, perhaps because she was unused to wearing long skirts, her heel caught in her hem, and she lurched unsteadily.

Lucas reacted instantly, righting her with a firm hand at her waist. Then slowly, inexorably, he pulled her closer until only a few inches separated them.

Anne felt the heat of his hand scorching her through the thin material covering her upper body. Her heart began to beat in double time. His fingers tightened at her waist. as though he were as affected by their nearness as she.

"I-I uh . . . wanted to thank you for coming to my rescue yesterday," she murmured uneasily.

"No need."

Luke's gaze dropped, touching on her breasts, and as though he had stroked them, Anne felt her nipples tauten.

A hot flush crept over her cheeks, and when she spoke, her voice was husky, as though she had just wakened from a long nap. "There is a need. I would have died out there if you hadn't intervened."

She licked lips that had gone dry at the thought, and his eyes narrowed, his hands tightening around her waist, his gaze riveted to her mouth.

Anne drew in a sharp breath, wondering how it would feel to have his mouth cover hers. All she had to do was tilt her head back, lift herself up on her toes and maybe. . . .

Suddenly, Lucas uttered a curse and released her. His lips thinned as he backed away, putting more distance between them.

Oh, God, he had apparently guessed her thoughts, and they were completely contrary to his own.

A flush warmed her cheeks. The man's mere presence was too potent for his own good.

Lowering her eyes, Anne forced her trembling knees to lock in place. Then, lifting her skirt so she wouldn't trip over it again and humiliate herself even more, she concentrated on putting even more distance between them.

"I . . . uh . . . have to go and . . . Mary needs . . ."

Oh, Lord, she silently groaned. *Leave, before you make a complete fool of yourself.*

Spinning around, Anne rushed toward the Baker wagon, and every step of the way, she imagined she could feel Luke's cold gaze on her. Nevertheless, when she reached her destination, she couldn't resist sneaking one last peek at him.

To no avail. There was no sign of him near the other wagon. A quick sweep of the area told her he had left the firelit circle.

Soon afterward, an old man tuned up his fiddle and played a jig. A young couple, both in their late teens by the look of them, clasped hands and began to dance in the clearing. The travelers watched and clapped their hands, stomping their feet to the music while cheering the dancers on.

"Come on, Mary." Henry Baker took his wife's hand. "We haven't danced a jig in many a day."

"Leave be, Henry," she said, laughing and tugging at her hand. "We're better off watching at our age."

"When I get too old to dance, just dig a hole and cover me up." He pulled her hard against him. "Now come on, woman. Or do I have to find me a sweet young thing to dance with."

"Don't you dare!" she said. "Not unless you want that sweet young thing to be snatched bald-headed! Anyway, I can out-dance anybody here."

"Talk is cheap." Henry laughed. "You got to show me."

Laughing and teasing each other, they joined the young couple in the clearing. But even as Henry whirled his wife around, the tune wound to an end.

"Play another one!" Henry shouted.

Obligingly, the fiddler began another tune, and several more couples joined the dancers.

"Miss Anne."

Anne turned to see James Odelbert holding out his hand. "Would you do me the honor of dancing with me?"

Completely caught up in the music, Anne placed her hand in Odelbert's much larger one. "It would be my pleasure, Mr. Odelbert."

Luke stood in the shadows and watched James Odelbert pull Anne toward the dancing couples. She was smiling at her partner, flirting with him, seeming intent on making him believe he was special to her.

Dammit! he silently cursed. She was just like Barbara! Like so many other women who teased and flirted, smiling at a man with eyes so innocent until he was nothing but a quivering mass of jelly.

But Lucas was on to her game. He had been caught in that trap once before, had already learned his lesson.

He watched the couple spin gaily around the firelit clearing, laughing, with Anne's skirts flitting high as Odelbert whirled her around again and again, and wondered why he felt a need to smash Odelbert's nose against his face.

Fool! He silently chastised himself. *She doesn't belong to you. So why does it matter what she does?*

She was a stranger, someone he had found in the desert and brought to safety. It shouldn't matter to him who she danced with. And yet it did matter. He found himself wishing he was the man holding her, wishing Anne was laughing with him in the same way that she was laughing with her partner.

A slight movement nearby told him he was no longer alone. He turned to upbraid the man, believing Jules had returned to torment him, but found himself facing Hawk instead.

"The woman is pleasing to the eye."

"Just like Barbara was," Luke muttered.

Hawk didn't have to ask what Luke meant. He had met Barbara, had known how Luke suffered at her hands. "The past is better left behind."

"I make damn sure I remember that particular past."

Lucas knew he should leave, yet his legs would not obey his command. They continued to hold him there, forcing him to watch the dancers whirling around the circle.

As the lively tune ended, the fiddler bowed, straightened his arm, then set bow to fiddle again, playing the first strains of a waltz.

James Odelbert took Anne's hand again, but before he could swing her into the dance, Thomas Warren tapped him on the shoulder. Words were exchanged, and Odelbert released Anne and, albeit reluctantly, stepped aside.

Not for long, though.

The dance had barely ended when James Odelbert reclaimed his dance partner. The fiddler began another tune, and as they swayed to the music, Warren stepped in again and tapped James on the shoulder.

"Damn!" Luke exclaimed. "She'll have them at each other's throats before she's through."

Feeling a tightness in his chest that could not be explained, Lucas spun on his heel and strode into the darkness.

"Where are you going?" Hawk asked, keeping pace beside his friend.

"I don't know," Lucas snarled. "But I'll be damned if I stand around and watch that woman turn two men who've always been friends against each other."

"Perhaps you judge her too harshly."

"The hell you say!" Luke glared at the other man. "I learned a lot from Barbara. And it was a lesson I won't soon be forgetting."

No. Lucas would never forget Barbara. She had stolen his heart, had given herself to him, and then when they had been caught together in a compromising situation by a man who turned out to be her fiancé, she had cried rape.

Horrified that she could say such a thing, Lucas had been frozen to the spot. It was almost the end of him. If he hadn't seen the six-gun in time, hadn't reacted so quickly, his life would have ended that day.

Even then, Lucas had been willing to forgive. He thought her fear had been responsible for the lies. That she hadn't meant what she said. She had, though. When Luke bought a ring and proposed to her, she had laughed at him, said she would never marry a man like him . . . a half-breed. A man who would always be shunned by polite society.

Half-breed! Even now the words stung.

But he had learned his lesson well. And he had learned to guard his heart. No woman would ever get so close to him again.

Not ever!

Anne didn't know how long she had been asleep when the noise woke her. She heard loud voices arguing somewhere nearby, then the sound of thuds as a fight broke out.

Wondering what was going on, Anne shoved aside the quilt and pushed herself upright.

"Stay where you are," a harsh voice commanded.

Anne recognized the voice instantly. It belonged to Lucas McCord.

Puzzled, Anne lifted her eyes to meet his. Although the campfires burned low, there was still enough light to see his expression. It was cold, as were his eyes . . . cold as a winter's day.

"What's happening?"

His lips thinned, flattening with distaste. "Just what you would expect."

"I don't understand."

"James Odelbert and Thomas Warren are trying to beat each other's brains out." Something in his voice told her he blamed her for what was taking place. But that was complete nonsense.

"Why . . . ?"

"Just shut up and go back to sleep!" he snarled. "Before you cause any more trouble."

Anne's lips tightened. "Surely you don't blame me for . . ."

Her voice trailed away as she realized the scout wasn't listening. Luke McCord's long strides had already carried him into the darkness beyond the wagons.

Anne's lips twitched in annoyance as she stared into the shadows, wondering where he had gone so quickly.

And why was he blaming her for the actions of two men who were strangers to her? She had done nothing to provoke the fight, knew she had not acted inappropriately with either of the men.

"Dammit," she cursed. "Who can understand men?"

Stretching herself out on the bedroll again, Anne yanked the quilt up to her neck, wondering if she would ever return to her own century. If not, tomorrow would be soon enough to learn the outcome of the fight.

Chapter Five

Dawn splashed a crimson hue on the eastern horizon as Lame Coyote bellied his way through the tall, waving grass that grew along the edge of the gully. A short distance away a rope corral had been stretched around a group of horses, while others, merely hobbled to keep them from straying, grazed nearby.

He had no interest in the hobbled horses; the mustangs in the corral were his target. And only a lone guard stood in his way.

As Lame Coyote edged closer to the horses, his gaze never left the man with the rifle slung across his shoulders.

The guard was no longer alert for danger, having been lulled, more than likely, by the peaceful night he had just passed.

Suddenly, the guard raised his head and sniffed the air like a wolf, and Lame Coyote hugged the ground, fearing for a moment that something had given away his presence.

"Coffee," the guard muttered, staring hard at the circle

of wagons a short distance away. "Hot coffee. Damn! I sure could use a cup of that."

Lame Coyote raised himself again, creeping closer and closer. Soon he would be near enough to strike . . . and then he would signal his brothers with the bird call they had chosen.

His lips curled in a quick grin as he eyed one particular horse. It was a magnificent steed, muscular and strong. And it would soon be his. Soon he would feel the mare's strength between his legs.

It was a good day for stealing horses.

"There, Miss Farraday. See? I told you they were roses." Jessie reached down and plucked the small pink-and-white flower from the patch growing low to the ground and held it toward Anne. "Smell it," she insisted. "Then you'll know it's a rose."

Anne sniffed the fragrant blossom and realized that it was, indeed, a rose. A wild rose.

"I thought wild roses only grew in the mountains," Anne said.

"Didn't you have none where you lived?"

"Not wild roses like these," Anne replied. "Only garden roses."

"Never heard of growing roses in a garden before," Jessie said. "We had some in a flower bed back home, though." She looked up at Anne. "Where do you come from anyways, Anne?"

"Texas. Dallas, Texas."

"I never heard of Dallas, but I heard about Texas. We lived in Missouri once," the child confided. "An' we got wild roses there. Lots of 'em. Just like these, too. Ma likes rose hip tea. And some of the bushes have rose hips on 'em. I saw lots of 'em in the gully where the women go to be private. Me an' Kate and Janie were playing there last night. Maybe we could pick some rose hips and take 'em to Ma. She sure does like rose hip tea.''

Rose hip tea. Although Anne had heard of the beverage, she had never tasted it. She found the idea intriguing. ''We have to hurry, though,'' she told the girl. ''I need to help your mother with breakfast.''

''Aw, Ma's used to cooking without no help.''

''Without *any* help,'' Anne said, automatically correcting the girl's speech. ''Anyway, there is no excuse for our not helping her with her chores.'' She looked toward the horses that were corralled nearby. ''Where is the gully you were talking about, Jess?''

''There.'' Jessie pointed toward the rope corral. ''Just beyond the horses.''

The guard stationed there had been watching them, Anne realized. She waved at him and smiled when he came within hailing distance.

''What are you two doing out here?'' he asked.

Jessie's piping voice rang out a reply. ''Morning, Mr. Harper. We're just gathering some rose hips for tea.''

The guard strode nearer. ''Don't suppose you'd have any coffee hidden on you anywheres?''

Jessie giggled. ''Nope. No coffee. But Ma's got some on the boil. We could bring you some in a few minutes. After we gather the rose hips.''

The guard turned and swept his gaze over the horses, then looked at the eastern horizon, where a thin slice of sun could be seen; then he turned back to them. ''No need to bother yourself, Jess,'' he replied. ''The night's done gone, and there was no sign of trouble. The horses oughtta do just fine without me now.'' He shifted his rifle slightly. ''I'll go in now an' get me some breakfast whilst there's time. Masters is dead set on us reaching the fort afore the week's out.''

With a quick wave of his hand, he strode toward the circle of wagons.

Jessie wrapped her hand around Anne's fingers and tugged her forward. "Come on, Miss Farraday. Let's gather some of those rose hips."

Anne quickened her stride, and moments later, they were slipping and sliding down the draw toward the rose-bushes on the bottom.

The draw was narrow and curving, and with the long grass growing along the edges, it offered a perfect place for children to play hide-and-seek.

As Jessie had stated, the rose hips grew in a plentiful supply. They wasted no time gathering them, and had already filled the basket they had brought when Anne saw a flicker of movement in her peripheral vision. She turned swiftly, studying the place where she had seen the blur of movement—the place where the draw curved out of sight—but there was nothing there.

Deciding it was merely the long grass waving in the wind, Anne lifted her long skirts and scrambled up the slope, her boots slipping and sliding on the shaley sides, then turned to help Jessie out.

The sight that met her eyes chilled her blood. A half-naked man leapt toward her, brandishing a tomahawk, while another, similarly clad, held Jessie aloft. The child's eyes were wide and round, her pupils dark with horror, and her face was ashen.

Jessie's captor held her in a cruelly tight grip, the fingers of one hand digging into her waist while the other covered her mouth to stifle her screams.

Anne's defense mechanism leapt into action. "Stop that!" she cried. "Let her go!"

The man nearest Anne lifted his tomahawk and arced it downward, a move that would have split her head in two had it connected, but she leapt aside swiftly, avoiding the blow.

As Jessie's captor ran down the gully, carrying the girl

with him, the man who had gone after Anne continued his attack. The tomahawk was too real to suit her, and she gathered her skirts high to keep from tangling her feet in the hem, and whirled around, kicking out her feet as she had been taught, using the training that she had acquired after having her purse snatched late one evening in a Dallas parking lot.

Her aim was accurate, and the weapon went flying. Another kick to the man's midsection sent him tumbling backward. Then, with a loud scream to warn the travelers of impending danger, Anne took up the chase.

Her years of training stood her in good stead. With her skirts lifted high, Anne raced swiftly through the gully, leaping over rocks and other obstacles as she raced to intercept the man who had carried Jessie away.

A heavy thudding behind her warned of danger. But before she could react, Anne felt a hard blow. Pain exploded through her skull, and her vision was clouded by a red haze that was quickly becoming thicker.

Anne felt herself falling and curled her body into a ball as she had been taught, rolling with the blow. Even so, she struck the ground hard enough to send her breath whooshing from her body. She fought to recover her breath as Jessie's terrified moans reminded her of the urgency of their situation.

Oh, God, please help us!

She needed to reach Jessica, needed to help her, but her legs were weak, refusing to comply.

Pushing herself to her hands and knees, Anne fought for the breath she needed. She sensed movement behind her, turned to face a new threat . . . too late . . . too late.

Through a red haze of pain she saw the warrior, looming above her . . . saw the upraised arm holding the tomahawk.

And then the arm descended.

* * *

Luke tightened the cinch around his mount's belly. As he did, the Lineback dun sucked in his breath.

"None of that," Lucas said grimly, delivering a sharp blow to the dun's side that expelled the air. "I don't have time to fool with an ornery horse this morning."

The dun shifted impatiently, as though to remind Luke that he had nothing to do with the lateness of the hour.

And it was late. The rising sun had already topped the horizon, and the wagon train should already be rolling across the prairie on its slow journey west.

But it was not.

It seemed everything that could go wrong had already done so. Frances Fitzhugh had been taken with severe abdominal pains during the night, and her son had sent for the doctor. And before Robert Wilson had seen to her needs, Major Ragsdale sent word that his daughter, Cynthia, was also unwell.

Since then, several others had complained of similar ailments, enough to keep the good doctor hurrying from one wagon to another.

In ordinary circumstances, the patient's wagon would have been left behind to catch up later, when the wagon train stopped for the night, but with so many travelers affected by the same ailment, the doctor must, of necessity, wait along with them.

It was the reason Masters decided to wait. The doctor must travel with the main group, in case others became ill.

And, as if that wasn't enough trouble to plague them, when Luke stopped by the Baker wagon, he was told both Jessie and Anne Farraday were missing.

Jessie's parents were naturally worried.

Mary explained that her daughter wanted to show Anne some roses she had found that were growing nearby. She had given permission for them to go, yet had expected them back long before she had finished making breakfast.

"And what worries me even more," Mary continued, "is something I heard . . . or thought I did."

"What was that?" Lucas asked.

"I didn't pay it no mind right then, thought it was just the children playing around the wagons, but the more I think on it . . . well, I just ain't sure anymore."

Lucas controlled the urge to shake the woman. "What did you hear, Mary?"

"I ain't rightly sure," she replied. "But it might have been somebody screaming."

Henry met Luke's eyes. "She didn't say nothing about that before," he said gruffly. "Might be just her worrying and all. Might be nothing to it."

Lucas nodded. "Might not be," he agreed. "But it needs checking out anyway."

"That's my way of thinking," Henry muttered, glancing uneasily at his wife. Then, "You shouldn't have let 'em go, Mary. Both of 'em should've been here helping you cook breakfast, instead of off somewheres looking at roses. I wouldn't have agreed to let Anne stay with us if I'd known she'd cause you grief."

"She's caused no grief!" Mary said quickly. "You know she hasn't, Henry. And she's been a big help to me. Always lending a hand where it's needed, and looking after Jessie . . ."

"Seems to me she wasn't looking after Jessie very good. Not when the two of 'em's turned up missing," Henry said evenly.

Tears filled Mary's eyes, and she turned away to hide them; but nothing about her escaped her husband's notice.

"Aw, Mary," he said, reaching for her and gathering her close. "Jessie's okay. There ain't nothing going to happen to our little girl. She ain't alone. She's got Anne with her, and that young woman has a lot of horse sense. They'll be along soon enough.''

Henry looked over the top of his wife's head and met Luke's eyes. "Lucas is gonna look for 'em. Ain't that right, Luke?''

"Sure, Mary," Luke said gruffly. "They probably just wandered farther than they meant to." And, if that was the case, Anne was going to get a good tongue-lashing when he found her.

Luke returned to where his horse waited. He checked his repeating rifle and shotgun before he mounted, even though he knew they were in battle-ready condition. Times like these a man couldn't be too careful.

Sliding the weapons back into their individual saddle sheaths, he was on the point of mounting when he heard the sound of hooves and turned to see Hawk approaching.

Hawk reined his mustang up beside his friend. "You're late getting away this morning," he said gruffly.

"Several folks have come down with the grippe." Luke's lips curled in a wry grin. "Maybe it was the deer you brought in last night." His eyes glinted with humor. "I thought you were mighty generous when you spread the meat around amongst the travelers. Come to think of it, you gave a good portion of it to Cynthia Ragsdale. And, considering how she always looks down that long nose of hers at you, you might've been tempted to season it with a little poison."

Hawk's black eyes narrowed. "You shouldn't jest about such things where you might be heard. Some of these people are just looking for a chance to blame me for whatever holds this wagon train back."

Luke sobered quickly. "I know. And you're right, Hawk. A wrong word spoken in the hearing of one person could spread like wildfire and cause endless damage."

Hawk shrugged. "It's the way of the paleface." He looked across the prairie. "This is the last trip, Lucas.

I'm tired of living among the white-eyes. In their so-called civilization. I have a yearning to live in the mountains.''

"I figured as much.'' Luke had seen it coming for a long time, had known that soon Hawk would not be riding with him. It was the reason he had decided to stay in Oregon himself. "But, whatever happens, Hawk, you'll always be welcome at my place.''

Hawk nodded. "I know.'' He looked toward the wagon train. "Masters should start the wagons rolling. It's not a good idea to linger long in one place.''

Lucas shrugged his shoulders. "Masters is aware of that. He doesn't like the delay any better than you do.''

"No. I guess not.'' He sighed heavily. "Go carefully today, my friend. Don't take too much on yourself.''

Luke frowned. "Do you expect trouble?''

Hawk shrugged. "Trouble is best expected, at all times.''

"We have two people missing, Hawk. If you know something about them, you'd best speak out now.''

"I know nothing of them.'' He looked toward the wagons where nothing seemed amiss. "Why have searchers not been sent out?''

"Because Mary Baker believes they wandered off while picking flowers. I was about to ride out and look for them, though.''

"Do you want me to search for them?''

"No. You ride on ahead and make sure there's no trouble brewing along the trail.''

The two separated then, Hawk riding west, while Luke circled the area around the wagon train with his mount, hoping the woman and child might have returned on their own.

But they were nowhere in sight.

Grimly, he began a close ground search, following their tracks into the gully nearby. Moments later he saw the basket they had used and the rose hips scattered over the ground. A closer search revealed moccasin prints.

"Dammit!" he cursed softly.

Lucas hurried back to the wagon train, intent on informing Masters of his discovery. But one of the wranglers was with the wagon master, and the news he carried did little to allay Luke's fears. It seemed half a dozen horses were missing.

"The Indians." Luke swore roundly. "They were after the horses, and they probably took the woman and child as well. How in hell did they get by the guards?"

But nobody had to answer his question. He already knew. Indians had a way with horses. And they moved so quietly in their moccasins that nobody had heard them.

The Indians had managed to steal half a dozen horses and kidnap a woman and child without anyone knowing what was happening.

With his lips set tight, Luke mounted his horse again and took up the trail.

Chapter Six

Jessie lay on the ground where the Indians had tossed her, like an unwanted sack of grain. The biggest savage, the one who had carried her off, had tied her hands and feet with strips of rawhide, restricting movement and preventing any possibility of escape.

She had been conscious throughout the long ride that had lasted until well after sunset, knowing that with each passing moment, she was being carried beyond any hope of rescue.

Ma and Pa would be worrying about her, wondering why she hadn't returned. But there would be nobody to tell them where she had gone.

She would never see them again.

That thought, painful though it was, caused no visible reaction; her face remained without expression, blank, completely emotionless.

Jessie was hiding, deep inside her mind where she could not be seen. And, beneath that outward mask, Jessie was a quivering mass of fear.

Her gaze had not left the Indians since her captor had tossed her on the ground. She had remained frozen as they went about the business of setting up camp, had remained that way, silent and unmoving, even when the big Indian with the red bandana across his forehead dropped Anne's motionless body beside her.

Miss Farraday.

She had been Jessie's only hope. But now that hope was gone . . . Miss Farraday couldn't help her or anyone else. Not when she was dead.

Dead. Like the baby bird Jessie had found back home. It had been like Miss Farraday. So silent and still. No, there would be no help from Miss Farraday, nor anybody else, because nobody knew she had been stolen. Pa would believe she had just wandered off . . . as she had done once before. They would search, but only within walking distance, and the Indians had taken her far, far away from the wagon train.

No. Her parents would never find her. She would never see them again.

Tears stung Jessie's eyes, and she blinked once . . . twice, to make them go away. She would not cry anymore. No, she would not!

The big Indian with the red bandana was looking at her, so Jessie quickly retreated within herself, hiding in the shadows of her mind. And there she remained, motionless, unblinking, afraid to come out lest they destroy her completely.

"The little one blinked," Running Wolf told the man who squatted beside him. "Perhaps she is not beyond recovery after all."

Gray Eagle's narrowed gaze skittered toward the girl who lay near the riverbank. He found no change in her at all. Her gaze was still unfocused, her face without expression.

Gray Eagle hoped the child had not retreated from reality, as he had seen others of her kind do, especially the young females. It had not been his intention to harm the child; he had only meant to silence her screams so the white-eyes would not be alerted.

He sighed inwardly. Many things had gone wrong this day. Too many things. And soon he must face the council of elders and explain his actions.

Would they agree that he had done only what was necessary? Or would they chastise him, as the shaman had chastised Red Fox when he had foolishly led an attack against an army supply wagon.

Three of their small group had been wounded in that raid before they managed to escape, and Red Fox was proud no more. He had been shamed by his defeat, and the shame would follow him throughout his life, for Black Bear was a constant reminder of his rash actions.

Black Bear. Once that warrior had walked proud, his head held high. Yet now that head was permanently bowed, his gait unsteady, caused by the bullet that had shattered his knee.

Yes. That raid had been a complete disaster. Many things had gone wrong that day. But Gray Eagle had been more cautious, and not one of his warriors had suffered a wound.

He looked across at the girl again . . . so still, and withdrawn. Then he looked at the woman lying motionless beside her. Not everyone had been so fortunate.

What would the council say if their young warriors, who had left the village to hunt game, returned not only with stolen horses, but with a dead woman and a child who had been driven completely out of her mind?

Whatever they had to say would not be long in coming, he knew, for tomorrow's sunset would find them in their

village. And soon afterward, the hunting party would sit
in council and explain their actions to the elders who
had already signed their mark on the white-eyes' paper,
thereby giving their word they would abide by the peace
agreement.

When Anne regained consciousness, she was aware of
pain, extreme pain that bombarded her senses, streaking
through her head from front to back. She groaned, opening
her eyes to stare down at the leaves and pine needles that
made up her bed.

The light was dim, flickering, as though she were in a
candlelit room, yet she could feel the cool breeze upon
her cheeks. She could feel more than that, she suddenly
realized. Her body ached all over, as it had done when
she had been tossed aside by the tornado.

Could it be possible. . . ?

No.

The cobwebs in her mind dissipated with a swiftness
that left her stunned. She remembered everything that had
happened. She had been kidnapped by savages, stolen
from the wagon train with Mary Baker's daughter.

Well, she damn well wouldn't take it lying down!

That thought caused a bout of hysteria that Anne quickly
controlled. The savages had no idea who they were dealing
with, but they would learn soon enough. Anne wasn't
some squeamish miss from the nineteenth century who
swooned at the first sign of trouble. She was a product
of a new breed of women who had learned to take care
of themselves.

Flexing her muscles, Anne realized she was trussed up
like a Thanksgiving turkey. Her hands and feet were tied
achingly tight. She bit her lower lip, stifling the groan of
pain threatening to erupt, then, with a rocking motion,
managed to roll onto her back.

Night stretched out above her, stars beyond counting spread out like glittering diamonds on a bed of black velvet.

Night. The day was gone, passed without memory. *Oh, God, how long have I been unconscious?*

And Jessie? Where is Jessie?

As she tried to curb her rising fear, a guttural voice sounded nearby, words that were incomprehensible to Anne. She turned her head and saw three Indians squatting around a small campfire. And their eyes were focused on her.

The largest man, who probably measured near six feet when he stretched his length to its full height, was barrel-chested, wide of shoulders and slim of hips. He wore his hair in two long braids, fastened at the ends with leather thongs.

"So you are finally awake," he said in perfectly good English.

Anne ignored his statement. "Where is Jessie?" she asked hoarsely. "Where is the girl who was with me?"

His gaze darted to a spot beyond her, then quickly returned to her. But it was enough. A quick look showed Anne the girl was nearby. Her hands and feet were bound, and her eyes were open, wide and staring.

"Jessie." Anne spoke softly. "Are you all right, honey? Did they hurt you?"

Silence.

Cold fear slithered down Anne's spine. Something wasn't right with the girl. "Jessie!" Anne's voice was sharp. "Answer me. Please. Are you all right?"

Continued silence.

Fury surged over Anne, swamping the fear as surely as water would have doused a flame. Anne glared at the big Indian. "What have you done to her?" she cried. "What in God's name have you done?"

* * *

"The woman is brave," Lame Coyote said in his own language. "She thinks only of the child."

"Yes. She is brave," Gray Eagle replied. "And she is a good warrior. She would bear strong sons. Together we could make many warriors for our tribe."

"Running Wolf captured her," Lame Coyote reminded.

"He wants nothing to do with her," Gray Eagle replied. "He has said so. He already has a woman in his lodge, and he has no time for another. Especially one who would cause trouble as this one surely would."

"Do you think the old ones will allow you to keep her?" Lame Coyote queried.

Instead of answering the question, Gray Eagle asked one of his own. "Who else has more right to her? Running Wolf has no wish to own her. And she cannot be sent back to her people. There would be too much danger involved for whoever undertook such a task."

"You are right. But who knows what the old ones who sit at council will decide."

"Yes," Gray Eagle replied. "Who knows?"

The woman had remained quiet throughout their conversation, but her eyes continued to flash her fury. And suddenly that anger erupted. "How dare you treat us this way!" Her blue eyes resembled the storm clouds that too often swept across the land. "Get over here and cut these damn ropes . . . or whatever it is you've used to truss us up this way."

He ignored her.

"Dammit! Can't you see the child needs me? She needs to be held and comforted!"

Gray Eagle considered her words. She might be able to help the child. And it was a fact that the council would look more favorably on his actions if the two captives were unharmed.

With his gaze locked on the woman's, he raised himself to his full height and drew his knife from its sheath.

Anne watched the big Indian draw his knife, and her pulse skipped a beat as fear slithered through her. What was in his mind? Was it his intention to slit her throat to silence her?

She watched him approach and bend over her. Her pulse pounded in her ears as her fear increased. His knife arced down, and she closed her eyes and waited for death. But it did not come. Instead, she felt the bonds on her hands fall away.

Realizing she was free, Anne opened her eyes and stared up at the big warrior, who was already striding away from her.

"Wait," she called. "My feet are still bound."

He ignored her, obviously intending to leave her that way to keep her from escaping. Anne wasted no time with useless words. Instead, she crawled to Jessie and took the girl into her arms.

Jessie was stiff, completely unresponsive.

Anne turned to the big Indian again. "There's no need to leave her this way," she said sharply. "Come free her."

He ignored her.

"Please," she said. "She is frightened out of her wits. And no wonder after what she's been through. What harm would there be in releasing her? She's only a child."

He seemed to consider her words for a long moment, then, with a quick jerk, strode toward them. Moments later Jessie was free of restraints.

Anne gathered the child close and held her, whispering soft assurances in her ear while she rocked back and forth. She knew the exact moment when she finally reached the girl, because Jessie began to tremble violently.

"It's all right, honey," Anne whispered. "I'm here with you. Nobody is going to hurt you." She shot a heated glance toward the big Indian. "Nobody!"

"Miss Farraday?"

Jessie's voice was so soft that at first, Anne thought she had only imagined it.

"You're not dead? They didn't kill you?"

Anne hugged the child tighter, reassuringly. "Oh, honey, no. I'm alive and so are you. And we're both going to be just fine." She cupped the girl's tear-streaked face. "Jessie? Did they . . . ?" She didn't know how to ask the question. If they hadn't raped the girl, she didn't want to put the idea in her mind that their captors might ultimately do so. "Honey, what did they do to you?"

"One of them slapped me and knocked me down. And he pulled my hair real hard and made my head hurt. But I can stand that." She shuddered, her small body shaking with fear as her tears overflowed again and washed down her face like rain. "I thought you were dead, Miss Farraday. I kept waiting for you to wake up, and when you didn't, I thought you must be dead."

"No, honey. I'm not dead. But they're going to wish I was before this is over." Anne turned her attention to the big Indian who had resumed his place beside the fire pit. Although both Indians there appeared to be ignoring their captives, Anne knew it was only pretense. The Indians were aware of every move she and Jessie made.

"Don't make them mad, Miss Farraday," Jessie pleaded. "They might hurt us."

"I'll be careful," Anne assured the child. She focused her gaze on the big Indian again. Since he had already obliged her by freeing the child, he might be persuaded to listen to reason. "You!" she said. "Come over here and loosen these damn rawhides on my feet. They're cutting off my circulation!"

He ignored her, as did the other man.

"I'm not sure he speaks English," Jessie whispered.

"He does." She spoke to him again. "You. Come over here and loosen these bindings! If you don't, then I won't be worth beans to any of you when you're ready to leave here!"

He looked at her again and suddenly straightened to his feet and crossed the distance between them. He hovered there for a long moment, his gaze holding hers.

"You are right, paleface," he said gruffly. "You would be worthless to us if you lose the use of your legs."

Then, drawing his knife once more, he leaned over and sliced through her bonds, leaving her legs free.

She winced as circulation began to return to her limbs. but her gaze never left his. "What are you going to do with us?"

"That has not been decided."

"Why did you take us?"

"It was not our intention to take captives. Merely to steal horses. But we could not leave you behind to raise the alarm." He took another leather thong that had been looped at his waist and held it toward her. "Hold out your hands," he commanded.

"If I promise not to run away, will you leave me free from restraint?"

"A white woman's promise means nothing," he said grimly. "You would escape the first chance you had. Now, hold out your hands."

He could have forced her, but she realized he wanted her acceptance of her fate. And for the moment, with the other warrior watching, she could do nothing else.

She held out her hands, noticing as she did that her wristwatch was gone. "Where is my Rolex?"

He didn't answer, just continued to wrap the rawhide around her wrists. Anne tried to separate the heels of her palms, hoping to leave enough room to manipulate her bonds when her captors were not looking. But he would have none of it. He lashed her wrists together, tight, but not as tightly as before.

"What are you called?" he asked suddenly.

"Anne Farraday," she replied.

"And the girl?"

"Jessie Baker."

"My name is Jessica," the girl corrected.

The big Indian grunted and turned away.

"Wait," Anne said. "What is your name?"

"Gray Eagle," he replied gruffly.

He returned to the fire where several rabbits had been cooking, leaned over and sliced off two chunks of meat and brought it to the captives. "Eat," he said, handing one to each of them.

Neither of the captives had to be told twice. Anne hadn't realized how hungry she was until she bit into the meat. It was apparent Jessie felt the same as she ate greedily, then gnawed at the bone until it was picked clean. When they finished their food, Gray Eagle brought them a waterskin and allowed them to drink from it.

The water was tepid, but it quenched their thirst. Anne leaned back against the riverbank and uttered a deep sigh.

"Maybe they ain't gonna kill us," Jessie whispered.

Anne smiled encouragingly at the child. "Of course they won't, honey. They are probably going to hold us for ransom. Your folks will be glad to give them whatever they want to get you back."

"And you, too, Miss Farraday. They'll pay for you, too."

They fell silent then, Jessie huddled close beside Anne, trying to keep the night air at bay and to gather strength from the woman.

The cool breeze blew Anne's tousled curls across her eyes, and she lifted her bound hands to push them aside. All the time she watched their captors, hoping to catch them off guard so she and Jessie might escape.

"We're gonna be all right, ain't we?" Jessie sounded lost, in need of constant reassurance.

"Of course we are, honey," Anne quickly assured the young girl. Her voice didn't betray her own fears. She was not so certain they could escape. The savagery of the attack had done what nothing else could do. She no longer doubted her circumstances.

However it had happened—by tornado, or the frivolous hand of fate—Anne was no longer in her own time. Impossible as it seemed, she had been thrown into the past to a place where no law prevailed, where only the fittest survived. And if she was to survive, she must accept what Fate had dealt her and learn to use her strengths to live in this harsh, untamed time.

The only thing that consoled her was the fact that the Indians had not been after the pioneers. Instead, they had been intent on stealing horses, not taking captives.

But that made no difference to their own plight. So far, the Indians had done them no permanent harm, yet how long would that situation last?

Anne looked up at the night sky again. The moon was full, surrounded by a profusion of stars. It was a night for lovers, for dreaming, yet for her and Jessie, the dream had become a nightmare.

There should have been dark clouds above, stormy, ominous in appearance, and the moon should have been red. Blood red. Yet it was not. The stars continued to glitter as brightly as diamonds, circling a big yellow moon.

A night for lovers.

For dreaming.

But the bindings on her wrists were real enough. The blood on her bottom lip where she had cut herself when she had struck the ground was real enough, although she wished to God it was not.

"I'm scared, Miss Farraday," Jessie said, wiping her

nose with the sleeve of her dress. "I want to go home . . . to Ma . . . and Pa."

"I know, honey." Anne stroked the pale cheek with the back of her hand. "But try hard to be brave." Anne had read somewhere the Indians admired bravery and were scornful of cowards. But how brave would she be if their captors decided to torture them?

Jessie began to cry harder, sobs shaking her slender frame. "They ain't gonna let us go, are they?"

The youngest of the braves, a man who appeared to be in his late teens, met Anne's eyes with a hard look. She returned his gaze unflinchingly, determined she would not look away first.

The big warrior, Gray Eagle, nudged his companion and spoke in the guttural language that was so strange to Anne's ears, and the impasse was broken.

A movement at the corner of her vision caught her attention, and she turned and saw another Indian approaching. He was dressed only in a breechclout, as were the others, and as she watched, he spoke in harsh-sounding words that appeared to bode no good for the captives as the Indians around the fire leapt to their feet and, as one, looked at the girl and the woman.

Anne's heart gave a lurch of hope. Was rescue at hand?

The warrior, apparently having done what he had come to do, turned around and disappeared into the forest, followed closely by Gray Eagle and the youngest warrior. That left only one man to guard the captives.

Anne considered the situation. Could she possibly free both herself and Jessie while the warrior was distracted? She flexed her wrists, attempting to loosen her bonds, but the rawhide was too tight. If escape was to be had, then it would be done with bound hands.

She bent over Jessie and whispered in her ear. "If I say go, you must rise and run as fast as you can. Do you understand, Jessie?"

The girl nodded, her eyes lighting with sudden hope. "I understand," she whispered.

Anne settled down to wait, and to watch for the chance, for that one moment in time when the warrior's attention was diverted. And all the while she wondered if she would have the strength needed if that moment should present itself.

Chapter Seven

The wind blew lonesome, and the sun rose higher and higher as Luke searched for the Indians and their captives. At times he followed the tracks left by the stolen horses; at others, like now, he merely guessed at the direction they had taken.

Although he tried not to think about what the captives might be suffering, the horror of their circumstances was constantly on his mind. Lucas knew the way of things. The child would probably be adopted into the tribe, but Anne was a woman . . . a paleface woman. She would be raped. Many times over. So many times, and so harshly, that she might not survive. And that would not be the end of her torture either. Too many women had lost both husbands and sons to the hated white-eyes. They had a way of revenging their loss on the white captives brought to their village.

Luke's body became rigid as he fought to control the impotent rage that swept over him at the thought of Anne's suffering. It was a fury so great that it threatened to consume him.

But Lucas could not give in to his feelings, could not allow them to make him careless. It was imperative that he find the captives as quickly as possible, before the Indians decided to make camp.

The warriors who had taken Anne and Jessie were as adept at hiding their tracks as were the Comanche who had taught him ways to find what other white-eyes could not see. But then, Lucas wasn't a white man. Nor was he an Indian. He was a half-breed. A product of two worlds.

Lucas had been a young boy when his parents died, and his mother's people had made quite an impact on his life. But even so, those years with his Comanche family had not erased the earlier years—with his parents—from his memory.

His mother. Asa Nan-i-ca.

Lucas remembered her laughter most. She had been happy in her marriage to the big Scot, John McCord. And that happiness had spilled over onto their young son, coloring his thoughts, making him believe he would one day find a woman who would give him what his mother had given her husband.

He had been ripe for the plucking when he met Barbara. A young fool who had fallen in love with a woman because of her laughter.

But no more. He had learned his lesson. He would never give his heart away again.

Luke's mount nickered softly, sidestepping as a rabbit darted across the path.

"Easy, boy," Luke soothed, leaning over to stroke the Lineback dun.

Then, narrowing his gaze, Lucas scanned the area surrounding him. He found nothing to show the Sioux had passed this way. Yet something told him they had. The landscape was changing. In the distance the ground appeared to rise in small mounds that would eventually prove to be mountains.

He must find the captives before they were taken there, else they might never be recovered.

It was the Comanche way to find a fast-flowing river and drive the stock through it, either upstream or down, for several miles, thereby making their trackers lose time by searching both directions.

The thieves had done that several times already, and Lucas had lagged farther and farther behind them. But his determination kept him moving, would not allow him to rest until he found the woman and child, whether dead or alive.

He had no need to worry his mount would give out beneath him. The dun was stronger than most horses. The get of a mustang mare and a Thoroughbred stallion, the Lineback dun stood over sixteen hands high, and had the strength and size of the stallion, yet the staying power of the hardier mustang horses that roamed the prairies.

A fact that had proved useful in the past.

Darkness covered the land by the time Luke reached the Platte River again. But the full moon above gave off enough light to make the going easy as he dismounted and allowed his mount to drink.

Lucas went upstream a short distance and stretched himself out to drink. And when he had done so, he dipped his canteen into the water and filled it to the brim.

The horse had already quenched his thirst and was tearing delicately at a patch of green grass.

"Hungry, boy?" Luke questioned.

The dun shook his head up and down as though to say

yes, and Luke reached down, tore up a handful of grass, and offered it to his mount.

The horse took the offering and munched contentedly.

Luke left the dun there while he climbed the riverbank and stared across the moonlit prairie, looking for signs of a campfire, which could be seen for miles around.

The wind moaned softly as it blew a tendril of dark hair across his face. It was a wild country, beautiful in its lonesome state, and the moaning wind held a sound of emptiness, making him think of far-off places where no white man had ever set foot.

Oregon.

Oregon was a place where a man could put down roots. A place where he could file on a section of land and know it would never be taken from him. The land. Land would never let a man down. Would never destroy his hopes . . . his dreams. It was the thought of owning his own land that drove Luke.

But first he had a job to do.

Lucas returned to his mount. Fort Laramie was only a few days distant. If he didn't find the captives soon, he would ride there and seek help. He could only hope the woman and child would survive that long.

The horse snorted and laid back his ears, and Lucas tensed, his gaze searching the purple shadows. Then he saw it, loping away into the darkness. A coyote.

Luke was on the verge of mounting when he noticed the dun favoring his right foreleg. "Trouble, boy?" he muttered, bending to find the problem. A moment later, when a pebble that had worked its way beneath the horse-shoe had been removed, he noticed the imprint in the ground.

"Dammit! A shod horse has been through here."

He began his search then, and soon found another track beside the flowing water. He would have to search both sides of the river again.

But that wasn't necessary, he realized, as he reached the other side and saw the tracks emerge from the water. The thieves had apparently decided they had laid enough false trails that no one would be following closely behind.

Luke's jaw set in a grim line. They would soon learn their mistake. He just hoped he wouldn't be too late to help the captives.

Anne's gaze never veered from the warrior who had been left behind. She waited quietly for a chance to escape, even as she wondered what had taken the others away from their camp. Although the savage remained silent, unmoving, she sensed his agitation.

Had someone from the wagon train followed them? she wondered. Was rescue, even now, close at hand?

Hope bloomed like a flower after a summer rain at the possibility, then just as quickly died.

If someone *was* coming, they were walking into a trap, because the Indians had been alerted.

But perhaps the rescue party was a large one; perhaps they had enough men and rifles to defeat the Indians if it came to a fight.

Even as the thought occurred, a piercing scream split the night. Anne's blood ran cold, and Jessie uttered a terrified cry and wrapped her arms around Anne's neck.

"What's happening, Miss Farraday?" Jessie's words were muffled as she clung tightly.

Although the cry had sounded like a terrified woman, Anne realized it could have been the cry of a puma as well. The scream appeared to have unnerved their guard, because his body was tense, his gaze sweeping the darkness as though he expected danger to erupt all around him.

Anne realized in that moment that she must act now,

while the warrior's attention was diverted. It might be their only chance.

And yet, how long would he be diverted? If they did not make good their escape, they would be dealt with harshly.

Her gaze swept the area, found the horses tethered nearby, and a plan slowly took shape in her mind. If she could find a stone and startle the horses into bolting, then escape might be possible.

A quick search of the area nearby revealed a large stone that should do. But she would have to hurry. If the other warriors returned, all would be lost.

She pushed at Jessie, silently urging her to pay attention. The child's grip tightened, then eased.

Pulling back slightly, Jessie tilted her head to meet Anne's gaze.

Silently, Anne mouthed the word, *Now!*

Jessie's eyes widened, then shifted to the warrior, who was still staring into the darkness where his companions had disappeared.

As Jessie edged quietly toward the purple shadows created by a nearby bush, Anne reached for the large stone, closing her fingers around it.

It would be an awkward throw, with the stone held between both hands. Oh, God, could she even do it?

She considered forgetting the whole thing. But only for a moment. Knowing she would have just one chance, Anne bunched her muscles and, using all the skill that she had acquired pitching softball, drew back her arms and threw the rock toward the largest horse.

Whoosh! The rock went straight to its target, striking the mustang with a soft thud, causing the horse to scream out its terror. It reared wildly then, striking out at the nearest horse with its sharp hooves.

The warrior's head snapped around, and he jerked

upright, his gaze fastened on the bucking, biting mustang that had appeared completely placid only moments before.

Shouting in a language that was incomprehensible to Anne, he leapt toward the horses, intent on calming them before they were injured.

It was the chance Anne had been waiting for. "Go, Jessie," she whispered urgently. "Run as fast as you can! I'll be right behind you!"

Then, gathering the hem of her long skirt between her bound hands, Anne followed the girl. Together, they raced along the riverbank, dodging between willows that were growing beside the river, pushing aside branches that sought to slow their progress, running as fast as their legs could carry them.

But Jessie was too young, her strength too little, to keep up the pace Anne set. And if they slowed down, they would surely be caught.

Even as that thought occurred, Jessie stumbled and went down. Anne's heart beat in double time as she bent to pick the young girl up.

Tears streaked Jessie's face. "I can't . . . can't run no more," she sobbed. "My legs h-hurt."

Anne brushed at the tears raining down Jessie's face. "We can't stop now, honey," she soothed. "Not yet. Not until we're safe."

"I can't!"

Realizing Jessie was completely played out, Anne searched the area for a hiding place, somewhere they could rest in safety, but there was nothing. Only the willows growing along the river.

"Jessie . . . honey. I'm going to carry you. But my hands are tied, so you mustn't move."

"Okay."

Using a fireman's hold, Anne put the girl across her shoulder, then straightened quickly. She loped forward, pacing herself as she had done so many times in the past.

She listened for sounds of pursuit, but knew that with her pulse thudding so hard in her ears, the warriors could be on them before she heard anything.

The extra weight was taking her strength, but she could not stop . . . dared not pause for even a moment lest they be captured again.

The path became darker as the willows and saplings grew thicker. Anne realized she should leave the river, should hide in the long grass growing on the prairie, but she dared not. The river was her only way of reaching civilization. Somewhere, up ahead, lay Fort Laramie. If she could stay with the river, she would eventually find the fort. And, hopefully, it would be before the Indians found them again.

If the wagon train had been closer to the fort, help from that quarter might have been available. But they had been too far away. There would be no troops coming to their rescue. Nor anyone else. No, their safety lay in her own strength. In her own abilities. That knowledge kept Anne moving, running along the riverbank. Her feet crunched over fallen leaves and twigs. Her heart pounded in her chest, her pulse pounded in her ears, and still she ran.

Fast.

Faster.

The ground seemed to tremble around her.

Were the Indians coming?

She chanced a quick glance over her shoulder.

It was a mistake.

She tripped and was flung forward, striking the ground with a hard thud that sent the breath whooshing from her body.

Anne lay there, motionless, struggling for air, knowing she had to rise again, to find the strength to go on. Somewhere close by she could hear Jessie sobbing. She wanted to reassure the child, but could only lie there, facedown, trying to breathe.

"Miss Farraday?" Jessie's voice quivered. "Are you hurt, Miss Farraday?"

Anne felt her chest expanding as air suddenly flowed into her lungs. She shoved herself to hands and knees, then used her bound hands to push her tousled curls out of her eyes.

Her mouth went dry as her gaze fixed on a pair of moccasin-clad feet.

Chapter Eight

It was over.

As surely as mice in a trap, they had been caught.

That knowledge dissolved Anne's strength, turned her knees into quivering lumps of gelatin. Fear coiled in her belly and spread out, tightening her chest and lodging in her throat, creating a knot that obstructed her breathing.

No use to fight anymore. It's over. They've won.

She had done her best, but her best had not been good enough. She had lost. She and Jessie. Lost.

Jessie!

"No!" she cried hoarsely. She couldn't give in so easily. It was not in her nature.

Anne allowed her anger free rein, knowing there was adrenaline in that emotion.

Keeping her head bent, pretending submission, Anne crawled upright, bracing herself on her toes. With her gaze fixed on the moccasined feet, she bunched her muscles, preparing to make her move.

"Miss Farrady," Jessie cried. "It's—"

Before the child could finish, Anne was reaching forward, curling her hands around the nearest ankle and jerking it hard. Then, while the warrior was off balance, she tightened her fingers in the hem of her skirt so it wouldn't trip her and surged upward, turning as she went and lashing out with her foot.

He was too agile by far as he leapt quickly aside, avoiding the blow that would surely have sent him to his knees had it connected with the soft flesh between his thighs.

But Anne wasn't finished. The world was a blur of colors, of green, purple and tan, as she whirled quickly, then struck out once more. The kick connected with his right hip.

Muttering hoarse curses, he leapt toward her, wrapping his long arms around her own, locking his fingers beneath the fullness of her breasts and jerking her hard against the length of him.

"Dammit, Anne!" he cursed. "Stop fighting me."

It was the use of her name, more than his demand, that was responsible for her sudden stillness. She looked over her shoulder and met Luke's dark eyes.

"Lucas?"

"Yes, Lucas!" he snarled. "Now are you going to settle down?"

She nodded and sagged against him, her strength sapped like dewdrops beneath the morning sun. "I didn't know it was you," she muttered shakily. "I thought it was the Indians . . ." Her voice rose as panic suddenly overwhelmed her. "We have to get away before—"

"Quiet, dammit! Do you want them to hear?" His gaze swept over her, taking note of the matted copper curls, the darkening bruise on her forehead, and his grip tightened as rage flowed through him. "How bad are you hurt?"

Why did he look so grim, so angry? Anne wondered. "Hurt?" she queried, puzzled. "I don't think—"

"I don't have time to check you over," he interrupted, drawing the long knife he carried at his waist. "Hold out your hands."

A moment later she was free.

He turned to Jessie. "You okay?" he asked softly.

She nodded, wiping at the tears that continued to rain down her face.

"You're safe now," he said gently, lifting her into his arms.

Holding the child against his massive chest, Lucas threw a quick look at Anne. "We don't have any time to waste," he said grimly. "Come on."

Without waiting for a reply, he turned and strode swiftly away, appearing to simply blend with the purple shadows of night.

Fear reared its ugly head as Anne stood frozen, staring at the spot where Lucas had been only moments before. *Oh, God,* she silently cried. *Where did he go?*

She searched the shadows. Nothing. No movement whatsoever. Not ahead of her, nor behind her. Knowing the Indians must be searching for them, and their fury when they found her would be immense, still she couldn't run, couldn't escape them again, could do nothing to save herself, only wait for whatever fate had in store.

Sweat broke out on her skin, beading her upper lip as she stood there . . . frozen to the spot.

"Anne! Come on, dammit!"

The harsh voice jerked her head around. Luke had returned for her. And he was alone. Her throat worked convulsively. "I-I thought you'd gone."

His voice gentled. "I wouldn't leave without you."

Miraculously, her knees unlocked, and she stumbled forward. Apparently not quickly enough for Luke, though. He curled an arm around her waist and lifted her against his right hip, loping swiftly into the night until he reached a thicket of willows where Jessie waited atop a large, dun-colored horse.

"Get on that horse with Jessie." His voice was gruff, yet low, barely distinguishable to her ears. "And if you hear anything at all, ride out of here as fast as you can."

"What are you going to do?" Anne asked huskily.

"I'm going to get another horse," he replied.

"But what about—"

"Dammit, woman! There's no time to explain. Just do as you're told!"

Without another word, he spun around and loped away, quickly blending with the shadows again.

Anne looked up at Jessie. "Scoot behind the saddle for a minute, honey," she said. "That way you can hold on to me."

"Are we gonna get away?" Jessie asked tremulously.

"Of course we are," Anne replied. "Lucas is with us now. He knows how to deal with the Indians."

"You really think so?"

"Of course I do."

"How long will he be gone?"

"Not long." *God, please don't let it be long.* "He's just going to get another horse. He—"

Anne broke off as a shot sounded in the distance. It was followed quickly by three more, fired in succession, one right after the other.

"Oh, God," she whispered. "They saw him!" She looked up at the girl. "You have to go, Jessie," she said urgently. "You have to leave before they find us!"

Even in the moonlight she could see the girl's face blanched white. "I don't know where to go!"

"Oh, God! I don't know either."

Suddenly, a horse and rider broke through the thicket. "Dammit, woman!" Lucas snarled. "Why didn't you leave like I told you?"

Relief swept through Anne as she quickly mounted. He was alive. Lucas was alive.

"I couldn't—"

"Dig your heels in that dun and get him moving!" he snarled.

Before she could react, he slapped the dun's rump, and the horse leapt forward with such speed that her heart dropped like a rock thrown into a pond. "Hold on to me, Jessie!" she cried. But she needn't have. The girl was clinging as tightly as a tick to a dog.

They burst out of the thicket, riding neck and neck, the smaller mustang with the big man atop keeping stride with the larger dun that carried double.

"Here they come!" Luke yelled. "Ride for your life!"

Heart pounding, Anne bent low over the horse, and planted her toes in the animal's side. The dun shot forward with amazing speed, and she rode as she had never ridden before.

The clatter of unshod Indian ponies behind them was almost deafening as she urged the dun to greater speed. A quick look back showed Luke following closely behind her. His six-gun was out, pointed toward the Indians. A shot sounded, followed by another, then another . . . random shots that appeared to accomplish nothing.

But she was wrong, she realized, as she saw a riderless horse. At least one Indian had fallen beneath Luke's six-gun.

A shiver of apprehension went through her as one Indian suddenly shot ahead of the others. There were so many. How had that happened? She had thought there were only four, but there had to be at least six of them.

It all seemed so dreamlike, yet she knew it was agonizingly real. They were alone, in the year of our Lord, 1851, far away from help of any kind, with only one weapon between them.

Even as the thought occurred, Anne became aware of

the rifle near her right knee. If she could get it out, load it and fire before the Indians were upon them, then perhaps . . .

The thought was interrupted by a volley of gunshots, so many shots they couldn't possibly have come from one weapon.

And, impossible as it seemed, the noise came from beyond them, farther up the trail where several willows formed a cluster.

The Indians swerved suddenly, reining their mounts away from their quarry. And the dun, as though given some silent signal, slowed to a trot, then stopped completely. He shook himself like a big dog that had just left the water, then lowered his head to the long grass and began to munch as though he had nothing better to do.

"Are you all right, Jessie?" Anne asked.

"Um humph." Jessie's deathlike grip loosened slightly. "What happened? Why did they go away?"

The answer came in the form of two mounted riders that left the willows and rode toward them.

"Who is that?" Jessie's body tensed, and her hands tightened around Anne's waist again. "Are they Indians, Mr. McCord?"

Lucas reined his mount beside them. "No, Jessie," he replied gently. "They're friends."

"Look!" the girl cried. "One of them is Hawk!" She sat up straighter, waving her arms above her head. "Hawk! Over here! We're over here!"

Anne's gaze narrowed as she watched the two men approach. The bigger man was obviously of Indian blood. The smaller, wizened old man sported a beard and mustache as white as the hair growing on his head.

"Howdy, son," the old man said. He spat a stream of tobacco on the ground, then squinted at Luke. "Looks like we got here just in time." He shifted his gaze to

Anne, appearing to take her in at one glance, then looked at the child. "You okay, young'un?"

"Yessir. They didn't hurt me none."

"That's good to hear." His shrewd gaze found Anne again, touched on her blood-soaked curls, then lingered on her bruised flesh. "It appears to me you got bunged up a mite, little lady."

"Just a little," she admitted. "But nothing serious."

"You got a doctor on that wagon train, Luke?" the old-timer asked.

"Yeah," Lucas growled. "We got one."

"Better have him look her over."

Luke's lips thinned. "I had every intention of doing just that," he replied.

"She got a name?"

Anne resented being talked around. "My name is Anne Farraday."

"Pleased to meetcha, Miss Farraday." He touched his forehead, as though tipping a hat.

"And I'm certainly glad to make your acquaintance," she replied. "You and your friend, Mr. Hawk, drove the Indians off. If you hadn't come when you did—"

"Lucas would have got you through safe enough," the old man replied. "We just made it happen faster." He reined his mount around. "You gonna stop at Fort Laramie, boy?"

Lucas nodded. "You gonna be around?"

"I'll be there."

The men moved a short distance away and had a brief conversation between themselves. Although Anne tried to hear what they were saying, their voices were too soft to be heard.

Moments later the old man rode away, leaving them, and they rode on, the men flanking the dun that carried Anne and Jessie back to the wagon train.

It was daylight by the time they reached the wagon

train. Lucas left them with Jessie's parents while he went to fetch the doctor. He waited long enough to know that neither Jessie nor Anne had suffered permanent damage, then left to resume his duties as scout.

When the doctor finished his examination, Anne looked for Lucas, needing to thank him for saving their lives. It was then she found that he had already left the wagon train.

She would thank him later, she silently vowed, unaware they would reach Fort Laramie before she laid eyes on him again.

And by then thoughts of what she had suffered at the Indians' hands would have been driven from her mind by a much larger problem.

Chapter Nine

Several days later, as they were cleaning up after the morning meal, Mary told Anne another fight had broken out during the night between James Odelbert and Thomas Warren.

Anne handed a dripping plate to Mary. "Those two were fighting? Again? I thought they were friends."

"They were." Mary frowned at the plate as though it were personally responsible for the fight. She wiped the last plate and stacked it on the others. "But when it comes to them wanting the same woman . . . well, I guess friendship don't mean as much." She lifted her gaze, sweeping it past the wagons to the prairie beyond. "I'd think they'd at least try to get along, though. With the Indian trouble—them kidnapping you and Jessie like they done—we all need to be pulling together, not fighting amongst ourselves."

"They were fighting over a woman?"

"Well, land sakes, Anne!" Mary exclaimed. "Didn't

you know that? Them two ninnys have been fighting over you since the minute Lucas brought you here!''

"Me?" Anne squeaked, losing her grip on the plate she had been holding. It sank beneath the soapy water again as she turned wide eyes on her friend. "But why— how—why would they fight over me? I haven't encouraged either one of them."

"Pshaw! Them two don't need no encouragement from you. The land is encouragement enough, child."

Anne felt as though she were Alice, who had gone through the looking glass and found nothing familiar beyond. Nothing Mary said made sense. "I'm completely at a loss, Mary," she said. "What does land have to do with me?"

"Why, Anne, don't you know?" Mary asked. "The land is the reason for everything we've done. It's the reason we come on this trip. The reason we been traveling so long. If it hadn't been for the land that's waiting for us up yonder, then we wouldn't have sold our homestead in Independence."

"You're talking about the land in Oregon?"

"Land sakes alive! Didn't I just say so? Of course it's the land in Oregon."

"I still don't understand what that has to do with me."

"No. I guess you don't. But it's simple enough. James and Thomas are both single men, Anne, and they are only allowed three hundred and forty acres each. But if they were married, they could claim twice as many acres. And since you're the only single woman on the train that hasn't already been spoken for, well, they've both naturally set their sights on you." She grinned ruefully. "And that's it in a nutshell."

"Well, for heaven's sake!" Anne exclaimed. "If I'd known what they were fighting about, all this trouble could have been prevented."

"How's that?"

"I would have made sure both of them knew I wasn't interested in marrying anyone. Those fools have been fighting over nothing."

"I wouldn't exactly call you nothing."

Anne laughed, a melodic sound that turned heads and lifted spirits, however momentarily.

Zeke Masters, however, who was engaged in conversation with Henry Baker nearby, frowned with disapproval. His task would have been easier if Anne Farraday had been some mousy woman with a quiet temperament. But she wasn't. Instead, she was a vibrant, lovely woman. And had become a problem.

His mouth flattened in a grim line. Something would have to be done about that particular problem as soon as they reached the fort.

Anne was completely unaware of the wagon master's presence, or his disapproval. She hastened to reassure Mary of her intent to stay single.

"If I ever marry, and I doubt that will ever happen, it will be to a man who loves me," Anne said. "Not because of the acreage that might come with me."

"Only a foolish woman would demand love before marriage," Mary replied. "A woman needs a man's strength to lean on. And James and Thomas are both honorable men. They would treat you right, expecting no more from you than a frontier wife should give to her man."

She looked toward her husband. "I didn't know my Henry when I married him. It was Pa who set the whole thing up. My folks never had much, but they scrimped and saved to set something aside each year for my dowry. Wasn't much, but it bought our farm."

A dowry.

Anne had forgotten the ancient custom. In the past a man married with an eye toward what his wife could bring to that union. Not for love, but for financial reasons.

Well, Anne wasn't about to marry for any such reason. She was an emancipated woman, and she would damn well stay that way. She would answer to no man.

Marriage to one of these Neanderthals? No, thank you!

She would find a way to survive here on her own, a way that allowed her to live her own way, subject to no man's whim. It wasn't that she minded cleaning up after a man, or the cooking or even sharing the most intimate parts of her life with him. No, the thought of having someone who cared for her, who loved her deeply, and wanted her love in return, was definitely to be desired. But to marry for any other reason was completely abhorrent to her senses.

"Why did you leave the farm, Mary?"

"It was Henry who wanted to leave. He's a forward-thinking man, my Henry. In Missouri, we would never have had much more than the farm. But he has big dreams. To have a ranch of his own, something to leave for our children and grandchildren. And the only way we could ever have more was to file on the free land." Her eyes shone with excitement. "Just think about it, Anne, six hundred and eighty acres. And plenty of trees to build a large cabin for our family. When we heard about the wagon train that was being formed, it seemed like a dream come true. Henry decided right then and there that we'd be with them when they left Independence." She spread her arms wide. "Now here we are, about out of supplies, weevils in the flour, low on salt and sugar, but still alive and kicking. And when we reach Fort Laramie, then we'll buy more supplies, and with God's help, they'll see us on to Oregon."

Mary's enthusiasm throughout the trip had never waned, although when her daughter had been kidnapped, she had feared for the child's life. But now Jessie was with her again. The good Lord was watching over them.

And with His help they would make it to the golden land of milk and honey.

With God's help.

Lucas sat on his mount on the southeast slope overlooking the two forts that were built only a mile apart. The afternoon sun that heated his flesh made the forts appear almost white, a sharp contrast to the tan of the tepees the Sioux had pitched nearby.

There was movement below, of men and women going about their daily chores, and children dodging among the lodges, laughing and playing games. Several camp dogs could be seen, limping, nosing about for scraps, and farther out, several horses grazed among the long, waving grass.

Beyond, the Black Hills climbed away, dark with their scrub cedar and pine, with Laramie Peak rising oversized among them. And somewhere, out of sight, were the Red Buttes and the Sweetwater and the Southern Pass and the Green, where he had spent several years as a trapper.

And on the near side of the pass, to the north, was Laramie.

Laramie. The gate to the mountains. There was danger there. Still. Not as much, perhaps, as there had once been, yet it was necessary for a man to keep a watchful eye out and a weapon ready. It was Indian land. Pawnee, Sioux, and farther on, Blackfoot.

Intruders were tolerated. Sometimes. The climate changed with the wind.

Nudging the dun with his knees, Lucas guided the horse toward Fort Laramie.

Anne was excited. A dance was being given in honor of the travelers who had camped outside the fort, and

Mary had insisted on making Anne a new dress for the occasion.

It was a beautiful gown, a vibrant blue color that exactly matched her eyes, and drew a man's attention.

With Henry escorting them, Mary and Anne entered the large room where the dance was being held. The band was playing a waltz, and several couples swirled and swayed to the music. Although Henry was eager to join them, he could not, in good conscience, leave Anne to fend for herself.

Spying a young lieutenant that he had met earlier in the day, he hustled the women toward him.

"Lieutenant Rogers," he greeted heartily. "Just the man I was looking for. I'd like you to meet my wife, Mary, and our guest, Miss Anne Farraday."

The lieutenant bowed to Mary. "Ma'am," he said, by way of greeting.

Mary smiled at him. "It's nice to meet you, Lieutenant. Have you been stationed here long?"

"Only for a few months," he replied, immediately turning his attention to Anne. His gray eyes were warm as they met hers. "It's a pleasure to make your acquaintance, Miss Farraday."

Anne smiled at the young lieutenant and offered her hand. Instead of shaking it as she had expected, he kissed her knuckles.

"I heard what happened to you," he said, "and I must say, you appear to have recovered from your ordeal."

She arched a puzzled brow. "My ordeal?"

"Yes." Something resembling distaste flickered in his gray eyes. "I heard you were captured by the Indians."

"Oh, yes," she agreed. "I was. Along with Mary and Henry's daughter, Jessica. But, happily, we were both rescued . . . by our scout."

"So I heard. Lucas McCord, wasn't it?"

"Yes. It was Lucas."

His gaze narrowed. "I'm not surprised he was the one that found you."

"Oh?"

"Who would know the habits of the redskins any better than a half-breed?"

Anne immediately took offense at the lieutenant's words. But before she could form a reprimand, Henry spoke up.

"If you'd be so kind, Lieutenant, I would like to dance with my wife."

"Certainly," Rogers replied. "My pleasure." He took Anne's hand. "If you will permit me?"

Without waiting for a reply, he pulled her out on the dance floor and swirled her around, dipping and swaying to the music.

Unwilling to make a scene, Anne held her silence, determined that when the dance ended, she would distance herself from the young lieutenant who appeared to hold himself in such high regard.

Although the dance floor soon became crowded, Anne knew the moment Lucas entered the room, and her gaze went unerringly to him.

He stood head and shoulders above most men, but it was not that which made him so easy for her to find. Nor was it the fact that he was undoubtedly the most handsome man there, with his coal black hair and tanned skin, and buckskins that stretched tautly over his well-muscled frame. It was a combination of things that set him apart from the others, the way he walked, the unconscious grace of his movements, something that few men ever acquired.

"Are you interested in him?" Lieutenant Rogers' voice was contemptuous.

Anne was jerked back to reality. The music had stopped. The dance was over. She pulled away from him. "That's none of your business."

His gray eyes narrowed. "You *are* interested, aren't you?"

She lifted her chin. "As I've already said, that's none of your business!"

Anne left him standing there and went toward Lucas. She had yet to thank him for coming to her rescue, and she intended to remedy that now. But she had only gone a short way when she felt a hand at her elbow and turned to see the fort commander.

Major Cleveland bowed to her. "Good evening, Miss Farraday."

"Good evening, Major," she murmured. "It's a lovely party."

"Indeed. May I have the pleasure of this dance?"

Damn! Was there a plot to keep her from speaking to Lucas?

Although Anne wanted to refuse the major, she knew it would be rude. So she nodded her agreement and held out her hand. The major proved to be a good dancer, and they twirled around the room, swaying to the music without speaking for several moments.

Then he broke the silence between them. "I have been thinking about your situation, young lady, and wondering how best to help you."

"My situation?"

"Yes. Masters approached me on your behalf. And I must admit the problem had me stumped for a while. There is, of course, no work available here for a young lady of good breeding. So it took some thought on my part. But I believe I have a solution to your problem."

"My problem?" Anne echoed.

"Yes. It's very likely you could find yourself a position as a lady's maid to one of our officers' wives. Mrs. Dowling, for instance, is breeding and would surely appreciate some help. And with so many unmarried men occupying the fort, some man will soon propose marriage and—"

Anne stopped dancing, and her lips tightened. "I'm not looking for a husband," she interrupted shortly. "And I have no interest in becoming a maid either."

"But my dear young woman," he protested. "There is nothing else for you to do here."

"I'm quite aware of that," Anne said stiffly. "But then, I don't intend to remain here. I plan on going on to Oregon with the wagon train."

"That is completely out of the question."

She arched a brow. "I hardly think that's up to you, sir."

"No. But it is up to Masters. And he says you cannot go with them. Not as an unmarried lady."

"Why ever not?"

"Surely that is obvious."

"Not to me."

"According to Masters your presence on the wagon train is causing dissension among the single men. And there is enough trouble to be found on the trail to Oregon without courting more."

Anne increased the distance between them. "Please excuse me, Major," she said stiffly. "I have to find Zeke Masters. We need to discuss this."

"It will do no good," Cleveland warned. "His mind is already made up, and I doubt anything you have to say will change it."

"Nevertheless, I must try."

Anne's heart beat with trepidation as she crossed the ballroom. What would she do if Masters refused to listen to reason? She didn't want to marry one of the travelers. But neither did she want to stay here. Oh, God, what on earth would she do if she remained trapped in the 1800s?

Suddenly, the hairs at her nape prickled, and she turned to see Lucas watching her from across the room.

Anne changed directions again, making her way through the crowd to where Lucas waited. And when she was facing him, she held out a hand. "Dance with me, Lucas."

For a moment it appeared he might refuse; then sud-denly, he relented, taking her hand in his much larger one. His palm was callused, warm, and his touch affected her in ways that no other man's had done.

As they moved across the dance floor, she spoke her thoughts aloud. "Did you know Zeke plans to leave me here?"

"I suspected as much."

"I can't stay here, Lucas!" She searched his gaze for some kind of understanding. "Surely you see that. I wouldn't fit in here. There's nothing here for me. No job. No way to earn my living. No future to be had."

He extended his arms and whirled her around, then pulled her close again. "I'm sure that given time, you could charm one of the troopers here into marrying you."

"I don't want marriage, Lucas!"

"Can't say as I blame you. But you might have no other choice."

"Oh, there are always choices," she said glumly. "The major told me I could probably find work as a maid."

He raised a dark brow. "He's probably right."

"I don't want to be a lady's maid."

The dance ended, and he escorted her off the floor. "You don't want to marry and you don't want to work for a living. Just what do you want to do?"

She turned angry eyes on him. "I don't mind working to earn my keep," she snapped. "In my world, I run a very successful design company. There's no future in being a maid."

"Careful," he warned. "We're attracting attention." He led her toward a secluded corner where the lamplight barely penetrated the shadows before he spoke again. "So you want something with a future?"

"Of course I do. Doesn't everyone?"

"Not necessarily," he replied gruffly. "And if it's a future you're interested in, then what's your objection to marriage?"

"I can't understand why everyone keeps trying to get me married!"

Something flickered in his dark eyes. "Everyone? Who's been trying to get you married?"

"Mary. And the major. And even Masters."

"You'll have to admit it would solve your problem."

"I don't want to marry without love, Lucas. And why should I have to?"

"Love is a myth," he said dryly. "It's only a word designed to confuse and trap men."

"Have you never been in love?"

His eyes became even darker suddenly, shadowed. "I thought I was. Once. But I was only a foolish young man who still believed in dreams."

"You don't believe in dreams now?"

"I believe in facing reality."

"And what is your reality?"

"Land. The good earth. Something the Indians revere. Like my Comanche brothers, I want to roam free . . . to live the life I choose without interference."

"The Comanche. Your mother's people." Mary had explained to Anne about Luke's upbringing.

"And mine. Make no mistake about that, Anne."

"Yet you choose to live apart from them."

"I'm an educated man," he said bitterly, "thanks to my father's brother. My mother's people are gone now, so there was no reason to stay there. Not when I know the Indians cannot win their fight against the white man. In the end they'll be driven off these lands, and they'll either be wiped out or forced to live on a reservation."

"Yes." *Sooner than you think.*

"I tried to make them understand what would happen if they continued to fight," Lucas continued, "but they refused to listen." He sighed heavily. "So I left them to search for my dream."

"And what is that?" she asked softly.

"Land. My dream is to own land. And that's why I'm going to Oregon. Somewhere out there is three hundred and forty acres just waiting for me to claim it."

An idea suddenly occurred to Anne. "Lucas," she asked hesitantly. "Is a woman allowed to claim land in Oregon?"

"I suppose so." His gaze narrowed. "Since a married man is allowed to claim twice as much land." He smiled thinly. "That's the reason you are so much in demand . . . the reason Masters won't let you go on with us."

She thought about that for a moment. "With a few acres of land I could earn my own living," she said musingly. "I know something about farming." Her stay at her grandparents' farm in east Texas would hold her in good stead in this day and age. "If I had my own land, then I wouldn't have to marry anyone."

"But you can't work the land alone." His eyes twinkled suddenly. "Perhaps you could find a man who would be willing to release you when the land was proved . . . and give you a portion of the land for your help."

"Would you do that, Lucas?" she asked quickly. "Would you marry me under those circumstances?"

Lucas was stunned by her proposal, but he quickly recovered. "You don't want to marry me," he said shortly.

"Why not?"

"I'm a half-breed, Miss Farraday."

She laughed at the absurdity of their conversation. "What difference does that make?"

"Anyway, I have no need for a wife."

"No. But you do want the land. And so do I. I wouldn't even take all my portion. A hundred acres would be enough to suit me. You could have the rest."

His eyes glinted. "Two hundred and forty acres for giving you my name? Nothing else?"

"No. Nothing else. It would be a good bargain for you." Silence stretched out between them. "Do you have someone else in mind to play that role in your life, Lucas?"

He studied her for a long moment, taking in her tousled nutmeg curls, her sky blue eyes and nicely rounded figure. If a man wanted a wife, he could do a lot worse than marry Anne Farraday. But he wasn't looking for a wife.

He was going to refuse her. She knew it, could see it in his eyes. "You wanted land," she reminded. "And most of my land would be yours."

"You really mean it, don't you?"

"Yes. I do."

Something undefinable swirled in the depths of his dark eyes, but it disappeared as quickly as it had come. "Let me think on it," he said slowly.

Anne lowered her lids to hide her disappointment. "Please don't take long, Lucas. If you don't want to help me out, then I may be able to strike a bargain with James Odelbert."

The sharpness of his tone caused her eyes to widen. "You shouldn't even consider Odelbert. He would never be satisfied with the marriage you have in mind. He's bound to expect children from a wife."

"That is out of the question!" she snapped. "It would be a marriage in name only. If James wouldn't agree, there's always Thomas Warren."

Lucas could see she was determined. And the thought of her approaching the other men and possibly finding one of them happy with the idea was not the least bit appealing to him.

He squared his shoulders. "You have no need to ask Odelbert anything. Nor Warren either. I've already decided. We will be married as soon as possible."

"And the marriage is to last how long?"

"Until my cabin and barn are built and two people are no longer needed—a year perhaps, maybe less—then you may select your acreage, and we'll start on your house. I will even give you a cow and a pig, and plow your fields the first year. Agreed?"

"Agreed," she said huskily. "A year then, and we will file for a divorce."

"There will be no divorce."

"But you said—"

"An annulment will cause less gossip than a divorce, and leave you with an untarnished reputation."

"Oh, I see." An annulment meant an unconsummated marriage. And he was right. In this day and age it would be less damaging to her reputation than would a divorce. But what about his reputation? Wouldn't an annulment be demeaning for a man?

But then, Lucas was no ordinary man.

"So we are in agreement?" Lucas asked.

"Complete agreement," she replied.

"Very well. There's an army chaplain here tonight. I will make the arrangements for the wedding."

"You mean now?"

"I see no need for delay. There will be too much to do in the next few days to organize a wedding."

"Like what?" she demanded.

His gaze narrowed on her face. "We leave in two days' time, and you'll need to make some purchases. There's supplies to be bought, both food and warm clothing. We can't rely on the other travelers for what we need."

"Of course not."

"Then you agree? We'll be married immediately?"

Immediately. The thought of an immediate marriage was somehow unsettling. Or was it the look in his dark eyes that made her feel that way? Those eyes were narrowed speculatively, as though he wondered about her motives. But why should that be? It was obvious that she had few choices. She was trapped in the past, her own time lost to her, perhaps forever. Since she had no intention of becoming a servant and living in another woman's house, she must, of necessity, wed.

She forced her lips into a smile that didn't quite reach her eyes, swallowed around the knot in her throat and murmured huskily, "Yes, Lucas. I agree."

An intent look flickered in his dark eyes, and he studied her for a long, silent moment. Was he already regretting his decision?

He stepped back, putting more distance between them, and when he spoke, his voice was harsh, grating. "I'll fetch the chaplain."

Then he left her standing there, staring after him, wondering if she had just agreed to something she might live to regret.

Chapter Ten

This was a mistake. A really big mistake.

She had to find Lucas, had to tell him she had changed her mind. "It won't work," she muttered crossly.

Everything was going too fast. She'd had no time to think things through. To consider every aspect of her situation.

Only moments after Lucas had gone to find the chaplain, Mary Baker and Sarah Thurman had arrived. They hustled her into a back room of the chapel and began stripping away her garments and replacing them with the wedding apparel that Sarah herself had used only two months before.

"Hold still, Anne." Mary tugged at the lace veil she was securing atop Anne's head.

But Anne couldn't hold still, couldn't allow this farce of a wedding to proceed. She tugged the veil off. "It won't work," she repeated. "I know it won't."

"Of course it will." Mary retrieved the veil. "Your

short curls won't be a problem. I have enough hairpins to make the veil stay in place.''

"I don't want it to stay in place!"

"I thought you liked my veil." Sarah Thurman's gray eyes looked suddenly hurt. "But if you don't want to wear it, dear, then . . .''

Now look what you've done, a silent voice chided. *Sarah has been nothing but kindness since Mary enlisted her aid, and now you've managed to hurt her feelings.*

Anne smiled to reassure the other woman. "It's a beautiful veil, Sarah. But I—''

"And so it is." Mary went about securing the veil again. "And it looks lovely with your wedding gown." Her admiring eyes took in the fragile creation made of ivory silk satin, cut in a long princess style. The bodice and the long, flowing sleeves were adorned with thousands of hand-sewn seed pearls. "Aren't you lucky, Anne, to be the same size as Sarah?"

"Yes, of course. The gown is very beautiful. And so is the veil. It's just that I'm having second thoughts about this whole thing. It was a stupid idea." She fidgeted beneath Mary's hands as the woman inserted another hairpin into the lace veil.

"It was an excellent idea," Mary said indignantly. "And the veil looks lovely on you." She stepped back to admire her handiwork. "Doesn't it, Sarah?"

"It most certainly does," Sarah replied. "And I have my mother's pin for you to wear. Something old, you know. And the veil is borrowed . . .''

"Everything is borrowed," Anne replied.

"Never you mind about that," Mary said sternly. "Now, we need something new and something blue."

"Mary," Anne protested. "This is really not necessary, you know. It's not a real marriage."

"Why, Anne Farraday," Mary said indignantly. "What a thing to say! Of course it's a real marriage. The chaplain is a man of God, and the chapel is a place of worship. And Lucas McCord is most certainly a real man.'' She winked at Sarah Thurman. ''Wouldn't you say so, Sarah?''

Sarah laughed heartily. ''I certainly would say so. And if it was me, I wouldn't do so much protesting either. Lucas McCord is handsome enough to turn any woman's head. Even mine, and me just married and all.'' She bent closer to Anne. ''Just don't go telling Jimmy that, though. He'd most certainly be jealous.''

Suddenly the door burst open, and Jessie scurried inside. In her right hand she clutched a bundle of flowers. ''I got them, Mrs. Thurman,'' she exclaimed. ''I picked the prettiest flowers I could find.''

''I see you did, Jessica.'' Sarah reached for the yellow and white roses and rearranged them before handing them to Anne. ''Here's your bridal bouquet, Anne, fresh from my flower garden.''

Anne felt her eyes flooding with tears and blinked rapidly to keep them from falling. ''Thank you, Sarah,'' she said huskily. ''It was sweet of you to think of it.''

''You're quite welcome,'' Sarah said gently.

''Now, we still have to find something new and something blue,'' Mary reminded.

''I got a blue ribbon that's new,'' Jessie said quickly, pointing at the wide satin bow that perched atop her curly head.

''Why, so you have,'' her mother exclaimed.

''Oh, but, I couldn't accept it,'' Anne protested.

''But I want you to have it,'' Jessie said, tugging hard at the ribbon. ''Please take it, Miss Farraday.''

She held the ribbon out to Anne, but her mother took it instead.

''Give me the bouquet, Anne,'' Mary said. Then she tied the ribbon around the flowers, leaving both ends hanging for a streamer. ''There,'' she said, thrusting the bouquet toward the reluctant bride. "That makes everything just right." She turned to her daughter again. "Jessica, go outside and let me know when the music starts."

"Music," Anne said faintly.

"One of the soldiers, Randy Travers, volunteered to play his violin," Sarah replied.

Tears stung the back of Anne's eyes as she looked at the two women who had gone to so much trouble to make her wedding so special. "I don't know what to say." She swallowed around a lump in her throat. "I thought it would be just the two of us. Just me and Lucas . . . and the chaplain, of course. I didn't expect all of this."

"All of what, dear?" Mary asked.

"This fuss."

"Pshaw!" Mary exclaimed. "A wedding is supposed to be fuss and frills. And since we don't have many frills, we have to go heavy on the fuss." She straightened the veil and met Anne's gaze. "Now, my Henry offered to give you away, and since you've been staying with us, it seemed only fitting. But if you'd rather have somebody else . . ."

"Oh, no!" Anne quickly protested. "If someone is going to give me away, then I'd rather it be Henry." *Since it can't be my own father. Oh, God, Daddy, I'll never see you again.*

For the first time she felt the pain of her loss.

The door burst open suddenly, and Jessie shoved her head into the room. "Pa's here!" Her blue eyes glowed with excitement. "He's come for the bride. And that soldier, Randy Something, is standin' behind the preacher and—"

"Chaplain, Jessie," Mary interrupted. "He's a chaplain."

"I thought he was a preacher. You said—"

"Go, Jessie," Mary interrupted. "Set yourself down on the first bench in the chapel and wait for me there."

"I'll go with her," Sarah said, following the child from the room.

Mary turned to Anne. "Are you ready, dear?"

No! Anne's mind protested. *Stop this, before it goes any farther!*

But Anne knew she couldn't do that. She was truly in the past, doomed to live out her life among these people. And she must conform to their standards or find herself an outcast.

"Yes," she said shakily. "I'm ready."

Trembling inside, Anne left the room and curled her fingers around Henry Baker's arm. When the wedding march began, she entered the chapel and began the slow march down the aisle.

What in hell are you doing? Lucas asked himself. He had been repeating that same question ever since he had come to the chapel and seen the gathering crowd. It seemed that everyone who attended the dance had left it to come to his wedding.

What was going on anyway? When had he lost control of the situation? He had expected to stand beside Anne while the chaplain read the words that would bind them together and make it possible for him to file on twice the acreage he could have as a single man.

But somehow, the word had gone out. A marriage was taking place. He had been deluged with questions. Nonsensical words. Did he want a formal service? Did he have a ring? Did he want music? Did he want flowers? A groomsman? A bridesmaid? Flower girl?

He'd had no time to reply, to even draw a deep breath, before Mary Baker was beside him, taking charge. And he had been so relieved that he had gone along with her arrangements.

But, dammit! This was too much! He felt like a fool,

standing here waiting in a chapel that was becoming smaller with each passing moment.

His gaze slid around the small room. So many people. James Odelbert was among the crowd, and so was Thomas Warren, a fact that brought Lucas a sense of satisfaction. At least with Anne now beyond their reach, there would be no more tension between the two.

Suddenly, the young soldier who stood nearby tucked his violin beneath his chin and played the first notes of the wedding march.

A stirring among the crowd sent Luke's gaze skimming the chapel, and he caught movement near the door. Then Anne stepped through on the arm of Henry Baker, and Luke's breath caught in his throat.

Anne bit her lower lip in consternation as her gaze slid around the crowded chapel. It appeared that everyone in the fort had decided to attend her wedding. Sarah had already taken her place in the front row, and Mary was sliding in beside her. Anne recognized Zeke Masters and the major, and other faces that she couldn't put a name to.

She looked farther, beyond the benches to the platform where the chaplain waited. Lucas was there. Lucas. The man who would soon be her husband. The man who was marrying her for two hundred and forty acres of land.

Swallowing around the lump that was growing larger with each passing moment, Anne fought against tears as the beautiful strains of the violin washed over her. She had never—even in her wildest dreams—imagined her wedding to be like this.

Anne felt a tug on her arm and realized in that moment that she had stopped walking. On leaden feet she moved forward again until they reached Lucas. His dark gaze swept over her face; then, in silence, he took her hand and placed it in the crook of his arm.

Henry stepped back, leaving Anne feeling as though she had just been abandoned.

One look at Anne's face told Luke that she was on the verge of backing out. He had seen her stop, recognized the look of panic that she couldn't hide. But dammit, the wedding must go on. They had come too far to stop now. He would look an even bigger fool if she ran from him. And that wasn't going to happen. He had already been through that once. With Barbara. And he had vowed never to let it happen again.

He slid a quick look at the woman who stood beside him.

God, she was beautiful.

Forget it, man! an inner voice said. *Barbara was beautiful, too. Even when she was laughing at you.*

The grip on his arm suddenly tightened, and Lucas realized the chaplain was reading the words from the Bible. Luke was only vaguely aware of the chaplain's voice until he heard the sound of his own name.

The chaplain was looking at him, apparently waiting for a response of some kind.

"Uh . . . I do!" Luke said firmly.

There was a tittering among the congregation, making him wonder if he had responded correctly.

The chaplain turned to Anne. "Now, Anne, repeat after me: I, Anne Marie Farraday, take thee, Lucas McCord, to be my wedded husband."

Anne repeated the words in a husky voice, then went on unassisted, "To love, and to honor . . ."

"And obey," the chaplain said softly.

"And . . . and obey," she said, chancing a quick look at Lucas, whose gaze seemed riveted on her.

"Till death do you part," the chaplain said.

"Till death do you . . . uh, do us part," she whispered shakily.

Oh, God, how could she promise such a thing, and then casually break that promise when the time came.

It's not like you're betraying him, an inner voice chided. *He agreed to the terms. It's what he wanted.*

"The ring, Lucas."

Anne was surprised when Lucas reached in his pocket and withdrew a ring. A moment later the ring embraced her finger.

"I now pronounce you man and wife," the chaplain said, smiling widely at them. "You may kiss your bride, Luke."

Anne's eyes widened in consternation as she stared up at her new husband. He looked like a man who was about to refuse, regardless of the watching crowd. But then, he gripped her shoulders, and the warmth of him radiated through the wedding gown and caressed her flesh. She licked lips that had suddenly gone dry at the same moment his head dipped down and his mouth covered hers.

Lucas felt the shock clear to the toes of his leather boots as he tasted the sweet warmth of her velvet tongue against his mouth. His arms tightened around her, and he slid his tongue around her mouth, tracing the outline of her lips.

Anne uttered a gasp as a tiny, shivery feeling uncurled in the pit of her stomach. Lucas was quick to take advantage, sliding his tongue inside her mouth to deepen the kiss.

Silk and satin, and the warmth of velvet. No other words could describe the feel of her against him.

Somebody cleared their throat. Loudly. Lucas found the noise intrusive, as was the laughter that quickly followed.

Forcing himself back to reality, Lucas became slowly

aware of his circumstances. He lifted his head, his gaze never leaving Anne, who clung to him as though she could no longer stand alone.

There was laughter in the chaplain's voice when he spoke. "I hate to tell you this, Lucas, but the ladies got together a reception, and they're expecting the both of you to attend."

Luke swore inwardly. He wanted nothing more than to carry his wife off to the nearest bed, but he had already made a big enough fool of himself. He forced his lips to curl into a smile as he was congratulated by his fellow travelers on his marriage.

He lost sight of Anne during the festivities, and finally, when he could stand it no longer, he sought out Mary and politely thanked her for her help. He had already turned to leave when her words stopped him cold.

"There's no need to go back to the wagon train tonight, Lucas. The major has arranged for you and Anne to spend the night in his quarters."

Spend the night with Anne? Although he felt stunned at the suggestion, Luke's feelings remained hidden, his face impassive. "That's not necessary, Mary. I'll just thank the major and go on—"

"Of course it's necessary," Mary chided. "You and Anne need some time alone. And your wagon is no place for any kind of privacy, Luke. Now, you just go on to the major's quarters. I sent Anne along a few minutes ago. She was looking kind of pale, and I knew she'd need a few minutes to change into her night wear."

"But, Mary," Lucas protested. "I didn't expect . . ."

"I know you didn't expect it, Lucas. You men don't usually think about what a woman needs on her wedding night. It was the reason we arranged it for you. A new bride needs time alone with her husband. And the major was perfectly willing to give up his quarters. Him being a single man and all, it was no real hardship for him. Now, you run along . . . Anne will be waiting for you.''

Anne stood alone in the major's quarters, staring at the nightgown Sarah had given her. It was a lovely garment, white, silky, and edged with the finest lace. It had been fashioned for lovers.

But how could she wear such a garment when she would be sharing a room with Lucas? It was an impossible situation. But she had no choice. She would either sleep in the nightgown or in the nude, because she had been brought here in her wedding gown.

If only the women hadn't insisted. She and Lucas could have gone back to his wagon, and nobody would have known about their sleeping arrangements.

No use crying over their situation, though. They had no choice except to go along with the arrangements that had already been made.

And the setup wasn't really so bad. She could use the bed, and Lucas could sleep on the floor.

With the sleeping arrangements settled to her satisfaction, Anne removed her wedding apparel and draped the garments carefully over a chair, hoping they wouldn't wrinkle too badly overnight.

She donned the nightgown and smoothed it down her body, noticing as she did that it clung to her curves like a second skin.

But that need not concern her, she knew. Not if she was already in bed when Lucas arrived.

Perhaps she should turn down the lamp, too.

Suiting thought to action, Anne reached for the lamp, then was distracted by a glitter of gold. Her ring. She brought it closer to examine it, something she'd had no chance to do earlier. Two hearts entwined on a circle of gold. How unusual.

Where did Lucas find such a romantic ring? And why? There's no love between us.

A knock sounded on the door, and she answered without thinking. "Yes?"

The door opened, and Lucas walked in.

Chapter Eleven

Lucas came to an abrupt halt, his body blocking the entrance as his narrowed gaze raked Anne with a look so hot it could have melted steel.

Her heartbeat accelerated, and a shiver coursed through Anne, beginning at the taut buds on her breasts and sweeping down to her toes. "Lucas." His name was a husky whisper on her lips.

"Go on, Luke," urged a laughing male voice from somewhere behind him. "Your bride is anxiously waiting for your manly attention."

Another male voice growled. "Judging from that kiss he gave her, I'd say old Luke is just as anxious as his bride."

Lucas stepped farther into the room and closed the door with a quick snap, shutting out the sound of raucous male laughter. He continued to watch her in silence, his body tense, his stance rigid, his face totally expressionless, except for his eyes which scorched her as they slowly traveled down the length of her.

The few times Anne had allowed herself to wonder about her wedding night, she had never imagined anything like this. Nor had she imagined a man like Lucas as her husband.

She felt heat washing over her and wished for a thick flannel nightgown to cover her body, instead of the thin, silky garment that clung like a lover's kiss to her curves, leaving little to the imagination.

"Lucas." Anne swallowed hard. "I . . . this wasn't supposed to happen."

"No," he agreed huskily. "It wasn't." His gaze lingered overlong on her bosom, where the fabric stretched taut against her swollen nipples, then slowly moved upward again to lock with hers.

She moistened suddenly dry lips with the tip of her tongue and saw his body tauten. She backed away, feeling suddenly threatened. "I-I thought we would be going back to the wagon train."

Lucas moved suddenly, and Anne felt so intimidated that she backed quickly away again. Her knees struck the side of the mattress, making further retreat impossible.

"We can't go back now, Anne," he said softly. "We have no choice except to stay here . . . together."

"But if we told them about the agreement . . . then maybe they would—"

"No!" he said shortly. "That's between the two of us, and it stays that way as long as we're together."

"But why, Lucas?" she protested. "They surely don't believe we married for love. We've only known each other for a matter of days."

He gripped her shoulders tightly. "We keep the agreement to ourselves, Anne," he said harshly.

"Lucas." Her voice was hesitant. "You do intend to honor our agreement, don't you?"

He released her abruptly, looking past her to the bed. "Which side do you want to sleep on?"

"You didn't answer me!"

"Which side, Anne?"

She flatted her lips. "Both sides," she snapped.

His heated gaze met hers. "Both sides?"

"Yes. If we must share the room, then you can sleep on the floor. There's enough extra blankets to make a pallet."

"Then, use them," he replied. "I'll take the bed."

Her gaze shifted to the bed that was covered with a colorful patchwork quilt. The mattress was springy, soft, probably filled with feathers. Her expression was wistful when she looked at Luke again.

"I have no objection to sharing it," he said mildly. "But only if you'll keep to your side of the bed."

Anne stiffened with indignation. "What, exactly, are you suggesting?"

He shrugged his massive shoulders, his expression carefully blank. "You're the one that's so worried about us sleeping together. I thought you might be afraid you couldn't keep your hands to yourself."

"Lucas McCord! You're no gentleman!"

"Never said I was. But I haven't slept on a bed for months. and I intend to remedy that tonight."

Without another word Lucas strode to the far side of the bed and pulled his buckskin shirt over his head.

"What are you doing?" she gasped.

"What does it look like?"

He unbuckled his gun belt and hung it over a nearby chair. Then his fingers went to the fastening on his britches.

"Don't! Please!"

His fingers stilled. "You'd rather have the light off?" Without waiting for a reply, he leaned over and blew out the lamp, leaving the room in shadows.

The mattress dipped as Lucas sat down. A heavy thud, followed by another, told her he had removed his boots.

Damn his ornery hide! He intended to deprive her of a soft bed. Well, she wouldn't stand for it!

Yanking back the covers, Anne slid between the crisp, linen sheets and stretched out as close to the edge of the mattress as she could possibly get without falling off. Then she pulled the quilt up over her shoulders and closed her eyes.

For a moment there was utter silence, as though she had surprised Luke with her actions. Then she heard the soft swish of clothing being discarded and felt the movement of covers being lifted. Then came a sigh of pure pleasure as he stretched his long length out on the mattress.

Anne held her breath, waiting for him to make his move. Her body was tense, her muscles coiled tight, ready to spring into action at a moment's notice should it become necessary. But as long moments passed, so did her tension, and soon, his even breathing told her she needn't worry longer. Lucas had fallen asleep.

Anne woke slowly, becoming aware of an incredible warmth surrounding her. She smiled, rubbing her skin sensuously against the soft, wooly blanket beneath her cheek.

She sighed with pure pleasure. It was wonderful to wake up in a feather bed, covered by a soft wool. . . .

Anne frowned. Her blanket felt different somehow, more like silk than wool. She opened sleep-drugged eyes and found herself looking at the bare, muscled chest that supported her.

"Good morning," a husky voice rumbled from somewhere above her head.

Anne sucked in a sharp breath as realization set in. She was in bed with Lucas. On *his* side of the bed. And she was curled against his chest. Her cheeks were hot as she lifted her eyes to find him watching her.

Her blush deepened at the look in his slumberous ebony eyes. "Oh, God, Lucas. I'm sorry." She pushed at his chest, trying to put some distance between them, but the action only served to bring her lower body closer against his. "I didn't mean to . . ."

"Don't apologize." His smile was slow and sensual, his breath warm against her face. "I like the feel of you in my arms." One hand lifted to stroke her nutmeg curls. "Your hair feels like pure silk."

Anne knew she should get out of bed, but his touch was so warm, so gentle. Anyway, she needed a few minutes to recover her senses.

He smoothed his palm down her back, and Anne felt herself melting against him, like butter beneath a flame. His hands continued the gentle movement, following the curve of her back, down to her hips, stroking softly, as though he was caressing a big tabby cat.

When his palm found the curve of her buttocks, her body arched against his lean hardness, and her fingers tangled in the thickness of his dark hair.

"Lucas," she murmured in unconscious longing. She wanted him to kiss her, ached to feel his mouth against hers.

Anne licked her lips, and Lucas' breath quickened.

I should never have kissed her.

He wanted to do it again, needed it as badly as a thirsty man needed water. And from the expression on her face, he was almost certain that she would have no objection.

Slowly, as though testing the waters, he lowered his head, giving her plenty of time to draw back if she so desired.

Her eyelids lowered, and she pressed taut nipples against his hard chest. That was all it took to make his manhood stand up and salute.

Uttering a low growl, he took her mouth, covering it

with hard possession. Anne shuddered lightly, then made a sound of pure pleasure.

Lucas had never known such pleasure could be had from a kiss. His heartbeat quickened; blood rushed through his veins, thundering in his eardrums. And his body, Lord, his body was hard, pulsing madly, demanding release.

Slow down. You're moving too fast.

Lucas wanted to ignore the silent warning, but knew he must not. He eased his hold and broke the kiss, tracing the contours of her mouth with the tip of his tongue.

Anne moaned softly and urged him closer again. He teased her lips apart and caressed the smoothness of her teeth, then probed farther into the delicious warmth beyond, savoring the taste of her as if she were aged wine.

She was assailed by delicious shudders that skittered through her as Lucas continued to woo her with his tongue. His right hand blazed a fiery trail as it found the curve of her breast and moved on to caress her nipple.

Anne's harsh breathing was matched by Luke's by the time he lifted his head and met her passion-glazed eyes. She couldn't speak, could only stare at him with unconscious longing. Her fingertips explored his unshaven face, rough with a new growth of whiskers. They must have scratched her softer skin, but she had no memory of it, only knew that she had reveled in the taste of his mouth, the crisp, clean scent of his skin, the sureness of his touch.

Lucas breathed in the sweet scent of her, folding her submissive body even closer, as her femininity branded him as surely as a hot branding iron would have done.

His lips found hers again, hard and demanding, his tongue a hot velvet predator that plundered the lush sweetness of her mouth. His rough hands moved over her, gliding over her rounded curves as he sought to conquer every enticing inch of skin that made her a woman.

Anne was almost mindless with pleasure, aching with

need. Lucas had set her afire. So easily. And the flames were licking over her, through her, penetrating deeply until they reached the apex of her desire.

She had no thought for agreements, no mind to stop what was happening between them. She could only ride the currents of desire, the pulsating sensations that reached the core of her sexuality.

Luke's lower body was demanding satisfaction, and he was experienced enough to know that Anne had become lost in physical pleasure. Her throaty moans of aroused abandon intoxicated him even more, urging him to take her without delay.

But there was that damned agreement standing in the way. He should never have agreed to such a thing. Anne was a beautiful woman with a lush body. Too lush. And she was his wife. He had a legal right to assuage his hunger, to quench the fire that was threatening to consume him.

Whoa, Lucas, a silent voice warned. *Stop what you're doing. You can't consummate the marriage.*

Lucas ignored the voice. His brain had turned to mush and his body had taken command. And that same body was howling, *To hell with the agreement!* Words meant nothing when his desires were so overwhelming.

And why should he fight those desires anyway? Who would be hurt if he surrendered to their demands? It was plain as day that Anne wanted him as much as he wanted her!

Realizing he could fight no more, he uttered a throaty growl and gave in to the desperate yearning. He shifted her closer until his throbbing heat fitted against the soft mound that promised pleasure beyond bearing.

Luke's low growl acted like an aphrodisiac on Anne, intensifying her own desire. She urged him closer, moving her hips with a frantic need that completely overwhelmed caution.

Then, suddenly, like a douse of cold water, a knock sounded on the door.

"Luke," a male voice called. "Time to get moving."

Lucas froze, his expression warring between frustration and bewildered confusion.

Anne's eyes widened with horror as realization struck her. "Oh, God!" she cried. "What are you doing?" She pushed frantically at him, struggling to free herself from his embrace.

His expression became hard, his gaze cold. "What am *I* doing? What in hell were *you* doing? You're the one that crawled in my arms during the night. This is *my* side of the bed we're on."

"Damn you to hell!"

Luke's eyes were hard. "Lady, I've already been there, and once was enough." He shoved off the bed and snatched up his britches, sliding into them quickly.

"Lucas! Come on!" the voice called again. Louder this time.

"I'm coming," Lucas growled. "Just hold your horses."

Fastening up his britches, he reached for his shirt and jerked it over his head. Then he strode across the room and yanked open the door.

Anne shrank against the mattress, pulling the quilt up to her neck with a grip so tight her knuckles showed white. But she needn't have worried. Lucas was blocking the opening with his large frame.

"Just give us a few minutes," Luke told whoever stood outside the door. "We're just waking up."

"Sure thing," the unseen man replied cheerfully.

Closing the door with a sharp snap, Lucas turned a hard look on Anne. "Don't read anything into what just happened. When a man wakes up with a woman in his arms, his body just naturally takes over."

Tears blurred Anne's vision, and she turned away to

hide the pain his words caused. Not soon enough, though, to stop a tear from escaping. It left a trail of moisture behind as it slid down her paper white cheek.

Lucas felt an ache in his chest and fought the urge to take her in his arms. When he spoke, his voice was harsh. "Get dressed, Anne. We have supplies to buy before we go back to the wagon train."

"I'll dress after you leave the room."

"Are you trying to convince me you're feeling shy?"

"I'm not trying to convince you of anything," she said shortly. "But I would like some privacy . . . if you don't mind."

"Of course." He pulled on his socks and boots, and buckled on his gun belt. Then he crossed the room and opened the door. "You have exactly ten minutes to dress," he growled. "Then I'll expect you downstairs."

Anne glared at the door he had closed behind him. She wanted to indulge in a temper tantrum, but knew she had no time to waste on anger.

Her feet had already touched the cold floor when she remembered her clothing had been taken away to be laundered.

Gathering the quilt around her shoulders, she opened the door several inches and peeped through. Her clothing was there, freshly washed and ironed, hanging on a peg beside the door as Mary had promised.

She dressed hurriedly, then quickly made the bed and stuffed the nightgown into her reticule.

Then she went downstairs to join her husband.

Chapter Twelve

Lucas felt a need to vent his rage, and it showed when he met Hawk entering the major's parlor with old Grizzly Barnes. "What are you doing here?" he demanded. "You're supposed to be with the herd!"

"Now, wait one damned minute, son," Grizzly growled. "Ain't no call to jump down Hawk's throat. Masters sent him here for a purpose."

"Yeah? And what was that?"

Although Hawk's face was without expression, there was a glint of humor in his eyes. "You have a hard night, Luke?"

Luke's hands clenched into fists, and he took a step forward.

Hawk laughed, holding his hands up and stepping out of reach. "What's the matter, Lucas? Didn't the wedding night go like you expected?"

"Shut up, Hawk," Luke growled. "And wipe that grin off your face before I do it for you."

"You're dead serious, aren't you?" Hawk's eyes were puzzled.

"You're damn right I am."

"Why did you marry her, Luke?"

"Because I—"

Lucas stopped short as the front door opened suddenly and the major walked in.

"There you are," Major Cleveland said heartily. "I wondered if you two were up yet. Thought you might be ready for some breakfast." His gaze swept the room, then returned to the scout. "Where is your lovely wife?"

"She's dressing. Ought to be down in a minute. I expect she would appreciate breakfast. As for me, though, I'm afraid I'll have to skip it. Too much to do before we leave. I'll just grab a cup of coffee at the mess hall and get on with it. I'd appreciate it if you would tell Miss . . . uh, my wife, to meet me at the sutler's store. We need to buy more supplies."

"Certainly."

After thanking the major for his hospitality, and trying to sound as though he meant the words he was mouthing, Lucas, followed closely by Hawk and Grizzly, left the house with ground-eating strides. He hoped, by putting distance between himself and his bride, he could rid himself of the frustration that continued to eat at him.

And the two men who had followed him, hoping for explanations, were doomed to disappointment. What had happened between Lucas and his bride would stay there. Between the two of them.

He had already done enough in the name of pride. And the sight of the single tear streaking down her face would stay in his memory, a reminder that nothing good could come of this marriage. Nothing but the land.

The land. He must hold on to that thought. He had married for the land. No other reason. They had both agreed. And when they had the land, it would be over. That was the way he wanted it.

So why in hell did he feel so alone?

The sutler's store stocked more goods than Anne had ever supposed they would. Every inch of wall space was covered with merchandise: harnesses, traps, pots, skillets, and rifles, and other items too numerous to name.

Tables were piled high with goods. Bolts of material were stacked next to men's clothing. Ribbons and scented soaps were piled together with army boots and gun belts. Jugs of sorghum stood on the floor next to barrels containing nails, rice, beans and flour.

The clerk was a middle-aged man, wearing a blue uniform to which a sergeant's patch had been applied. He leaned against the counter and watched Anne as she wound her way through the multitude of supplies.

"Help you, ma'am?" he asked gruffly.

"I need some supplies," she said quietly. "But I'm not sure about what I need or how much."

"You with the wagon train camped outside the fort?"

"Yes."

"Headed for Oregon Territory?"

"Yes."

"Then, I 'spect you better concentrate on replenishing what you already got."

"That's the problem," she said ruefully. "I don't know what we have." She went on to explain. "I just married last night, and my husband—"

"Well, glory be," he exclaimed, coming around the counter to examine her closely. "You must be the little lady that ever'body's talking about." He smiled widely at her. "And now I can see what they meant."

She stiffened. "I beg your pardon."

"Not meaning any dishonor, ma'am." He scratched

his graying head. "Folks is just talking about how you could put the sun and moon to shame. And dang me if they ain't plumb right."

"Why, thank you . . . I think."

"Now I see what your trouble is, and I'm just the man who can help you out."

"You can?"

"Da—" He caught himself. "Uh, dang right, I can. You married Lucas McCord, and he's a bachelor, ma'am, and as such, he won't be carrying any frills along with him. So you gotta buy the frills and folderols as well as replenish the supplies he brought along with him."

"Oh, uh, I don't think Lucas meant me to buy any frills," she said quickly. She was almost certain he wouldn't expect her to spend his money that way. "I'm not sure how much money we have to work with, so I'll just stick with the usual stuff. Like, um . . ." She looked around the room, spied a barrel of flour, and went on, "The flour! I'm almost positive we're going to need more of that. And bacon!" The women seemed to cook a lot of bacon, so it was almost a certainty they would need some. "You know the kind I mean, don't you. It's salty and sliced real thick. And let me think . . ." She stuck her forefinger in her mouth and nibbled on the nail for a minute. "Biscuits," she said abruptly. "I'll be making biscuits, so we'll need some baking powders, and some—"

"Got no baking powders. Got baking soda, though."

"That will do, then. And we'll need shortening for the bread. No! That's not what they use. Lard! We'll need some lard. And some beans. Lots of beans. And . . ." *What else would Mary buy?*

The thought had no more occurred, than Mary opened the door and walked in.

"Anne," she said, hurrying over. "Lucas told me you'd be here. He thought you might need some help."

"Oh, Mary, thank goodness you've come!" Anne exclaimed. "I don't know what to buy."

Mary slapped her own supply list down on the counter. "Just double whatever is there," she told the sergeant. "And while you're filling the orders, we'll look at some female fripperies."

"Oh, no," Anne said quickly. "I can make do with my jeans and the dress you so kindly gave me."

"No. You can't either." Mary's expression was stern. "You're a married woman now, and your husband will expect you to make him proud. Anyway, you're going to need some heavy clothes to keep you warm next winter."

Anne was aware of that fact, yet she had no idea of Luke's finances and was reluctant to use the money on herself. But Mary was insistent. A heavy coat was added to the pile, as well as a bolt of fabric, several spools of thread and a package of needles.

Stacking the dry goods near the counter, Anne turned to Mary, who stood just behind her. "I hope Lucas doesn't think I've gone overboard with—" She broke off with a soft cry as she spied a rocking chair that had escaped her notice, placed as it was behind several barrels of nails.

"Oh, look, Mary," she exclaimed, hurrying toward the chair. "Isn't it the most beautiful rocking chair you ever saw?"

Tears stung her eyelids as she ran a caressing hand over the smooth, unvarnished wood. It was identical to the chair that adorned her grandmother's parlor, with the slat back and arm supports. The maple and oak that formed the chair were designed to last for centuries.

"Want me to add it to the tally?" the sergeant asked.

"Oh, no." Anne's voice softened. "I was just admiring it. My grandmother used to have one just like it. She made cushions for the seat and back."

While they were still admiring the rocker, the doorbell jangled. Anne looked up to see Lucas entering the store.

His gaze went straight to Anne. "Are you done?"

"Yes. I'm finished." She hurried to the counter. "I hope I haven't overdone it."

He looked with approval at the stack of supplies, then added several packages of seed, a bridle and several boxes of ammunition. "How much?" he asked the sergeant.

The sergeant tallied up and gave Lucas the total, then said, "The little lady was taken with that rocker over yonder, Lucas. You want me to include it?"

"No," Anne said quickly, hoping Lucas wouldn't notice the flush of embarrassment that suddenly stained her cheeks. "It's too much."

She needn't have worried, though. He paid her no attention, nor did he even glance at the rocker in question as he paid the sergeant.

"Sure you don't want the rocker?" the sergeant persisted.

Lucas looked at Anne then, but she quickly shook her head. "No."

"Good enough, then. We already have a load." He turned away abruptly, stooping to heft a fifty-pound sack of flour to his shoulders. "The wagon's outside, Anne. You can bring some of the smaller parcels along."

As Anne filled her arms with supplies, she noticed Mary lingering beside the rocking chair.

"Such a shame about the rocker," Mary murmured. "Especially since your grandma had one like it. That kinda made it special somehow."

Anne wished she had never noticed the rocking chair, much less mentioned its likeness to the one in her grandmother's parlor.

She left the store and stacked her parcels neatly on the wagon, even though she knew Lucas would more than likely rearrange everything before he was done. While she finished stacking them, Lucas entered the store again and returned with two barrels, one over each shoulder.

Setting them down, he stopped her from reentering the store with a hand on her forearm.

"That's all the small stuff." Wood scraped against wood as he lifted the barrels into the wagon. "We'll be leaving soon as I'm done, so if you've got any good-byes or thank yous to say, best get them done with now."

"I hadn't really thought about it, but I guess I should thank Sarah Thurman for her help with the wedding." She eyed the loaded wagon. "Are you sure you don't need any more help?"

He grunted. "Go on," he said.

Anne left him to search for Sarah. When she had finished thanking the lieutenant's wife, and they had hugged each other and said their good-byes, Anne returned to the wagon to wait for Lucas. He was just leaving the store with the rocker she had admired over one shoulder.

"Lucas?" She eyed the rocker, then met his eyes. "I thought you said . . ."

"Man can change his mind, can't he?"

Anne couldn't speak around the lump that had lodged in her throat. And despite her efforts at control, tears blurred her vision.

Fool, she silently chided herself. *It's just a chair. Nothing to get so emotional about.*

But it wasn't really the chair that caused her tears, Anne realized. It was the fact that Lucas obviously cared enough about her feelings to buy the rocker for her.

"That's the last of it," he said, examining the knots that would keep the chair secured. "Now climb up on that wagon seat and we'll head on out."

"What about Mary?"

"Henry's coming to pick her up. They'll need to load their supplies, but I expect they won't be too far behind us."

Anne wondered how she was supposed to climb onto the high seat. But before she could figure it out, Lucas picked her up and sat her atop the high perch. Then he climbed aboard himself and snapped the whip in the air above the mules. "Ho, mules," he yelled. "Get along there."

The wagon wheels began to turn, and the wagon lurched, then moved slowly forward, across the parade ground and through the open gates. Soon they were leaving the fort behind.

The days passed quickly now, since Anne was in charge of driving the supply wagon now that Jules Turner was no longer with the wagon train. The first day Lucas had spent with her, teaching her to handle the mules. And, although he rarely spoke, except to give her instructions, she began to look forward to the hours they spent together.

He never showed, by deed or look, that he was tempted by her nearness. And that fact piqued her. She was always aware of his presence, conscious of his manly scent, the warmth of his body as he sat beside her on the high wagon seat and taught her how to keep the mules moving when they would have balked.

Just the thought of the kisses he had bestowed upon her was enough to set her body tingling. And she thought about that morning often, even though he had apparently put it from his mind.

As suddenly as it had begun, their time together was gone. Lucas decided she had learned enough to handle the team and went back to scouting, a job he had delegated to his friend, Hawk, since leaving the fort.

Although Anne didn't see Lucas for several days, Hawk made a habit of stopping by each night to keep her company.

It was Hawk who had returned from a scouting trip and told her that Luke would be gone for several days, searching the trail for signs of trouble.

"Is he worried about something?"

"No," Hawk replied. "But a man can't be too careful out here."

Tired of eating alone, Anne invited Hawk to eat with her. He made such a fuss over her biscuits that it soon became a habit. But when it was time for bed, she was left alone. And in those moments before sleep came, she thought about what might have been.

It was a week later when she woke to the smell of freshly made coffee. She breathed in the scent and smiled. It could only be Mary, waking her with an early morning cup, as she had done once before.

"Good morning, Mary," Anne said cheerfully, pushing aside the quilt that covered her, and stretching her arms wide. "You're going to spoil me if you keep doing things like this."

"Doing things like what?" drawled a purely male voice from close by.

"Lucas!" she exclaimed, a smile curling her lips. She had no thought of hiding her pleasure at seeing him. "When did you get back?"

"Late last night." He studied her from beneath hooded eyes. "You seem mighty cheerful this morning."

"I feel wonderful." *You look wonderful,* she thought. "I must have had a good night's sleep."

"Yeah. You must have. Too bad I can't say the same for myself."

He had slept better on the trail, and he'd had damned little sleep then. But when he had returned and seen her sleeping so peacefully, he had wanted to crawl in the bedroll beside her and do what he had promised himself he wouldn't do. He couldn't make love to her . . . not if they were going to get an annulment. And the thought of being tied for life to a woman . . . any woman . . . was enough to put a damper on his passion.

"Drink your coffee," he said, holding out the cup he

had poured for her. "Then you can rustle up some grub while I shave these whiskers off my face."

Pouring hot water into the wash pan, he turned his attention to shaving.

Anne sipped her coffee while her husband shaved, stroking his face carefully with the straight razor. She had never imagined shaving could be so erotic.

Suddenly, he looked up and caught her watching him. "Something wrong?" he asked.

"You . . . you missed some soap," she replied.

"Where?"

She picked up the towel and wiped away the dab of soap, then stepped back with a smile. "There. It's gone now."

"Thank you," he said huskily. "A man could get used to having a wife real easy."

At the heated look in his eyes, she backed hastily away, remembering how near they had come to breaking their agreement the morning after they were married.

Would it be so awful if the agreement was broken? a silent voice asked.

Yes, common sense replied. *Lucas made it plain that he needs no wife, nor does he want one. He wants the land. And when the necessary building and planting is done, he expects you to go your own way.*

And when she went, she had no intention of leaving her heart behind.

"Something wrong?" he asked again.

She shook her head, her tousled nutmeg curls bouncing as she did so, then turned away so he wouldn't guess her thoughts.

"Anne."

She looked back at him. He was watching her with hooded eyes. "Are you sure there's nothing wrong?"

"Of course not," Anne replied quickly. "I just realized I was wasting time. I haven't even started breakfast yet, and before I finish the morning chores, Zeke Masters will be riding alongside the wagons, hollering at anybody who's not moving along fast enough.'' She grimaced. ''I swear that man has eyes like a hawk. If I make a wrong move, he's right there beside me.''

''Zeke's all right. A good wagon master who knows his business.''

''I agree. He is a good wagon master.'' She brushed a lock of hair aside and summoned up a quick smile. ''Breakfast won't take long, so if you've got anything else to do before then, you'd best hop to it.''

He reached for his gun belt and buckled it on. ''I'll report to Masters while you're making breakfast. Shouldn't take long, though. Nothing much to report.''

''That's good, isn't it?''

''Damn straight.''

Luke made his report to Masters, then joined Anne for breakfast. He wanted to linger awhile, yet realized it would be impossible. Masters would be along soon, making sure everything was in order before they went on their way.

Albeit reluctantly, he saddled up and nodded to Anne, refusing to claim the lips that were so damned kissable.

Those same lips curved in a half smile as she watched him leave, and as he rode away, he looked back and saw her hand drop to her side.

Had she been waving at him?

For some reason that thought pleased him.

His wife, waving good-bye, her gaze never leaving him until he was out of sight.

There was a time when he had dreamed of such things. A wife standing in the doorway, waving good-bye as he rode out to tend stock.

But dreams were for children. They had a way of making a man vulnerable.

Lucas had learned that the hard way.

Chapter Thirteen

The wagon train moved slowly through the valley, the travelers unaware of the lone horseman who sat motionless on a distant peak.

A breeze teased the man's long hair, blowing it softly against his naked chest, but his black eyes never wavered from the wagon train.

Rawhide tassels and squirrels' tails adorned the lance that thrust skyward from his right hand. Arrows fletched with owl feathers and tipped with carved stone filled the quiver he wore across his back. The arrows had been fashioned by his own hand, designed especially to fit the short bow slung across his left shoulder.

Although wearing only the loincloth that protected his manhood, buckskin leggings and moccasins, Chase the Wind barely felt the wind's cold embrace. He was used to it, had been riding these ridges for many moons, watching as the white-eyes continued to invade Indian lands.

But it could not be allowed to continue.

The council must be made to listen this time.

His face was devoid of expression, giving no sign of the rage that simmered just below the surface. The only outward sign of emotion was his whitened knuckles as his hand tightened around the lance he carried.

His gaze never wavered from the long line of wagons as he measured its length. A large one, more wagons than he had ever seen together at one time. It was a clear violation of the peace agreement.

The elders were wrong.

There could never be peace between the People and the white-eyes. The generals—the ones they called the Great White Fathers who sat in a place called Washington—made promises. Their emissaries, the Yellow Legs, signed peace treaties, promising to limit the flow of immigrants through Sioux land. But before the ink had time to dry, they organized more wagon trains.

It had to be stopped.

Now! Before there were too many to fight.

Chase the Wind reined his pony, a mountain-bred mustang, around and sent it down the steep slope. He would return to the village, would approach the council again. And if they did not agree to act, then he would do so himself.

He was not without followers. There were many others who thought as he did. Others who had cause to hate the false-tongued palefaces.

As he descended the slope, his lips curled in a grim smile. The white fathers in Washington would soon learn the Sioux were not fools. And they would come to regret their actions.

Chase the Wind would make sure of that.

Zeke Masters had been riding point when he saw the rider coming in fast. He reined in his mount and raised his hand to shade his eyes against the glare as he studied the rider's horse.

It was a big animal. At least sixteen hands high.

"Must be Lucas," he muttered. "That has to be his horse. And there must be something wrong, the way he's riding that dun."

A feeling of dread settled over Masters as he spurred his mount forward to meet the man who had hired on as scout. The dun was lathered from having been ridden so hard, and as the two men reined up beside each other, dust boiled up and settled on the dun's sweat-dampened hide.

Masters pushed back the brim of his hat, his narrowed gaze taking in the dun's lathered condition. "What's wrong, Lucas?"

Lucas told the wagon master about the Sioux warrior he had seen watching the wagon train.

"One warrior?"

"Yeah."

Zeke frowned. "I don't see the problem."

"He rode straight to his village."

"Might not mean nothing. We have a peace treaty with the Sioux."

"Which has already been broken. By both sides."

"You saw the village?"

"Yeah. I was between him and the village. I saw where he was headed and crossed the mountains to take a look." His gaze went past Masters' shoulder, toward the upper end of the valley, and in his mind's eye, he saw the village again. It had been a large one, more than a hundred dwellings.

"How many tepees?" Masters asked.

"More than a hundred."

Masters whistled through his teeth. "Which means there could be twice that many hotheaded warriors, primed and ready to stop us."

"Yeah."

"They could do some serious damage . . . if they've a mind to."

"Yeah," Lucas said again.

"How far is that village?"

"Twenty, twenty-five miles. Maybe less."

"Where?"

"Straight ahead."

"Gawdamighty!" Masters exclaimed. "All they have to do is wait for us to come to them!" He rubbed the bridge of his nose. "What are we gonna do, Lucas?"

"We leave the valley now."

"Now?" Zeke looked at the mountains, rising on both sides of them. "We'd be dead meat if we're caught climbing the mountain." His gaze returned to Lucas. "We might be safer in the valley, where we can move faster . . ."

"You know the wagon train could never outrun their mustangs."

"The wagons won't go no faster on the mountain, Lucas."

"No. But we can defend them better. With men riding the ridge on three sides, the Sioux would have a hard time surprising us. And a few men could keep them from climbing the slope after us."

Masters scratched his nose again. "Sounds logical. But it ain't gonna be easy riding those mountains."

"There's a plateau beyond that rise." Luke pointed at a mound rising in the northwest. "No water, though. You'll be making a dry camp up there."

"Better a dry camp than losing scalps," Masters growled.

Lucas narrowed his eyes on the wagons, trying to identify his own, knowing that Anne would be driving the mules. But the distance was too great, and there was nothing to set his own wagon apart from the rest.

"She's managing the team like a trooper," Masters

said, guessing the direction of the other man's thoughts. "Nary a complaint neither. That's one fine lady you married, Luke. A lady any man would be proud of."

Luke made no reply to the other man's praise, nor was one expected. "I'll ride on ahead," he said grimly. "If there's trouble, I'll fire off three shots."

Masters nodded. "Ride careful," he said, then reined his mount back toward the wagons that had never paused in their slow journey across the valley.

The terrain had changed drastically since morning. The river valley was narrower, the mountains closing in around it. And each passing mile saw the wagon train on higher ground.

The sun was halfway across the sky when the wagon ahead of Anne stopped rolling.

"Whoa, mules!" she shouted, pulling hard on the reins to stop the stubborn creatures from plowing into the other wagon.

Her arms ached with the strain of driving the mules, and the sun was hot against her skin. She wondered about the delay, yet was quick to take advantage, knowing they might move again at a moment's notice.

Reaching for the canteen she kept beneath the seat, she unscrewed the lid and drank deeply. The water was cool, having been kept in the shade, and it tasted sweet, refreshing.

James Odelbert, who had the wagon just behind hers, loped toward her. "What's going on?" he asked, pausing to gaze up at her.

"I don't know," she replied. "Maybe somebody broke a wagon wheel."

James moved away and looked toward the lead wagon, then returned to Anne. "Zeke Masters is headed this way," he said. "And he's stopping to talk to folks along the way."

"Wonder what's going on?" Anne said uneasily.

James smiled up at her. "Guess we'll find out soon enough."

As Anne waited anxiously, wondering what was holding them up, she remembered the Indians who had taken Jessie and her captive. Her pulse skipped a beat as a jolt of fear swept through her.

"James." She swallowed around the salty taste of fear. "You don't suppose we're being attacked? Do you?"

He reached up and patted her hand. "Naw," he said gently. "They wouldn't dare attack us, Anne. There's too many of us. Too many rifles." His fingers curled around her hand, and he squeezed gently. "If they come at us, we'd chew 'em up and spit 'em out!"

That was the way Masters found them. Her leaning toward James, him holding her hand, their eyes locked together.

"Dammit, James!" Masters glared at the man who was so engrossed in his scout's wife. "What in hell are you doing here?"

James jerked away from Anne, his movement guilty in the extreme. And the blush that stained his cheeks only magnified that fact. "Uh . . . nothing, Masters. I was just—just trying to figure out what was going on."

"Like I'm trying to do?"

"Uh . . . um, I—I guess I'd better get back to my wagon."

"Might be a damn good idea."

Anne wondered at James's embarrassment, but only vaguely. Uppermost in her mind was worry about the Indians. Masters apparently guessed her thoughts because he hurried to reassure her. "Nothing to worry about, ma'am. Just wanted to alert everybody to what's going on."

"Is there some kind of trouble?"

"No. Just being careful. We're gonna be leaving the Platte River soon, Miss Farra—excuse me, Mrs. McCord." He smiled at her. "I keep forgetting. Don't know why, neither. Since it hasn't been more'n an hour since I talked to your husband."

Anne's heart gave a sudden leap. "You saw Lucas?"

"Yep. Surely did. And that's the reason we're leaving the valley. There won't be no water where we're headed, so you're gonna need to fill every available container before we go on."

Anne nodded. "All right." She wrapped the reins around the hook used for that purpose. "How long will we be here? Should I unhitch the mules?"

"No need," he replied gruffly. "We won't be here that long."

He reined his horse around, obviously bent on advising the next wagon in line, but Anne stopped him with a question.

"Is Lucas coming to the wagon?"

"No, ma'am," Masters said. "I wouldn't think so. Last time I saw Lucas, he was riding back the way he'd come."

Anne swallowed her disappointment and climbed inside the wagon to look for empty containers she could fill with water. But she looked in vain. The only empty containers she found were the dishpan and bucket, and the cooking utensils, none of which would hold water with the wagon lurching up the side of a mountain.

Even though she had capped off the water barrel hanging on the side of the wagon before they had left that morning, she checked it again. The water level hadn't dropped even one inch.

She looked outside, hoping to see Masters and ask his advice, but he was nowhere in sight. She looked toward the river and saw Mary Baker and Jessie carrying several containers between them.

As though she sensed eyes on her, Mary turned around and spied Anne. "Hurry up, Anne," she called. "We won't be stopping for long."

Knowing the necessity of having plenty of water, Anne ducked inside the wagon again and opened the barrel containing nails. She dumped the nails into the wash pan, replaced the lid, then climbed out of the wagon and hurried toward the river.

Soon they were back on the trail again, climbing higher with each passing moment. The wagon lurched and swayed, moving over rocks and debris as the mules strained to pull their load up the slope. Anne wondered if the contents of the wagon would stay put until they reached the peak. She prayed they would, because there was no place to restock their provisions. If they lost the supplies, they would simply have to do without.

It seemed an eternity had passed when they finally reached the top. And, amazing though it seemed, they had done so without mishap.

Exhaustion weighed heavily on Anne, and her muscles ached with strain. Yet the wagons kept rolling along, moving over the boulder-strewn plateau at a snail's pace as Masters tried to put some distance between them and the slope where enemy horses might soon appear.

The sun went down, stealing the warmth from the land. The wind was brisk, the night air cold, and Anne shivered beneath its touch.

Darkness was descending over the plateau when Masters finally sent out the call to make camp.

Anne's fingers were numb with cold as she took her place in the circle of wagons. But there was work to be done, mules to be unhitched and taken to pasture, a fire to be built and supper to make.

Oh, God, she silently cried. *When will it be over?*

The wind gusted suddenly, flattening Anne's long skirt against her legs and making her tremble with cold. She

Take advantage of this offer to enjoy Zebra's newest line of historical romance novels....Splendor Romances (formerly Lovegrams Historical Romances)- Take our introductory shipment of 4 romance novels -Absolutely Free! (a $19.96 value)

Now you'll be able to savor today's best romance novels without even leaving your home with our convenient and inexpensive home subscription service. Here's what you get for joining:

- 4 BRAND NEW bestselling Splendor Romances delivered to your doorstep every month
- 20% off every title (or almost $4.00 off) with your home subscription
- A **FREE** monthly newsletter, *Zebra/Pinnacle Romance News* filled with author interviews, member benefits, book previews and more!
- No risks or obligations…you're free to cancel whenever you wish…no questions asked

To get started with your own home subscription, simply complete and return the card provided. You'll receive your FREE introductory shipment of 4 Splendor Romances and then you'll begin to receive monthly shipments of new Zebra Splendor titles. Each shipment will be yours to examine for 10 days and then if you decide to keep the books, you'll pay the preferred home subscriber's price of just $4.00 per title plus $1.50 shipping and handling. That's $16 for all 4 books plus $1.50 for home delivery! And if you want us to stop sending books, just say the word…it's that simple.

Check out our website at www.kensingtonbooks.com.

4 FREE books are waiting for you!
Just mail in the certificate below!

If the certificate is missing below, write to:
Splendor Romances, Zebra Home Subscription Service, Inc.
P.O. Box 5214, Clifton, New Jersey 07015-5214
or call TOLL-FREE 1-888-345-BOOK

FREE BOOK CERTIFICATE

Yes! Please send me 4 Splendor Romances (formerly Zebra Lovegram Historical Romances), ABSOLUTELY FREE! After my introductory shipment, I will be able to preview 4 new Splendor Romances each month FREE for 10 days. Then if I decide to keep them, I will pay the money-saving preferred publisher's price of just $4.00 each... a total of $16.00 plus $1.50 shipping and handling. That's 20% off the regular publisher's price plus $1.50 for shipping and handling. I may return any shipment within 10 days and owe nothing, and I may cancel my subscription at any time. The 4 FREE books will be mine to keep in any case.

Name _____

Address _____ Apt. _____

City _____ State _____ Zip _____

Telephone ( ) _____

Signature _____
(If under 18, parent or guardian must sign.)

SN119A

Terms and prices subject to change. Orders subject to acceptance by Zebra Home Subscription Service, Inc. .
Zebra Home Subscription Service, Inc. reserves the right to reject or cancel any subscription.
Offer valid in U.S. only.

A $19.96 value.

FREE!

No obligation
to buy
anything,
ever.

climbed into the wagon and found her leather jacket before she began the task of unhitching the mules.

Her fingers were stiff and refused to cooperate. She was on the verge of desperation when James Odelbert stopped by. "Let me do that for you," he said gently.

"You have your own work," she protested.

"I have to take my mules out anyway." He pushed her hands away from the harness. "Yours might as well go with mine."

She summoned up a smile. "Thank you, James."

"That short coat you're wearing can't be very warm, Anne," he said gruffly. "Don't you have anything better to wear?"

"I do have another coat," she replied. "I bought it at Fort Laramie. But it's packed away in a trunk beneath a mound of supplies."

"Wrap up in a blanket," he advised. "We're making a cold camp tonight."

"Why?"

"Haven't you noticed there's no wood up here?"

Anne hadn't noticed, but she did so now. There were no trees, no bushes, no growth of any kind. The plateau was made up of fields of slate and strewn everywhere with large boulders.

Nor was there a sign of buffalo chips, the old standby when wood was unavailable. It was more than obvious that James was right. They would have a cold camp tonight.

Wrapping a blanket around her shoulders, Anne wondered how she would assuage her hunger. She had eaten the last biscuit for lunch, and her stomach was complaining loudly.

She had been foolish not to make more biscuits.

The clip-clop of shod hooves, along with the squeak of saddle leather, caught her attention, and she looked up to see her husband approaching.

"Lucas," she exclaimed, hurrying toward him. "I didn't think you'd make it back tonight."

He took one look at her, then swung down from the dun and unfastened a bundle from his saddle.

"If you brought rabbits, then you wasted your time," Anne said, shivering beneath a blast of cold wind. "We don't have anything for a fire."

"I didn't bring rabbits and you *didn't* have anything." As he opened his bundle, she realized why it had appeared so unwieldy. Lucas had brought wood along with him.

He knelt to build a fire. "I knew you'd be cold," he said gruffly. "Fill the coffeepot with water while I light a fire."

Eager for something hot to drink, Anne hurried to obey. She found the coffeepot she had left close to hand, then opened the nail keg, intending to take water from that.

The keg was empty.

"Darn it!" she muttered.

"What's wrong?" Lucas asked.

"I filled this keg with water earlier," she explained, lifting the empty keg to show him. "But there's not a drop of water remaining."

"You filled the nail keg with water?" He laughed abruptly. "Didn't you know a nail keg's not tight enough to hold water?"

"No. I didn't."

"Well, you do now." He frowned at her as a thought occurred. "What did you do with the nails?"

"I put them in the wash pan."

"Good. I was afraid for a minute there you might've thrown them out." He strode toward her. "Give me the keg, Anne. It's gonna need drying out before we put the nails back inside."

Feeling like a complete fool, Anne handed him the keg, then found the coffee beans and dumped them in the coffee grinder.

After putting the coffee on to boil, Anne sliced salt pork and placed the slices in a heavy skillet to fry, then made biscuits—a double batch this time—and set the Dutch oven over the coals.

Realizing the coffee was done, Anne poured two cups and handed Lucas one before settling herself on a rock beside the fire. As she sipped her coffee, she watched Lucas work on the nail keg. She had really goofed on that one, but he had only laughed at her mistake.

He was a good man, would make some woman a good husband, and she had begun to wish their marriage was real.

She had never forgotten his kiss, or the taste of him. And she had thought often about the way it would have been if they had married under other circumstances.

Lucas was aware of Anne's eyes and wondered if her thoughts had wandered along the same path his had taken. He had tried to forget how she had felt in his arms, but the memory would not be denied. He remembered the sweet, womanly scent of her, the curves that fit his body so naturally they could have been made just for him.

Just the memory caused his body to tighten. His head lifted, and their eyes met, and held. He cleared his throat. "You have any trouble with those mules tonight?"

"No." Anne smiled at him. "James took care of them for me."

Lucas tensed. "Odelbert?" he growled.

"Um hum." Anne turned the pork over and checked the biscuits, which were browning nicely. "I thought we should thank him by sharing our meal with him."

"Is that right?"

Something about the tone of his voice jerked her head around. "You don't mind, do you? James brought no wood, and he'll be making a cold camp tonight."

"He told you all that ... before he took the mules out?"

"He just said we'd be making a cold camp." She wondered what had come over him. "Lucas! Surely you don't begrudge the man a hot meal!"

Lucas sent a long look around the circle of wagons. "There's other campfires. Other hot meals to be had."

She rose to her feet and put her hands on her hips. "I don't know why you're acting this way, Lucas, but James went out of his way to help me when my fingers were so frozen they couldn't work the leather harness. Now, if you begrudge the food he would eat, then he can damn well have mine!"

Lucas was struck dumb by her anger. She was beautiful, with her windswept curls framing her glowing skin, her eyes brilliant with emotion, and her rounded breasts heaving with each breath she took.

He wanted to embrace her, wanted to cover her mouth with his own, to penetrate her sweet warmth and possess her thoroughly.

And dammit! Why shouldn't he? She was his wife. In every way but one.

But he was bound by that promise . . . that damned agreement they had made.

So his hands were tied. At least for the moment. He would be damned, though, if he would let another man sneak by him and capture the prize that belonged to him.

He forced his tense body to relax. "You're right, Anne. We do owe James. Dish up some of that pork and a couple of them biscuits. And pour some of that coffee, too."

Anne's smile brought sunshine to a dark night as she hurried to obey. And when she had dished up the food and poured the coffee, Lucas took them to Odelbert's wagon, catching him on the verge of leaving.

"Thought you'd like a hot meal," Lucas said shortly.

"Now, that's damned nice of you, Lucas," James replied, reaching for the steaming food. "Henry Baker was just over here with an invitation to supper, but this is even better. Won't be needing to visit when the meal's over.''

He sipped the hot liquid and expelled a sigh. "Anne makes a mighty good cup of coffee. You're a lucky man, Lucas." He broke open a biscuit and shoved the salt pork inside, then bit into it. "Yeah," he went on, chewing steadily. "A mighty lucky man to have a wife like that.''

"Yeah," Lucas agreed. "Kinda think so myself." He leaned against the wagon wheel and sipped from his own cup. "A man gets lonesome out here sometimes, Odelbert. And lonesome makes a man do some mighty strange things."

Odelbert paused in the act of taking another bite. "You got something on your mind, Lucas?''

"Just my wife, James," Lucas replied, watching the other man steadily. "And make no mistake. She is my wife.''

James laughed abruptly. "You're warning me off, Lucas?''

"Do you need warning off?''

"No. I know whose wife she is. And I never was a man to poach on another man's property. But I never could stand by and watch a woman struggle with work a man should be doing neither, Lucas. Not when I could help it.''

Lucas straightened. "Fair enough. And that help will be much appreciated. Now that we understand each other.''

Anne was dishing up the meal when Lucas returned to their wagon and handed her the empty plate and cup. "Thank you, Lucas," she said. "I know James appreciated that.''

"Yeah. He seemed to.''

After they had finished their own meal, they sat

together, each busy with their own thoughts as they
savored the last of their coffee.

Anne thought about the coming night, how the cold
would invade her bones after she went to her solitary bed.
The thought sent a shiver across her flesh.

"Cold?" Lucas asked.

"No. But I will be when this fire goes out." She smiled
at him. "I haven't thanked you for bringing the wood,
Lucas. I had no idea it would be so cold tonight, or that
there would be nothing with which to make a fire."

"I realized that," he replied. "That's why I brought
the wood. Anyway, those biscuits of yours are worth
coming back for, Anne." His gaze darkened. "I should've
said something before . . . about your biscuits."

"It's never too late," she teased.

"No . . . well, um, dammit, Anne, you make the best
damn biscuits I ever tasted!"

Anne flushed with pleasure. It was evident he was
sincere. "Why, thank you, Lucas. That's the nicest thing
anyone has ever said to me."

Anne was glad she had spent so much time with her
grandmother on the east Texas farm, learning how to
cook in the old-fashioned way.

Lucas had become silent again, his gaze fixed on the
flames that leapt and swirled inside the circle of stones. He
looked like a man who had something weighing heavily on
his mind.

"Is something wrong, Lucas?" she asked quietly, her
thoughts returning to the Indians who had taken her captive. "Is there trouble ahead of us? Have you seen the
Indians again?"

Instead of answering her questions, he said, "I wasn't
thinking about the Indians, Anne. I was thinking about
tonight, about the cold wind . . . and how it would affect
our sleep."

"I thought about that, too."

His dark eyes captured her blue ones. "It's going to drop below freezing tonight," he said softly. "And we won't be able to keep the fire going."

"I know."

"It would be warmer if we slept together."

Slept together? Like they had on their wedding night? Just the thought of being in his arms again was enough to quicken her heartbeat, to make her blood race through her veins.

A flush spread over her cheeks, and when she spoke, her voice was husky with feeling. "Yes. I guess it would be warmer."

"Then, you agree?" His eyes were hooded as he watched her closely. "I thought you might dislike the idea, that you might think I was using the cold for an excuse to sleep with you."

The wind gusted, and Anne shivered beneath its icy touch. "I'm not a complete idiot." Her voice trembled, whether from cold or the thought of them lying so close together, she didn't know. "The only way we'll be able to keep warm tonight is to share our body warmth."

Lucas studied her bent head. It was going to be a hard night, he knew, in more ways than one.

I should never have kissed her, he told himself. *Then I never would have known how sweet she tasted.*

And yet he had done so. And he had never forgotten that kiss, no matter how hard he tried to put it from his mind. The coming night would be pure torture, but he damn sure wouldn't be cold.

Chapter Fourteen

As they went about preparing for the coming night, the wind gusted sharply. It howled around the wagon, tearing at Anne's clothing with icy fingers when she tossed their bedrolls beneath the wagon.

The wagon shifted slightly as Lucas climbed inside. A moment later he emerged with a canvas tarp slung across his shoulders.

"What are you doing?" she asked.

"Making a windbreak." Lucas fastened the top corners of the canvas on the bed of the wagon, then secured the bottom against the wagon wheels and weighted it down with rocks.

With the wind subdued, if only slightly, Anne spread Luke's bedroll out to its full width, then used her own to cover it. By the time she had finished preparing the bed, she was shivering uncontrollably, and her teeth were chattering like a pair of castanets.

A quick look was all Lucas needed to realize how severely the cold was affecting her. He swore softly.

"Climb in that bed, Anne," he ordered. "I'll be with you in a minute."

Anne never even considered undressing. Even if she had been sleeping alone, she would have kept every layer of clothing on. She would need her garments to keep warm throughout the coming night.

But the boots would have to go.

She jerked them off, tossed them aside, and crawled into the bedroll in her coat, long dress and stocking feet. Then she lay there shivering, her body chilled to the bone.

Suddenly Lucas was beside her.

"Sh-should I sc-scoot over?" she asked through chattering teeth.

"No. You take this side. It faces into the circle. I'll sleep on the backside."

Bent on keeping himself between her and a possible attack, Lucas crawled on his hands and knees until he was near the canvas; then he unbuckled his gun belt and left it near at hand.

Anne pulled the cover around her ears to shut out the cold wind that continued to find its way around the tarp. She heard a thud and knew that he had discarded one boot. Another thud was followed by a grunt. Then the covers lifted, and Luke slid in beside her.

She felt the warmth of his body as he settled in the bedroll, but the cold had penetrated so deeply that her teeth continued to chatter.

"Scoot over here," Luke commanded.

Without waiting for her to comply, his strong arms reached out and pulled her against him, tucking her gently into the saddle of his hips in an intimacy that would have embarrassed her in other circumstances. At the moment, though, Anne had no thought of anything save the heat radiating from his large frame.

Lucas sighed deeply as Anne settled against him. He was aware of her firmness, of her gently rounded buttocks that were snug against the part of him that was most a man. Even as that thought occurred, Lucas could feel himself growing hard, swelling beneath the womanly curve of her buttocks.

Damnation, he silently cursed.

Lucas expected her to pull away from him at any given moment, but she remained where he had put her, pressed firmly against his manhood, either uncaring of the state he found himself in, or waiting silently for him to make a move on her.

And it wouldn't be hard to do. Somehow, his hand had wandered to the underside of her gently curving breasts. All he needed to do was move his arm a few inches higher and he would hold that sweetness in his palm.

Would she object if he did? It was a certainty that making love was an excellent bed warmer. Many times he and Barbara had—

Barbara!

For a moment he had actually forgotten about her. And that was a damned stupid thing to do. He had to keep her in mind or he would wind up making a fool of himself all over again.

Just the thought of Barbara's laughter, the way she had ridiculed him for daring to believe she could ever love a half-breed, was enough to dim his passion.

Remember her, he told himself. *Never forget about Barbara.*

Even as Luke told himself that, Anne sighed heavily and shifted, her buttocks moving against his staff, and it rose magnificently, rigid and straight, like a soldier who stood at attention.

Think of Barbara, an inner voice whispered.

Lucas did, forcing his thoughts away from the woman in his arms, making himself remember instead the other woman's laughter as she had refused his ring.

Instantly the starch left his rod, and his tension drained away.

But Anne was unaware of his turmoil. She sighed deeply, luxuriating in the warmth that surrounded her, feeling the arms of Morpheus opening wider, beckoning her into a welcoming sleep.

Yet she couldn't quite reach that state. There was something intrusive, something hard, digging into her rib cage.

She arched her back, hoping to escape the troublesome object, and as she did, her hips were shoved closer against the warmth that felt so good on her backside.

"Dammit, Anne," Luke growled. "Keep still!"

"I can't, Luke."

"Why in hell not?"

"There's something hard under my ribs." Anne moved backward again, her fingers searching for the object that was keeping her in a restless state.

Luke swore roundly. "Dammit, woman! Are you deliberately trying to arouse me?"

"What?"

"Never mind," he growled. "Are you sure there's something under there?"

"Of course I'm sure," she snapped. "I think it's a rock, and it keeps digging into my ribs. It hurts, Lucas!"

"That's not the only thing that hurts!"

Suddenly, with a harsh curse, he flung the covers aside and sat up, bringing her with him. "Show me where the damn rock is," he snarled. "If there's actually one there!"

She looked at him in confusion. "Of course there's one there. Why would I lie about a thing like that?"

"How the hell should I know?" he asked sharply. "Maybe you decided a hundred acres weren't enough. Maybe you want half of everything I've got."

"Half of . . ." She looked at him in confusion. "What on earth are you talking about?" When he didn't answer, she said, "Never mind. We can carry on this conversation beneath the covers. After I move the rock."

Anne pulled aside the bottom bedroll and searched for the intrusive object. Moments later her searching fingers closed over the rock, and she held it out triumphantly.

"See. I told you it was there."

"Are you going to save it or throw it away?"

"Why should I save it?"

"Never mind," he said wearily. "Just get under the covers before we both freeze to death."

She stretched out on the bedroll again, and he tucked the covers in around them, then circled her with his arm and snugged her close.

"Lucas," she said, "what did you mean about me wanting half of what you had?"

"Never mind," he said gruffly. "I made a mistake."

"But—"

"Anne." His voice held a warning. "Go to sleep. Tomorrow will be another long day."

Silently vowing to ask her questions again later, Anne closed her eyes and relaxed against him. Moments later she was sound asleep.

Nothing showed in Chase the Wind's expression as he left the council lodge and strode across the compound, headed for Stalking Wolf's tepee. But those who knew him realized his anger at the council's decision.

They had refused to act, had told him to leave the white-eyes alone.

But he refused to heed their words.

Chief Running Fox spoke against fighting the white-eyes; he refused to allow them to move against the wagon train.

But the old man was wrong in his beliefs. He was too old to lead them now, worried too much about the consequences of a raid. The Sioux needed a strong leader, a leader like himself, or Stalking Wolf.

Chase the Wind had seen that warrior's fury, knew how he felt, because he felt the same way. Yet he could use that anger, could make it work for him. Anger was like coals, he knew. They needed only a few twigs to create a small fire that could eventually—if left alone to spread—destroy a whole village.

And he would be the twigs added to Stalking Wolf's coals of fury.

The wind moaned loudly, as though in pain, and he looked up at the night sky where the stars twinkled merrily overhead and Sister Moon showed only a thin smile to those below.

Suddenly, a hand gripped his upper arm, and he swung around, fists clenched, prepared to deal harshly with whoever dared to touch him.

White Cloud's face was expressionless as he examined his son's features. "You waste energy with your anger that could be put to better use, my son."

"They are wrong," Chase the Wind said tightly. "How can they not see that?"

"The elders have lived many summers beyond yours," White Cloud replied. "They are the chosen ones, the wisest of us all. They have learned it is foolish to fight a useless battle."

"It doesn't have to be useless," Chase the Wind said grimly. "Our people speak of the great leader—chief of the Ottawa tribe—who lived many lifetimes ago." Although he could not speak aloud the man's name since he had long since passed from this life, his father would know that it was Pontiac of whom he spoke. "The chief's word was carried to all the tribes throughout the land," he continued. "And when they banded together they were as one nation, fighting against a common foe."

"I have heard the story, my son. I was the one who told you."

"But not the only one. It is not just a story told to children at night. It happened, Father. That chief had a great vision, and he was a mighty warrior. Not only the Ottawa tribe listened to him, but all the Peoples of all the nations. They listened to his words, and the warriors came together to conquer the white-eyes."

"And did they do so?"

Chase the Wind's eyes burned hotly, and he did not answer the question since they both knew the outcome. "They burned many forts," he said fiercely. "And they killed many white-eyes."

"But did they conquer them?"

"The warriors held the forts at bay," Chase the Wind said grimly. "The People struck together and took the forts when they were not expecting trouble, and—"

"But did they conquer the white-eyes, Chase the Wind? Did they drive the white-eyes from our lands? Did they send the palefaces back across the big water where they came from?" His hard grip and his dark eyes demanded an answer to his question.

"They almost did!"

"But they did not!" White Cloud said. "The white-eyes still travel across our land, and the People cannot stop them."

"But—"

"Hear my words!" White Cloud said harshly. "We have fought against the white-eyes for many years, as our fathers did before us. And for every soldier we slay, two more take his place. Their numbers are greater than ours, their weapons are better, and the People grow tired of living in fear."

His voice was suddenly that of an old man as he searched for the words that would sway his son. "It is time we learn, my son. We must give way where we cannot stand firm. There is a time for fighting and a time to let go. The time to let go is now.''

''No,'' Chase the Wind said sharply. ''I will not stop fighting those who steal our lands.''

''Then, you will fight alone.''

''No. There are others who feel as I do.''

''A handful of hotheaded warriors like yourself,'' White Cloud said. ''How can you hope to win such a fight against so many when there are so few of you?''

''Perhaps we cannot win,'' Chase the Wind said sadly. ''But at least we will have tried. And when we are done there will be fewer white-eyes to steal our land.''

''Is there no way to convince you?''

''No.''

''Then, so be it.''

They parted, and Chase the Wind continued across the compound, searching for the young warriors who were brave enough to ride against the white-eyes with him.

The search didn't take long. As he had told his father, there were many others who thought as he did, and they were more than eager to strike against the wagon train.

It was only a short time later when Chase the Wind and his followers left the village, heading for the wagon train, eager for the coming battle.

Chase the Wind knew they should reach the travelers before first light. And by the time Father Sun showed his face on the eastern horizon, he would see the enemy defeated ... at least, some of them. And he would be well pleased to see the white-eyes on the ground, their blood flowing around their pale bodies.

The warrior smiled at the thought.

His father was right. He could not slay all the white-eyes; but he could make them fearful of the Sioux warriors, and perhaps that fear would keep them from sending more wagon trains into the land of the People.

*   *   *

Lucas woke quickly, aware of the total silence around him. The sky was awash with stars, and an errant cloud obliterated most of the moon.

The wind had died down, leaving the mesa hushed, quiet. But was there something unnatural about that very stillness?

Where were the creatures that occupied the night?

No crickets broke the silence. No night bird sounded. There was no beat of owl wings as it swooped through the night searching for food. Even the stock that had been kept close by were silent.

Carefully, Lucas reached for the pistol he had left close to hand, then covered Anne's mouth to keep her silent when she woke. Bending low, he spoke softly against her ear.

"Anne."

She sighed, then stirred against him. Suddenly, as though startled into awareness, her lashes lifted, and she stared up at him in fear.

He shook his head quickly, placing a finger across his lips to quiet her, then released her mouth. She watched him in silence as he slipped from the covers, then handed her a pistol.

Her gaze slid to the weapon, and her eyes widened. But she apparently understood, because her hand closed quickly around the six-gun.

Anne gripped the weapon tightly, her searching gaze sweeping the area around them.

From what direction would the danger come?

Feeling more certain with each passing moment that danger was closing in around them, Lucas went to warn the others.

Holding the pistol grip securely, Anne moved quietly, aware of the need for absolute silence. Her heel tangled in the hem of her long skirt, making her wish for her jeans.

Trying hard to control her fear, Anne searched the shadows with narrowed eyes, watching for the slightest movement that would warn her of approaching danger.

Was she safer beneath the wagon, or would it be better to take whatever shelter the wagon wheels afforded?

The canvas offered no shelter at all, she decided, and at least the spokes of the wagon wheels might deflect an arrow aimed at her.

She crawled quickly toward the wagon wheel, then carefully examined the six-gun. Although Anne knew it was the usual practice to leave one chamber empty, she found that Luke had loaded them all.

Anne was settling down for a long wait when Luke returned.

"What's going on?" she whispered.

"Indians," he replied. "Get ready."

"Get ready for what?"

Before he could reply, a scream split the silence.

Chapter Fifteen

A cold chill slid over Anne, dimpling her arms with goose bumps. "What was that?" she whispered.

"Get down!" Lucas growled, shoving her low against the wagon wheel.

The thought of disobedience never entered Anne's mind. Her fear was too great, almost overpowering as she crouched against the wagon wheel, seeking whatever shelter it would provide from an unseen enemy.

We'll get through this, Anne silently told herself. *We have better weapons. Rifles and six-guns. They'll be using arrows and spears.*

Whump, whump, whump. Three arrows, one following quickly on the other, struck the rim of the wagon wheel. The iron rim deflected the first two arrows, and they fell harmlessly to the ground. But the third arrow was buried in the wood, mere inches from Anne's face.

While the feathers in the arrows were still quivering, a ululating shriek came from somewhere beyond the wagons.

"Eeaaahhh!"

More shrieks joined the first one. War cries. A cacophony of sound that swept over Anne in waves, rising and falling. She realized it was the Indians' way of unnerving their enemies.

"And guess what?" Anne muttered, positioning her six-gun. "It works."

Anne tried to ignore the sounds, concentrating instead on the darkness beyond the circle of wagons. A shadow shifted, and she narrowed her gaze on the spot.

"Lucas! I think I saw something move out there."

"Let them get closer before you start shooting."

Anne remembered a line from an old movie. "Don't shoot until you see the whites of their eyes," she recited.

"Not that close," Lucas growled.

She felt the urge to giggle, and realized she was on the verge of hysteria. If that noise didn't stop before long . . . if something didn't happen out there, she was going to go stark, raving mad.

Even as that thought occurred, all hell broke loose.

The shrieks intensified. Dark shadows rose from the ground, leaping forward with a speed that was completely unnerving.

Crack! crack! crack! Shots blasted the air, mingling with the sound of Indian war cries. A woman screamed within the circle of wagons, a long, painful cry.

"Eden!" a deep voice shouted. "Oh, my God! She's been hit! Doctor! Send for the doctor! Those damned redskins killed my wife!"

Anne tried to ignore the sounds, concentrating instead on the leaping shadows in the darkness, shadows that rose long enough to shoot deadly arrows at the pioneers before blending into the night again.

Knowing she must do something, that she must help fight off their attackers, Anne narrowed her gaze on one particular shadow. When it moved, she squeezed off a shot. A hoarse cry sounded, and the shadow dropped, disappearing into a wrinkle in the ground.

Another shape took the place of the first one, and Anne squeezed the trigger. Missed. Fired again. Once. Twice. The shadow faltered, then leapt forward. She could see the warrior clearly now. Could make out his features. She fired again . . . the Indian faltered. Then came on. Anne's finger tightened on the trigger. *Click.*

"Oh, my God!" she cried. "Lucas! I'm out of bullets."

He spared her a quick glance, then said, "Here!" thrusting out a handful of bullets before sending off another shot.

A hoarse cry sounded nearby, and Anne jerked around to see a warrior stumble and fall. It was the same one Anne had been shooting at.

Instantly, hot lead whined like angry wasps around her. Her eyes widened with disbelief. "Lucas! They have guns! Rifles!"

For some reason that thought was completely unnerving. Anne's fingers trembled as she broke open the pistol and began inserting the bullets in the chamber.

A bullet whined nearby, then struck the metal lining the bottom of the wagon and ricocheted, sending fragments of wood scattering everywhere. Pain stabbed through her left thigh. Stinging. Burning! Numbing.

Somewhere in the back of her mind Anne realized splinters from the wagon bed had penetrated the soft flesh of her thigh. But the pain was negligible. A mere nuisance when compared to their very survival.

Shoving the last bullet into the chamber, she snapped the cylinder in place, then turned . . . to see a wiry warrior leaping toward her.

Anne froze in place, momentarily forgetting what she had learned in her self-defense classes. She was unable to cry out, unable to squeeze the trigger, knowing with a certainty that her end was near.

She could see his eyes, dark orbs rimmed with white, staring at her from a red-streaked face that must have come directly from her nightmares.

The whites of his eyes.

Time to shoot! Time to shoot! Shoot him, Anne! Squeeze the damn trigger!

As she watched, openmouthed with horror, unable to move a muscle, the warrior lifted his tomahawk, then brought it straight down in a blow designed to split her skull wide open.

But Anne's survival instincts suddenly kicked in. She dropped and rolled away, and as he came after her, she braced herself on her elbows and kicked out, up, striking a hard blow against the soft flesh between his legs.

The warrior grunted, his knees giving way beneath him.

Anne leapt to her feet, then cried out as pain blurred her vision, forcing her to her knees. The warrior's face was livid as he leapt forward, knocking her down and locking his hands around her throat.

Lucas was unaware of Anne's plight until it was almost too late. He didn't know what caused him to turn, yet turn he did. And when he saw the warrior on Anne, choking the life out of her, he reacted instantly, lunging forward as he yanked his long blade free of its sheath.

With the heel of his hand, Lucas shoved the warrior's head back. The two men stared at each other. Then Luke's blade swept across the other man's neck, slicing the flesh from ear to ear.

Blood spurted forth as Lucas pushed the man aside, then knelt over his wife. Her eyes were closed. She was motionless. Still as death.

"Anne," Lucas groaned, pulling her against him. "Oh, God, no!"

He was vaguely aware of the battle raging around him, yet made no effort to loosen his hold on his precious burden. And she *was* precious to him, had been for some time, although he had been unaware of that fact.

And to lose her now. . . .

Before the thought was finished, Anne sucked in a gasping breath, and her eyes flew open. She breathed again, coughed, then sucked greedily at the air.

Luke's heart swelled with relief that she had been spared. And with that knowledge came rage, blind fury, aimed at the Indians who had forced this fight on them. Two quick strides and he had rifle in hand, ready to rejoin the battle. Then he became aware of the silence. Somehow, within the last few minutes, the battle had ended.

Sighing with relief, Lucas straightened his long frame and leaned his rifle against the wagon wheel. The first light of day was quickly approaching, chasing night shadows away. No wounded or dead had been left behind, save for those that had penetrated the circle of wagons.

"Lucas."

The word was only a whisper, but it was enough to catch his attention. His quick stride crossed the distance between them, and he knelt beside Anne, lifting her into his arms.

"Oh, God!" she rasped hoarsely.

And then she fainted.

Panic washed over Lucas as he knelt to examine her. Her throat was bruised, already darkening. It must be painful in the extreme. But would it cause her to faint?

His gaze traveled over her, his hands following the path of his eyes. Her arms were intact, no broken bones. No bruises that he could see. He worked his way down her torso, found no problem until he encountered the dampness. Sticky, yet hard to see on the dark fabric. Blood?

A hand peeled back her skirt, but her legs appeared unharmed. Higher. Her knees were intact, shapely. And her thighs—

Damnation! She's been shot!

Anne moaned softly as he was examining the wound. The bullet had pierced her thigh several inches above her left knee. And there was no exit wound.

Anne woke to excruciating pain.

Her eyes flew open, and she screamed, piercing sounds that revealed her pain, her terror. And that same terror surged outward with fists flailing.

"Hold her!" a deep voice shouted.

And they did. Her captors pinned her to the ground, and she tried to kick them; but her legs were held fast while one of her captors sawed steadily through her leg with a dull-bladed knife.

"No, no!" she cried, thrashing wildly as she tried to throw her captors off. "Please! For God's sake, don't use the knife!"

Lucas' face hovered above hers. "He has to use it, Anne." His voice was gentle. "There's no other way. Be patient, darling. It will be over soon."

"Don't let them do this!" she cried. "Stop them, Lucas!"

The knife bit deeper, and she shrieked as pain burned through her flesh, white-hot pain that would not be denied. The sharp blade moved again, and she uttered another shriek and strained mightily at her bonds. Her back arched, her shoulders left the ground, and then she fainted.

"Thank God," Lucas whispered hoarsely.

Despite the cool morning air, sweat beaded Luke's forehead. He released his grip on Anne's wrist for a moment and smoothed his thumb over the tender flesh.

"She couldn't have stood much more," Hawk said gruffly.

"I know." Lucas swallowed hard, his gaze going to

the man who was digging the bullet out of Anne's thigh. "How much longer is this going to take?"

"Don't rush me," Robert Wilson snapped. "Do you want this knife to slip?"

"It damned well better not slip." Luke's voice held a threat.

"Easy, Lucas." Hawk held Anne's ankles firmly against the ground. "The doctor is doing the best he can. Better grab hold again. I think she's coming around."

"Damnation!"

"Got it!" Wilson exclaimed. "Here, Lucas."

He dropped the slug in Luke's palm, then threaded his needle. "Hold her while I stitch the wound."

Lucas barely had time to grab her wrists before Anne came fully awake. Her blue eyes were startling in their brilliance as she took in the situation at a single glance. "Turn me loose," she demanded, her tone angry, furious.

"I can't, honey," Lucas said softly. "The doctor has to stitch your leg up."

"Damn you!" she cried. "I won't be held down this way. Turn me loose!"

Robert Wilson spoke up, obviously intent on clarifying things. "You took a slug, Anne. I had to dig the bullet out."

"And *he* held me down."

"He had to. Still needs to. This wound won't heal without stitches."

"Then, sew it up!" she snapped. "But don't have him hold me down again!"

Wilson grunted, then, "Turn her loose, boys. The lady thinks she can take it."

Hawk's face entered her line of vision, and she read sympathy in his dark eyes. "Don't blame Lucas, Anne. He only did what he had to do."

"Anne . . ." Luke's voice was soft, gentle. "It was necessary."

She turned her head away from him. "Go away, Lucas."

Something flickered in his dark eyes, but only momentarily. His features became expressionless as he straightened himself, then strode quickly away.

Hawk was recruited to drive Anne's wagon since she was in no condition to do it herself. The wagon train had come through the Indian attack relatively unscathed but for a few injured pioneers, so they continued slowly on their way, trying to put the horror behind them. And Lucas, having obviously taken her at her word, had left to scout their backtrail, looking for trouble.

Anne realized her anger had been completely unwarranted. Lucas had only been trying to help. But coming as it had when the nightmare was still fresh in her mind, her sense of betrayal had been almost overwhelming.

Still, she had already begun to put the whole incident in perspective by the time the wagon train resumed its slow journey across the plateau. And now she wished it was Lucas beside her, guiding the team around the roughest spots as Hawk was doing.

Lucas didn't return that night, and Hawk prepared their evening meal, since Anne couldn't move around freely. He did allow Anne to stir up a batch of biscuits, though, bringing the ingredients she would need to where she sat beside the fire.

The meal was barely done when Zeke Masters came around to see if she needed anything, and Doc showed up to examine her wound.

Hawk watched from a distance as Wilson cleaned the wound and changed the bandage, but his obvious disapproval at such intimate contact between Anne and the doctor made the man hurry with his examination.

After Robert Wilson left, Hawk dished up the food and handed Anne a plate and a cup of hot coffee.

She sipped the hot liquid and simply looked at her food. For some reason she had no appetite. She sighed heavily and set the plate aside.

"You need to eat."

"I'm not hungry, Hawk." She took another sip of coffee and thought about the man who was her husband. "I thought Lucas might come back tonight."

"He's watching our backs," Hawk replied. "Making sure the warriors who attacked us won't be coming again."

Fear made Anne's voice husky. "Do you think they will?"

"No." He squatted down on his heels, and commenced eating.

Anne watched Hawk eat with obvious enjoyment, eyeing him over the rim of her coffee cup; then she decided to get some answers to a few of the questions that had been plaguing her.

"How long have you known Lucas?"

"Since he came to live in our village when he was a boy."

"You're Comanche, aren't you?"

He nodded, his gaze on the beans he was shoving into his mouth. He quickly washed the mouthful down with a gulp of hot coffee, then took another huge bite.

"And when was that?"

Caught in the act of shoving a biscuit into his mouth, he looked at her, a frown deepening his forehead, as though he were puzzled.

"When was what?"

"You said he went to live in your village. When was that?"

"When his parents died." He looked thoughtfully at the biscuit he was holding. "We were very young then."

"Am I asking too many questions, Hawk?"

"No. But I cannot remember the time. Many seasons have passed since then." Hawk used the Indian way of counting time. "It seems like Lucas and I have always known each other." He shot her a quick look from dark ebony eyes. "You knew his mother was a Comanche woman?"

"Yes. Someone did mention that."

"And you are not bothered by his heritage?"

"Of course not!"

Her answer came so quickly, and carried such surprise that he would even believe otherwise, that Hawk felt good about her relationship with his friend.

They might make something of their marriage if Lucas could ever forget the past. But he would not allow himself to forget.

Perhaps it was best if Anne knew what she was up against, that his friend's heart had been locked in chains and the key thrown away since his relationship with Barbara Fairchild had come to an end.

He opened his mouth to tell her about Barbara, then quickly shoved a biscuit in instead. The secret was not his to tell. If Lucas wanted her to know, then he would tell her himself.

Anne continued to ask questions about Luke's past. Some he answered, and others he did not. She appeared undeterred by the unanswered questions and willing to leave it at that.

Which suited Hawk just fine. He would not like making an enemy of Anne, he decided, not when she made such light, fluffy biscuits that literally melted in his mouth.

Lucas was a lucky man. Luckier than he would ever know. And when—if—he carried out his decision to get his marriage annulled, Hawk just might be waiting somewhere nearby, ready to pay the bride price that would make her his own.

With that end in mind, Hawk met her gaze, and his lips curled into a rare smile. "Good biscuits," he said gruffly. "You will make some man a fine wife."

Anne laughed, and Hawk found the sound as pleasing as a cool creek on a hot summer day. In fact, many things about her pleased him. And if Luke was fool enough to let her get away, then it was nobody's fault but his own.

"I am already a wife," Anne reminded gently. "Lucas and I are married. Had you already forgotten that?"

"Perhaps it is something I would like to forget," Hawk replied, picking up the honey pot and pouring a generous amount over the last biscuit. His gaze never left hers as he bit into the treat. "Ummm," he said. "Very good, indeed. I would fight every bear on this mountain for such a treat."

She laughed again. "Hawk! I don't believe there are any bears on this godforsaken mountain. But it was a nice thing to say anyway."

"I thought so, too." He laughed huskily, and his dark eyes actually twinkled.

Anne was enjoying his company, probably far too much, she guessed. But she hated eating alone, as she had done most of the time since marrying Lucas.

She watched in silence as Hawk finished his meal and poured them another cup of coffee. It was a companionable silence, though, enjoyed by both individuals. And then it was over. Hawk tossed the dregs of his cup aside, then rose to his full height and brushed the crumbs off his buckskins. "I'll clean up, then bed down for the night."

Anne watched him wash dishes and put them away in a neat stack. Hawk would make some woman a good husband whenever he decided to marry.

After Hawk finished cleaning up, he circled Anne's waist with a long arm while she limped to the bedroll he had already spread out beneath the wagon. "Do you have everything you need tonight?'' he asked gruffly. ''Should I send Mary Baker to you?''

Again, Anne was struck by his consideration. But Mary had already stopped by while Hawk tended the stock, and her private needs had been seen to. ''She's already been here, Hawk, and I don't need a thing now. Don't worry about me so much. I'm doing fine.''

But she'll be sleeping alone, a silent voice reminded Hawk. She wouldn't be if she belonged to him.

Hawk would not ordinarily have allowed himself to have such thoughts about another man's woman, but the circumstances were unusual in this case.

· Luke had assured him that he wanted no wife, that they were married in name only, and that meant that within a year of reaching their destination, Anne would be free to find another husband.

And, Hawk again vowed, when that day came, she would find him waiting nearby.

Chapter Sixteen

It was three more days before Lucas rode into camp.

His unshaven face was haggard, his dark eyes bloodshot from lack of sleep. And he was eager as hell to see his wife.

It didn't help his frame of mind to see Hawk kneeling beside her bedroll, applying a wet cloth to her forehead.

"You look like bloody hell, Lucas," Hawk said, sparing his friend only a quick glance before returning his attention to the woman who appeared to be asleep.

Luke's woman. His wife.

"What's wrong with her?" Lucas asked gruffly.

Hawk pinned Luke with a hard gaze. "She got shot!"

"Dammit! I know she got shot, Hawk. But she should be recovering by now." He dropped to his knees beside her and stared at her flushed face. "Why isn't she?"

"If you'd stayed with her instead of running off like some young buck who'd had his feelings hurt, then you wouldn't have to ask another man what was wrong with your wife."

Luke's hands fisted, and he glared at Hawk. "Dammit, man! Do I have to chase down the doctor to find out what's going on here?"

Hawk relented. "The wound's infected."

"Infected? Then, where's the damn doctor? Why isn't he taking care of her?"

"Calm down, Lucas. The doctor's already been here and gone. He's got other patients to tend to. Eden Roberts, for instance. She's in bad shape. She may not pull through."

"And Anne? What does the doctor say about her?"

"Said to lower her body temperature. That's hard to do in the heat of the day."

"How long has she been like this?"

"I think it started last night. But I didn't know there was anything wrong until late this afternoon. She fell off the wagon and tore the stitches."

"Damnation, Hawk! I told you to look out for her!"

"And that's what I'm doing," Hawk replied calmly, dropping the wet cloth in the wash pan nearby. "But I've been wondering where you got off to, Lucas."

Hawk squeezed the excess water from the cloth and was about to place it on Anne's forehead again when Lucas snatched it away from him. "I'll do that," he snarled. "As to where I've been, I rode to the fort."

"To see the major?"

"Yeah."

"What did he say?"

"Not much. They've had some trouble from the Sioux. But only now and then. Only a few bucks stealing horses and the like. But nothing to raise alarm. At least not until now." Lucas smoothed the cloth over Anne's forehead, feeling alarmed at the heat radiating beneath his hand. "Maybe we better have the doctor look at her again."

"He said he'd stop by later," Hawk replied. "Is Cleveland going to take action against the Sioux?"

"He's planning to send an emissary to the Sioux village, hoping to—" He broke off as Anne's eyelids fluttered open and she stared up at him with fever-clouded eyes.

"Lucas." Her voice was raspy, hoarse. "You came back."

"Of course I came back," he chided gently. "Did you think I wouldn't?"

She grasped his hand. "I didn't mean it, Lucas." Moisture flooded her eyes and leaked out the corners.

He swallowed around a lump that suddenly clogged his throat. "Mean what, honey?"

"Those things I said. I thought I was being tortured, and that you were holding me so the Indians could cut off my leg." She shuddered, but whether from memory or a sudden chill, Lucas had no way of knowing.

"It's okay, honey," he said, smoothing back her hair. "I understand." God, her skin was so hot, so dry. He met Hawk's concerned gaze. "We need something to lower her temperature."

"The doctor left quinine."

"Why in hell didn't you give it to her?"

Hawk paid no attention to Luke's anger, knowing it was worry that rode his friend. "The medicine cannot be administered too often," he explained. "I hoped the wet cloth would be enough."

Even as they watched, Anne's eyes were glazing over again. "It's so hot, Lucas," she moaned. "Turn the thermostat down. Make it cooler."

"What's a thermostat, honey?"

"You know." Her eyelids dropped against her cheeks, then flew open again, and she licked her dry lips. "I'm so thirsty."

"Give me the medicine, Hawk, and bring her a dipper of water."

Moments later he slid an arm around her shoulders and held her upright while he fed her a spoonful of quinine.

She shuddered at the bitter taste and gulped thirstily at the water that followed. Soon she fell into a restless sleep.

Lucas sat beside his wife, administering to her while Hawk prepared a hot meal for them. Then the two men spoke together about the battle and its results and Major Cleveland's intentions. It was late when Hawk finally took his leave.

Spreading his bedroll beside Anne's, Lucas heaved a sigh of utter exhaustion and stretched out beside her. He intended to catch only a few winks of sleep, just enough to ease the burning in his eyes. But his body had other things in mind. Too long denied the rest it needed, he had barely closed his eyes when his brain shut down and he fell into a deep, restful sleep that lasted throughout the night.

Anne watched Lucas sleep with a feeling of peace. She had awakened almost an hour before, her nostrils twitching at the aroma of hot coffee.

She had protested lying abed when Hawk presented her with a cup of the hot liquid, but when she had tried to rise, she found herself as weak as a kitten and quickly gave in to his persistence.

And now she lay replete, her breakfast devoured, content to watch her husband sleep beside her.

Her husband! She wished Lucas was truly her husband, in every sense of the word. But he was not, and never would be if things continued as they were.

But suppose he changed his mind. Maybe he wasn't any happier about their agreement than she was.

She remembered how tender he had been with her in her fevered state. He had called her honey, as though he really cared for her.

It might mean nothing though. She had heard him use that same endearment when he had spoken to Jessie after he had rescued them. But that fact didn't have to stop her from wishing. From hoping.

While she was still pondering that over in her mind, Luke's dark eyelashes quivered, like a bird readying itself for flight. Then his eyes snapped open, and he stared at her with bemusement.

Her lips curled in a soft smile. "Good morning, sleepy head."

He uttered a hoarse curse and jerked upright. "Dammit! It's morning."

"So it is." Her vivid blue eyes flashed with amusement. "Any objection?"

"Yes," he said wryly, flashing a quick glance at Hawk, who was pouring another cup of coffee. "I meant to watch over you last night."

"I didn't need watching over," she said cheerfully. "But thanks for the thought anyway."

He grunted, running his fingers through his dark hair. "You're mighty cheerful this morning."

"Surprised?"

"Yeah. Considering how sick you were last night." He took the coffee Hawk proferred, his attention never wavering from the woman who was his wife. "Is your leg bothering you?"

"Not much. But I'm weak as a kitten. There's an advantage to that, though."

Lucas sipped at his coffee before inquiring. "And what is that?"

"I got to lie abed while Hawk made my breakfast." She flicked a quick look at the big Comanche warrior who stood watching them. "Will you stop hovering and sit down for a few minutes, Hawk? You've been flitting around this wagon like a butterfly since before I woke up. And even butterflies have to rest sometime."

Hawk seated himself on a crate and threw a look her husband's way. "Sassy, isn't she?"

"Damn straight she is," Lucas muttered, eyeing her over the rim of his cup. "Sounds like she's well enough to handle that team of mules."

"Not yet, I'm afraid," Hawk replied. "She's still lying on that bedroll because she was too weak to stand up. Guess I'll have to drive the mules for a few more days."

"Wrong," Lucas said shortly. "You'll be acting as scout while I tend my wife."

Anne had never been sure of Hawk's position on the wagon train, but supposed he had been hired on as scout, along with Lucas. That supposition was quickly set to rights.

"You're the scout, Lucas. I only came along for the ride."

"Are you refusing?" Lucas asked softly.

"Nope." Hawk chuckled. "Just clarifying things." He looked at Anne. "Guess I'll be heading out to, um . . . do Luke's job . . . make sure he won't lose it while he's tending to other things."

"Get out of here, Hawk," Lucas growled.

Hawk grinned at the man who had the distinction of being his only friend, as well as the husband of the woman he desired. "I'm going," he replied. "But I'll be around for Anne's biscuits when she's up to making them again." He straightened his long length. "Best damn biscuits I ever tasted. A man would ride a long ways for a biscuit like hers, Lucas. You might think about that."

Lucas had thought about it—long and hard—while he was riding to the fort and back. But he wasn't very happy to know that Hawk had been thinking of those damn biscuits of Anne's as well. And, if Lucas wasn't mistaken, those light, fluffy, melt-in-the-mouth biscuits of hers wasn't the only thing about her Hawk found attractive.

Maybe, Lucas silently told himself, he would just forget that damned agreement.

It had been a stupid idea anyway. Anne was a beautiful

woman. And she was his wife. He had rights. Husbandly rights. And just because he hadn't chosen to exercise them before didn't mean that he couldn't do so.

His gaze found her mouth. Her lips were perfectly formed . . . pouty lips, the color of a ripe strawberry. So kissable.

Lucas had never forgotten the way she had tasted. Her mouth had been so sweet. So moist. Just the thought made him ready, wanting, needing.

He never should have kissed her.

God, why *had* he kissed her?

He raked a frustrated hand through his hair again. How was he supposed to deal with this longing, this aching need that demanded satisfaction?

"Lucas? What's wrong?"

"Nothing," he lied, forcing a smile to his lips. "I was thinking about everything that needed to be done before we leave here."

"I wish I could help." She hated the thought of causing so much trouble.

"You can help best by staying put, Anne. You had a high fever when I rode in here last night. It will take some time to recover your strength."

"I guess so." She plucked at the bedroll with restless fingers. "I just hate to be a problem."

"You're not. Did Hawk feed you yet?"

"Yes. And he made me eat every bite." It was an exaggeration, since she had been so hungry.

Luke's lips curled wryly. "Yeah. You already told me how good he was at looking after you." He stretched and arched his back, then headed for the iron skillet where his own breakfast waited.

Lucas ate hungrily, then cleaned and put everything away. He was loading the wagon when the doctor stopped by to examine his patient.

"Looks like she might be over the worst part," Wilson

said, securing a fresh bandage over the wound. "Just be sure and keep her down for a while, Lucas. That wound needs time to heal."

"I'll be sure and do that," Lucas said seriously.

He went about making room for Anne in the back of the wagon, and a short time later the wagons moved out, continuing their slow journey westward.

The landscape was rapidly changing. They had left the mesa, and in the distance, jagged peaks soared majestically, rising thousands of feet above sea level.

After two days of riding in the back of the wagon, Anne was glad to be allowed on the high seat beside Lucas where the view was so much better.

Game had become plentiful, and each day the hunters rode out, returning with deer, elk and turkeys slung across their saddles. And, since there was no way of preserving the meat except for smoking it—and there was no time to do that—each family received a portion of whatever was brought in.

One particular evening, as they lingered over a second cup of coffee, Lucas asked the question that had been bothering him for several days. "What is a thermostat, Anne?"

She looked curiously at him. "It's a heat regulator. Something that controls the temperature inside a building."

A heat-controlling device? Lucas smiled at the thought. His wife certainly had an imaginative mind. "And how does this . . . uh, regulator work?"

Shrugging her shoulders, Anne replied, "I don't know. And I never really thought too much about it. The electrical wires that run between the units—the air-conditioner and the furnace and thermostat—are responsible. Somehow." Her gaze was puzzled. "Where did you hear about thermostats anyway?"

"You mentioned it"

"I don't remember doing so." She was silent for a long moment, then, "I wish I could explain the whole process better, Lucas, but I'm afraid I'm a pure dunce where mechanics are involved."

She brushed aside a tangled, nutmeg curl, tucking it behind her ear. During the trek her hair had become longer, and she hadn't had the time, or the inclination, to borrow a pair of scissors for a trim.

"We need a pair of scissors," she muttered, tucking another long strand behind the other ear.

"Why?"

"Why do we need the scissors?" At his nod, she replied, "I need to cut my hair."

"No."

"What?"

"Don't cut your hair." Then, as though the matter had been settled, he said, "Tell me something about yourself, Anne. Do you have brothers or sisters?"

"No." She smiled at him. "I am an only child. My mother died several years ago, and my father moved us to Dallas. It was closer to his work. I hated it, though. It was too crowded to suit me. But I was able to spend summers with my grandparents. They owned a farm in east Texas." In her mind's eye she could see the farm, could see her grandmother feeding the chickens and clucking sympathetically as one particular hen tried to steal all the corn.

"I loved spending time with my grandparents. Gramps would take me out to Lake of the Pines for a week at a time." Anne laughed happily. "He believed in using that Golden Age Pass of his as often as possible."

"Golden Age Pass? What is that?"

"The Golden Age Pass is a card issued to Senior citizens so they can use the parks without paying an entry fee. It's just one of the perks of growing old.''

"Perks?''

"Uh . . .'' She searched for a way to explain. "Perks are . . . a plus, as opposed to a minus. One of the good things about growing old.''

"There is nothing good about growing old, Anne. Age often brings wisdom . . . in most cases. But it also brings weakness. Of body and sometimes of mind. And we live in a world where only the fittest survive. Too often, especially during harsh winters, the old and feeble are left behind when nomadic tribes move their village. No.'' He shook his head. "There is nothing good about growing old.''

"Not now,'' she agreed. "Not here, in this time of yours, but where I come from. In my time . . . the future . . . things have changed. We've learned the benefit of exercise. Of eating the right kinds of foods to keep our bodies healthy. People live longer in the future.'' She leaned forward, her expression earnest, wanting him to understand. "Things are so different here, Lucas. In your time, women are literally worked to death. They die so young, either in childbirth, or by disease their bodies are too weak to resist. But things change over the next century. Drastically.

"Machines will be invented to wash and dry clothes. Machines will wash and dry dishes. They will clean floors. Microwaves will cook a whole meal in a matter of minutes that would take hours, or even the whole day, to cook here.''

His lips curled into a smile that suddenly erupted into laughter. She was so intense that he could almost believe her. Almost. "And what do the women do while these . . . uh . . . machines do all the work for them?''

Her blue eyes glinted as humor mingled with disappointment. "You don't believe me, do you?''

"Did you really expect me to?"

"I hoped you would." She smiled wryly. "It would have been nice to talk about my past—and your future—sometimes."

"I have no objection to talking about whatever you desire, Anne," Lucas replied. "Just as long as you keep your imaginings between the two of us."

"This is not imagination, Lucas." Anne's lips stretched thin, and anger darkened her vivid blue eyes. "I am not a half-wit. Nor has my brain been cooked by the sun, as a few others have suggested."

"Yet you maintain you come from some distant future."

"Not just some distant future," she replied. "But a particular time. The year of 1999."

"Oh, yes. You did say 1999, didn't you?" Lukc sipped his coffee, watching her over the rim. "If that's true, Anne, then you must know what's going to happen in the future."

Anne felt a flicker of excitement. Was Lucas finally receptive to her words? He gave every appearance of being so. What had he asked her? Oh, yes. "I do have knowledge about some of . . . the future," she replied.

"Tell me, then." His voice was a soft purr, not unlike a cat just before it pounces. "Will we reach Oregon Territory safely?"

"I don't know that!" Her tone was completely exasperated.

"Why not?" he asked. "You claim to know the future, yet you can't answer such a simple question?" Lucas had no idea why he was so inclined to torment her, only knew that it was so.

"I *am* from your future. But I don't know every detail that happens between now and then. I know several wagon trains went to Oregon, but I don't know any particulars about any of them. Of course, there was the Donner party." Where had they been going? To Oregon? Or had it been California?

"The Donner party?"

"Yes," she replied. "More than half of their members were lost when they were trapped by snow in the Sierra Nevadas. That happened in the mid-eighteen hundreds. I'm not sure of the year." She shuddered. "History books say they ate human flesh to survive."

Something flickered in the depths of his dark eyes. "That tragedy is told throughout the land. It happened five years ago."

"Oh. Well, there's the Civil War coming up," she said. "The war between the states. And there's the gold strike in California . . . but that's already happened, hasn't it?"

"Yes. There has been a gold strike there. You say there will be a war between the states?"

"Yes. Between the North and the South. The bloodiest thing in history. Brother fought against brother, father against son. And even though we've gone through two world wars since then, the Civil War is the most abhorred."

"Two world wars? The whole world was at war?"

"Twice." She went on to explain, and when she was done, he remained silent, staring into the flames that danced and twirled around the wood.

Lucas almost believed her. There was something in her eyes when she spoke of the war, something that went beyond pretense.

"I've thought about the whole thing since coming here, Lucas," she said softly. "Thought about it many times. And I've wondered if the Civil War could be prevented by foreknowledge, or if I should even try changing history, no matter how horrifying the events. But how could I possibly prevent something so terrible from happening when no one will believe me? Even Mary thinks I've gone completely bonkers the few times I've talked about the future." She shrugged her shoulders. "So I just keep my mouth shut."

"A wise thing to do," he said gruffly. "Your words only confuse people."

She speared him with a hard look from cold eyes. "You still don't believe me, do you?"

"No. I'm afraid I don't. Nobody has the power to predict the future."

"I'm not predicting the future. I'm only telling you what happened in my past."

"What you believe happened."

"Is there a difference?"

He shifted impatiently. "Yes. There most certainly is a difference."

"I know what I know," she said defiantly. "And *every-one* doesn't believe I've lost my mind."

He raised a dark brow. "Someone believes you? Who?"

"Hawk believes me."

"He said that?"

"Not in so many words. But we had occasion to talk together when he was looking after me, and he didn't ridicule my words."

A muscle twitched in Luke's jaw, and he stared at the biscuits Anne had put aside in case Hawk rode into camp. He would be damned if he would let the warrior eat biscuits that his wife had made. If Hawk wanted to eat biscuits, he could get his own wife.

Luke snatched up the biscuits and rose grimly.

"Why are you taking the biscuits?" Anne asked.

"They're for my horse."

He stalked away, leaving Anne to watch with her mouth open.

* * *

Anne had settled in for the night when Lucas returned to the wagon. Although her bedroll was beneath the wagon, as was her usual practice, she had spread Luke's blankets beside the fire.

She was aware of him pausing, of his long silence; then he snatched up the bedroll and spread it beside her own.

Moments later he stretched out on the pallet and pulled her against him.

"Lucas!" she gasped. "What are you doing?"

"Getting ready for bed," he replied.

"But . . . why are you here next to me?"

"You're my wife," he said grimly. "And from now on you'll sleep beside me . . . whether or not it's cold."

"But what about our agreement?"

"The agreement hasn't been broken. The marriage is still not consummated." Anger, not good sense, was responsible for his next words. "Nor will it ever be."

"Oh."

She had hoped otherwise.

Although Anne felt sure she would never be able to sleep, not with the tension that vibrated between them, the heat radiating from his body was soothing to her nerves, and she soon drifted off.

She was deep in the arms of Morpheus when he shifted her closer. "Luke?" she mumbled sleepily.

"Who else?" he asked through gritted teeth.

Anne sighed sleepily and curled herself against him. Her hand slid around his neck, her fingers tangling in his hair, and she sighed again.

Swearing beneath his breath, roundly cursing himself for a fool, Lucas moved his hand upward until he could cup the round firmness of her breast.

A fire streaked through him then, lodging in the core

of his strength and spreading outward. And, even as he told himself to put her from him, he pulled her hips closer against that part of him that burned so hotly.

He was rigid with desire, yet Anne slept on, completely unaware—and more than likely uncaring—of his need, or his pain.

Lucas wondered how long he could go on like this. He fought against his desire with every fiber of strength he possessed, yet it was not enough.

His mind told him to leave her alone, yet his body forced him to reach out to her.

His mind told him she was just like Barbara Fairchild, yet his body refused to listen.

Slowly he came to realize that there were differences between the two women.

Barbara had thought only of herself.

Anne was concerned about others.

Barbara would have fainted at the first sight of blood, yet Anne had fought bravely beside him.

Barbara was selfish.

Anne gave of herself, lending a hand wherever needed.

They were both beautiful women, unused to the rigors of frontier life, yet Anne was willing to learn, to do her part, rather than wait for others to do for her.

Perhaps Anne was not like Barbara after all.

Lucas held her firmly against him and wanted nothing more than to bury himself in the soft folds of her body. He wanted to taste her sweetness, to feel her respond to his possession.

And yet, if she did respond, he would never be able to keep that damned agreement. If he gave in to the yearnings of his body and caressed the softness that was pressed so close against him, he would never leave this bed without making her his wife in every sense of the word.

He was tempted. Lord, how he was tempted.

Lucas swallowed hard, fighting against his body's

needs. As though acting without thought, his hand slid downward, coming to rest on the soft curve of her buttocks. He pulled her closer against the pulsing hardness that fought against confinement.

If only he could—

"Lucas?" Anne muttered sleepily. "Are you having trouble sleeping?" She shifted closer, her taut nipples rubbing against his chest. "Is there anything I can do to help?"

"Yes," he rasped harshly. "You could help me. But I'll be damned if I let you!"

He shoved her away from him roughly. "Dammit, woman!" he swore. "Why in hell must you tempt me so?"

Startled, Anne came completely awake. "What?" She stared up at him with luminous blue eyes. "What are you saying, Lucas? What did I do?"

"Nothing!" he snapped. "You damned well did nothing. And that, my dear wife, is the whole problem."

She stared at him, feeling utterly confused at his words. "Lucas? What's wrong?"

But Lucas had nothing more to say.

In fact, he was so unwilling to speak that he carried his bedroll into the darkness that surrounded them, leaving Anne to lie awake long into the night, wondering what he was so upset about.

Chapter Seventeen

"Oh, my Lord, Anne! Would you look at that!"

Anne had no need to make reply. She was looking. Everyone on the riverbank was looking. And not a soul among them was happy with what they saw.

"We can't cross that," a woman nearby protested. "The river's too wide and the water's rising too fast and it's bound to be too deep in the middle."

"What if we lose the wagon?" said another.

Anne turned to look at the woman who had spoken. She was a pretty woman with blond hair that she kept tied back at the neck. The family—they had several young children—rarely mixed with the other travelers, yet they seemed friendly enough when approached.

"Zeke Masters knows what he's doing, Sarah Jane," her husband soothed. "He wouldn't take the wagons across if it was dangerous."

"But Elijah," she protested. "He may not know. And everything we own is in that wagon. The furniture. And pictures. And my grandmother's china! Oh, God, Elijah! I couldn't bear to lose my grandmother's china!''

"Good Lord, Sarah Jane!" Mary scolded. "I can't believe you're moaning over a set of dishes when there's more here at stake."

A flush swept over the young woman's face, and she looked away, settling her gaze on the river again.

Anne felt sorry for the woman. She was just as worried as the others around her, but she kept her opinion to herself. Sarah Jane's husband was right. Zeke Masters knew his business. He would keep them safe.

But he didn't know the river was in a flood, a silent voice reminded. *He told us it was wide and shallow.*

Perhaps it was wide, and maybe it was shallow enough to cross, but Anne didn't want to be the one responsible for driving their wagon safely across.

"Lucas should be doing this," she muttered.

"What did you say, dear?" Mary asked.

"I said Lucas ought to be the one driving his mules across the river."

Mary patted her arm. "You'll do just fine, dear."

Suddenly the wagon master strode among them. "That's enough gawking, folks," he said in that booming voice of his. "You know what you're up against now, so load up and let's hop to it."

Muttering among themselves, the travelers dispersed, moving to their respective wagons and climbing atop their high perches while they mentally prepared themselves for the journey across the wide river.

Anne lingered on the riverbank, eyeing the muddy water with trepidation. Was it possible? she wondered. Could she really cross the river without losing the wagon?

"What are you waiting for, Anne?" Zeke Masters shouted. "Get on that wagon, woman! Or you'll lose your place in line!"

His words sent Anne scurrying toward the wagon. She

couldn't afford to lose her place in line. The first wagons would have an easier time crossing the river.

By the time she had climbed to her high perch on the wagon, there was a loud commotion down by the river.

"Get those ropes tight!"

"Grab that lead mule's reins and pull him up!"

"Don't let 'em stop in the middle, boys! Keep 'em moving along!"

The shouted orders continued, coming one right after another as the men worked together beside the mule teams to keep the wagons moving along.

Anne's fingernails dug anxiously into her palms as she watched the men work. The wagons squeaked and groaned as they crawled slowly across the swelling water. There was a shout of jubilation as the first wagon reached the other side.

"Dammit! We made it!"

"That's just one wagon, boys!" Zeke roared. "Get your butts back here and let's get the others across!"

Anne's stomach was queasy. There were only two wagons in front of her now, and one of them was already entering the water.

Anne gathered the reins in her right hand while her left hand clutched the wagon seat with a white-knuckled grip. She couldn't do this alone. No way. The mules were stubborn. They would balk at the first sign of trouble, and she would be stuck in the middle of the river.

What was Zeke thinking of anyway? He should have circled the wagons on this side of the river. They could wait for the water to subside.

Yes. That would be the way.

Anne shifted her gaze upstream. The river looked even wider there, almost double in size.

Oh, God, she couldn't do this!

Settle down, Anne, a silent voice urged. *You can make*

it across. The other wagon did. And the men are there to help if there's any trouble.

Even as she reassured herself, she heard the shouts of triumph that told her another wagon had reached the creek bank safely.

And then it was her turn.

She didn't need to urge the mules forward; they followed the wagon ahead of them, keeping in line as they had done ever since leaving Fort Laramie. But even as that thought occurred, the lead mules reached the muddy water and stopped abruptly.

Fear surged through Anne. The mules apparently had more sense than the humans who drove them. They realized they couldn't make it to the other side, so they refused to even try.

Anne sent her gaze skittering across the muddy water, to the man whose word was law. Maybe he would allow her to stay on this side, to wait for Lucas or Hawk, whoever returned first.

Suddenly Masters' attention was focused on her. But instead of the sympathy she had expected, he was cursing roundly.

"Dammit, Anne, drive them mules in the water! You're holding up the wagons!"

Anne swallowed around her fear and cracked the whip over the backs of the mules. "Eeeyahh! Get along there, mules," she hollered.

The mules lumbered forward, straining at the harness as they pulled the wagon into the churning froth that was lapping at their hooves.

Nothing she had ever dealt with had prepared Anne for this. Not even the Indian attack. At least then there had been something substantial to fight. But nothing could stop a river when flooded.

Water lapped thirstily around them as the mules continued to plod through the muddy river, dragging the wagon slowly behind them.

Swallowing around her fear, Anne snapped the whip in the air again, watching the water surge higher around the wagon wheels. She could feel the power generated by the current as the water rushed past her. She could feel the wagon swaying beneath its own weight as the mules strained to keep their burden moving forward.

They can't do it, an inner voice cried. *They'll never make it to the other side. If you keep on going, you'll lose the wagon. Better to abandon the wagon now, to lose it in the flood, than lose your life.*

Anne tried to ignore the silent voice.

Snapping her whip again, Anne yelled encouragingly at the mules, knowing she could not abandon the wagon. Even if Lucas didn't need the supplies, she would probably drown before she reached the other side.

The water rose higher as they reached the middle of the river, and the wagon lurched sideways, lifted by the churning brown waves.

Fear was Anne's constant companion now. It shivered through her, settling in a tight knot in the pit of her stomach, before spreading out and moving up into her throat.

Water splashed higher, dampening the hem of her skirt. But she paid no attention, knowing there was far more at stake than a wet skirt.

The water was rough, relentless, and it continued to rise swiftly. The wagon swayed constantly, lurching forward behind the mules that would surely balk at any given moment.

And if they did, she would lose the wagon, and perhaps, her life as well.

Anne refused to drown.

"Eeeeyahhh!" she yelled again, snapping the whip as close as she could get to the mules without actually touching their ornery hides. "Get along there, you stubborn devils!"

The wagon lurched forward again, then suddenly stopped. Smack dab in the middle of the river.

The wagon slid sideways, caught by the current. "Oh, God!" Anne muttered, cracking the whip over the mules' backs. "Get along there, mules!"

The mules didn't budge, and Anne's fear was a tangible thing. She wasn't going to make it.

Then suddenly, help was at hand. Amazing though it seemed, Hawk was beside the wagon. "Give me the reins and hold on," he shouted above the roaring water.

Anne quickly handed them over, then gripped the wagon seat with both hands, determined to keep herself in place. Hawk would know what to do. He would see her safely across the river.

Riding ahead of the mules, Hawk forced them forward. The mules strained against the harness, and the wagon wheels began to turn again. The wagon lurched, swaying sideways, then steadied.

Hawk stayed with the mules, urging them forward even after they had reached firmer ground. And when they were finally on the other side, he returned to the wagon, looking up at Anne with concern. "Are you all right?"

"Yes. Thank you, Hawk. I wouldn't have made it across if you hadn't come along."

"No thanks needed," he said abruptly. "You can relax now." He reined his mount around, intent on helping the others who might need it.

Exhaustion weighed heavily on Anne as she drove the team to higher ground, joining the other three wagons already there. Her muscles ached with strain, and there was a knot between her shoulder blades.

Anne wanted to rest, to close her eyes and sleep, but that was impossible, she realized. It was only midafternoon. Zeke wouldn't call a halt to their journey before sundown.

She was wrong, she discovered, when only moments later, Hawk reined up beside her. "We'll be making camp here tonight, Anne," he said. "Move over and let me handle those mules for you."

"What about the other wagons?"

"Masters is leaving them on the other side for the time being."

"What's going on here?" demanded a harsh voice.

Anne turned to see Colby approaching. His gaze flickered between them suspiciously, as though he suspected them of some devious plot.

Ignoring him, Anne climbed down from the wagon, leaving Hawk to deal with the man and his suspicions.

They made camp that night with six wagons on one side of the river, while the rest camped on the other side. It was obvious to everyone there that they wouldn't be going anywhere for a while. Not until the water subsided enough to allow the other wagons to cross.

It was a beautiful place to camp, with willows growing beside the river and, farther on, a thicker growth of pines and fragrant cedars. Even the ground itself was covered with lush grass and wildflowers.

But Anne was too weary to admire her surroundings. Too weary even for food. She cooked anyway, though. Hawk deserved a hot meal for seeing her safely across the river.

Hawk had finished his meal and they were lingering over coffee when Lucas rode in.

His shoulders were slumped with weariness as he dismounted beside the wagon and ground-reined the dun. His long strides carried him swiftly across the distance, and Anne could see the tired lines radiating out from the corners of his eyes.

"Did you leave any of those biscuits for me, Hawk?" His voice was a combination of teasing and something else that was not so innocent. Something grim. "I've been a long time without hot food in my belly, and I wouldn't take it kindly if you've devoured everything my *wife* cooked up."

"There's plenty left," Hawk replied. "Though it's more than you deserve." He swallowed the last of his coffee and tossed out the dregs, then unfolded his long length. "Guess I'll see to the dun. He looks like he's been rode hard."

Lucas grunted. "He was." He took the plate Anne had piled with food and squatted down beside her. "You okay?" he asked.

"Yes," she said softly, her gaze feasting on him. It had been three days since she had seen him, and she wondered where he had been sleeping. "I had some trouble with the crossing. But Hawk helped me."

Lucas pinned the other man with a hard look. "Seems to me he stays mighty close these days."

Hawk lifted a dark brow. "Would you rather have lost the wagon . . . and your *wife?*" Like Lucas, Hawk stressed one word.

"No. And thanks for your help, old friend." Lucas took spoon in hand and tended to the business of eating.

Hawk unsaddled the Lineback dun, then took reins in hand. "I'm staying out there tonight, Lucas," he said. "Keep a sharp eye out here."

Luke's head jerked up, and he met his friend's eyes. "Something going on I don't know about?"

"Just a precaution. I saw a Ute hunting party a few miles north of here."

"Did you tell Masters?"

Hawk nodded. "He knows. It's the reason he was so determined to get the wagons across the river. He was hoping to put more miles between us. But he's taking precautions."

Fear shivered through Anne as she remembered the Indian attack and its results. "Will there be trouble?"

"I doubt it," Hawk replied, smiling at her. Then he strode away into the gathering darkness, taking the dun along with him.

Lucas concentrated on filling the empty space in his belly. At least he gave every appearance of doing so. But he was aware of each move Anne made as she went about the business of cleaning up and putting things away.

He had missed her. Too much. He watched as she added another log to the fire, saw how her bodice stretched taut across her breasts, outlining the round globes of feminine flesh beneath.

An urge came over him then, almost overpowering in its intensity. He wanted to strip her naked, to caress her breasts with his tongue and teeth until her nipples were firm with desire and she was squirming beneath him, begging for what he wanted to give her.

Such a foolish notion, he knew, forcing his eyes away from her and back to the food that was needed to replenish his energy.

Anne was aware of his gaze as she washed and dried the dishes and utensils. When she had finished packing them away, she turned to leave, bent on finding her bed as quickly as possible.

"Don't go," Luke said quietly. "I'm tired of my own company, Anne. Stay and have coffee with me."

Anne smiled at him, secretly delighted that he wanted her company. "I'll get another cup."

"No. Sit down," he ordered. "You can share mine."

She found it strangely erotic to drink from Luke's cup, knowing his lips had been there before hers. She almost swore she could taste him on the rim.

As for Lucas, he fought the urge to reach out, to take her sweet body into his arms, to cover her soft mouth with his. He needed to hold her and be held in return.

But he could not . . . dare not, lest his emotions overpower him and he find himself making love to her. To do so would be heaven. To bury himself in her sweet body, to feel his staff in her warm sheath, just the thought caused such a surge of desire that he shifted to hide his need.

They spoke together quietly, talking about the trail they had already passed over, and the one yet to come. And then he was describing the cabin he meant to build when they reached Oregon.

"It will be small at first." His expression was relaxed, his gaze thoughtful as he stared into the flames. "Just one room. But others can be added later when we need more space."

We. Anne found herself desperately wanting that home, needing to stay with him, yet she had agreed to a parting of ways. It had been a devil's bargain she had made, she realized now. But she must abide by her word.

Sorrow weighed heavily on her shoulders by the time she sought her bed. And she didn't see Luke's yearning gaze follow her all the way.

Tears rained down Bright Water's face as she raced through the forest. Her breath came in short gasps, and her blood pumped heavily through her veins. *I must get help,* her mind screamed. *Must find the shaman. Only he can help Black Crow.*

The land rose sharply upward, and she clutched the babe tighter in her arms, knowing that she must not lose her balance lest she hurt the child. She stumbled, then quickly righted herself. She must go on, must get help.

Yet even as she continued her onward flight, her mind told her it was no use. The village was so far away, would take half a day or more to reach, even by swift pony . . . and she was afoot.

Coward! her heart screamed. *You should have helped*

Black Crow when the Ute warriors attacked him, instead of hiding as he ordered.

Even as the thought occurred, she realized she could not have helped her husband. Not against the four attackers. If she had not fled, then she and her baby would both be dead . . . like Black Crow.

Like Black Crow. *Her husband.* Dead.

It was true. Running would not change the facts. The shaman could not help her husband. She had seen the killing blow dealt him, yet her eyes had denied it. She had waited, hidden in the bushes, while the Utes fell upon her husband, slashing at him with knives until there was no sign of movement.

And when it was over, they took the horse and rode away, either unaware, or uncaring, of Bright Water and the babe who were hidden in the bushes nearby.

There had been so much blood. So much. And her husband had lain so still, almost unrecognizable in death.

Bright Water's knees weakened at the memory. She had barely reached the top of the gully before her strength ran out. As her babe let out a wail, she crumpled on the ground, unaware of the flowers that grew nearby, unaware as well of the danger that coiled beneath them.

Until she heard the warning rattle.

Chapter Eighteen

The sun was a crimson ball riding the eastern horizon when Anne opened her eyes the next morning. Yawning widely, she stretched her arms above her head and shivered delicately.

The morning air had a definite chill to it, making her want to linger in bed, something she hadn't been able to do since she had been chewed up and spit out of that damned tornado.

A smile curled her lips as she thought about her life in the twentieth century. She had worked hard at her job and found satisfaction in that work.

But, surprising though it seemed, she didn't miss that old life. She derived more satisfaction out of her accomplishments here, simple things like preparing a meal for her husband or crossing a river without losing the wagon . . . or her life.

Of course, she'd had some help crossing the river, but Anne was satisfied she had given a fair accounting of herself before Hawk arrived.

Hawk.

The warrior was an enigma. And so was Lucas.

Before she could pursue that thought, the aroma of strong, hot coffee wafted over her. It was almost overpowering, as though someone were waving a cup back and forth somewhere nearby.

She turned lazily to see Lucas squatting beside the wagon, doing exactly that. She smiled into his laughing eyes, then focused her gaze on the steaming cup.

"I don't suppose that coffee is mine."

He grinned at her before lifting the cup to his own mouth and taking a long, leisurely drink, as though intent on teasing her. "Now it is," he said, handing the cup to her.

"Thank you," she murmured.

With Lucas watching her closely, Anne turned the cup and placed her lips in the exact same spot where his had been only moments before. Something flickered in his dark eyes as he watched her drink from the cup, and she felt heat coil through her belly.

"Breakfast is about ready," he said huskily.

"You're going to spoil me."

He grinned wryly. "I could change places with you. Or better yet, I could just join you there and to hell with eating."

Her cheeks caught fire. "Lucas," she scolded. "There's no privacy here."

The words had no sooner left her mouth when Lucas took off like a scalded cat, leaving her to wonder why he had done so.

Anne finished her coffee, then crawled out of bed and saw to her morning ablutions while Lucas finished making breakfast. They ate in silence since neither of them were inclined to make conversation. That soon changed, though, when Hawk stopped by.

"Did you leave anything for me?" he asked Lucas.

Lucas nodded at the iron skillet where he had left a portion of fried potatoes, salt pork and biscuits. "Help yourself," he grunted.

Hawk did so. Then, with breakfast in hand, he squatted down beside them to eat. "The stock was restless last night," he said gruffly, shoving a forkful of potatoes in his mouth.

"You think there's trouble afoot?"

Hawk picked up a biscuit and frowned. "Might be. Or it might have been just a hungry coyote looking to fill his belly." He threw a hard look at Lucas. "Anne never made these biscuits." There was accusation in his tone as well as a good measure of disgust. "This bread is hard as a rock."

Anne couldn't help the giggle that erupted. She agreed wholeheartedly with Hawk, but unlike the Comanche warrior, she had chosen to keep silent about Luke's bread making.

"You don't have to eat them," Lucas said mildly.

Almost defiantly, Hawk shoved the biscuit in his mouth and chewed with great exaggeration. "My belly needs filling," he explained, making a show of washing the bread down with his coffee.

"You talked to Masters yet?" Luke asked.

Hawk nodded. "The river crested during the night, but it will be a while before the water goes down enough for the wagons to cross. Might be two or three days."

"Does that mean we're stopping here for a while?" Anne asked eagerly. She had clothes to wash and mend, and so far, there had been no time for such things.

"Looks like it," Lucas replied. "So we might as well make ourselves comfortable."

Anne had no objection to that.

The men talked quietly together while she cleared away the breakfast dishes and put away the food. But soon

Hawk bade them good-bye and left to do whatever men do when they find themselves at loose ends.

Tossing the dregs from his cup, Lucas dropped it in the empty dishpan, then leaned into the wagon, picked up a box, and set it on the ground.

"What are you doing?" Anne asked curiously, peering over his shoulder at the boxes and crates and barrels of supplies.

His fingers curled around a rocking chair leg, and he dragged it forward and set it on the ground beside her. "Getting this for you."

Anne was so pleased that she stood on tiptoe and kissed his cheek. "Thank you, Lucas," she murmured.

Although the kiss was nothing more than a peck, Lucas felt the effect clear down to his toes. He fought the urge to clasp her to him, to claim her lips with hard possession. He was on the point of doing so, and damn the consequences, when she stepped back and carried the rocker to their makeshift table.

"There," she said. "Now, doesn't that look homey?"

Lucas found the notion completely ridiculous. A circle of wagons could never be called a home. A home was a place where a man could close a door, shutting himself away from prying eyes. A home was a place where he could make love to his wife in complete privacy. Where he would not have to hide his feelings, or his body when it demanded satisfaction.

As it did now.

And a home was a place where others would not enter unless they were invited. A place where he wouldn't have to put up with the likes of Colby, who was fast approaching his wagon.

Lucas ignored the man and leaned into the wagon again, reaching for the harness that needed mending, and hoping that was enough to dissuade Colby from stopping by.

He should have known better.

"Howdy, Lucas." Colby leaned against the wagon and watched Lucas untangle the harness he had thrown there several days before. "I see you've already heard the news."

Lucas turned to face the wiry man, the worn harness dangling from his right hand. "What news is that?" he asked shortly.

"The news that we'll be staying here awhile."

"Hawk did mention that when he stopped by."

Colby followed Lucas to the campfire and settled himself in the rocker, making Luke's mouth flatten with displeasure.

"Well, what do you think about it?"

Lucas shrugged. "Masters knows his business."

Colby grunted, then said, "I wouldn't say no to a cup of coffee if offered one."

"We finished off the pot," Luke said shortly.

Colby's gaze shifted to Anne, who was going through one of the boxes Lucas had unloaded. "Reckon your woman could have another pot boiling soon enough."

"She could." Luke's voice was hard. "If either of us wanted some. But we don't. And you might remember something, Colby."

"What's that?"

"Anne is not just my woman. She's my *wife*. And as such, she's entitled to respect." His voice became softer, yet it was cold as ice. "It would be to your benefit to treat her accordingly."

Colby tensed, his angry gaze narrowing on Anne, as though suspecting her of something devious. But when he spoke again, his voice, as well as his expression, was mild. "I ain't looking for trouble, Lucas."

"Then, what are you looking for?"

"Support," Colby replied. "Masters is bent on making us wait here until the river goes down."

"Sounds like a damn good idea to me. There's no way the other wagons can cross the river now."

Colby gave up all pretense of affability. "Hell's fire, McCord! A man like you oughtta know we ain't got no time to waste!"

"A man like me?" Lucas queried softly.

"Yeah. You bein' a breed an' all."

"Nobody can predict how long a river will be in flood." Luke's face was impassive, save for the muscle that twitched in his jaw. "Not even a half-breed."

Colby didn't appear to notice. "Maybe not. But you know we ain't got no time to lose. The south pass could be closed by the time we get there, and you know damn well we don't have the supplies to wait another year before crossing the mountains!"

"Zeke Masters knows what he's doing, Colby. That's the reason he's wagon master. I suggest you leave the decision making up to him."

With a muttered oath, Colby jerked upright, leaving the rocking chair swaying beneath him. "I should've known you'd side with him. You don't care if we ever reach Oregon, do you? And why should you? You ain't nothing but a damn half-breed."

Anne had been content to stay out of their discussion, but no longer. She turned on Colby with the fury of a mother cat whose kittens were threatened. "How dare you call him names!" she spat. "Luke's twice the man you are, you pompous little twerp. I ought to—"

"Keep out of this, Anne!" Lucas snarled.

"No!" she cried. "I won't! I'm tired of his name-calling. Tired of him trying to stir up trouble." Her anger was a tangible thing as she held the intruder's gaze. "Go back to your own wagon, Colby, and keep away from ours!"

The man was plainly furious. "Is she giving the orders around here now?" he asked spitefully. "Somehow, that doesn't surprise me none. It takes a real man to keep a woman in line."

"That's enough!" Luke's voice was carefully controlled, which made it all the more menacing. "Get out of here, Colby, before I decide to take you apart with my bare hands."

Whatever Colby was, he was no fool. He scurried quickly away, putting distance between himself and the man who gave every impression of a prowling cougar.

Lucas waited until the other man was out of hearing; then he dragged Anne behind the wagon. "Don't you ever do that again!" he snarled.

Anne flinched from the look in his eyes. "He insulted you, Lucas."

"And it was my place to do something about it . . . if I wanted to. Which I did not." He looked furious enough to eat nails. "You made me look a fool, Anne. Like a man too weak to stand up for himself."

"But I never meant—"

"Dammit!" he barked. "I didn't ask for your help. And I sure as hell didn't want it!"

Tears stung the backs of Anne's eyes, and Lucas swore roundly as they overflowed and rained down her face.

With a muttered curse, Lucas flung her from him and strode quickly away from her. Moments later she saw him riding out of camp.

"That's it, Lucas," she muttered, wiping away the tears that continued to dampen her cheeks. "Just ride on out when the going gets rough."

Anne wished she could leave as well, that she could find a quiet place, away from prying eyes, where she could come to grips with her trampled emotions.

Her gaze found the heavy growth of willows standing nearby, and she decided a brisk walk was just what she needed.

As she had hoped, she felt a sense of peace beneath

the willow trees. She strolled through them, stopping to gather wildflowers on occasion, as she wandered farther and farther away from the others.

Anne had no notion of how far she had gone when she found a spring—only a seepage really—that bubbled out of the ground. And beside the spring grew a large patch of watercress.

She gathered some of the greens, then continued walking along the game trail the animals had worn smooth in their quest for water. Her thoughts were on Lucas, and the harshness he had displayed when she had only meant to chastise Colby for speaking so badly of him.

What had she done that was so wrong anyway?

Every time she thought they might be getting close, something always happened to turn him into that cold stranger that she so despised.

Tears stung her eyes again, and she struggled to bring her emotions under control. Crying would do no good. She had learned that long ago. And, as Gram used to say, it did no good to cry over spilt milk.

When Gram was alive, Anne had never felt alone. As she did now. So alone.

Stop it! Anne silently chided herself. *You're acting like a fool. So Luke is angry. So what? People have been angry with you before, and you've survived. Time to quit feeling sorry for yourself and get on with your life.*

Sighing heavily, Anne was on the point of returning to the wagons when she saw a patch of scarlet growing at the edge of the trail several yards away.

Was it wild roses?

Before she had time to reconsider, Anne hurried toward the bright patch of color growing near a deep gully. She was leaning over to examine the flowers when a thin wail, carried on the breeze, stopped her. Straightening her body, Anne continued to the edge of the gully.

The sound came from below, she realized, and it

reminded her of an animal in pain. The cry was so weak that had it not been for the breeze, Anne might not have heard it.

Knowing she couldn't leave without tracing down its source, Anne slid down the slope, amidst a rattle of shaley rock, looking for whatever had made the sound. But there was nothing to direct her, no sound except for the rocks sliding beneath her own feet.

Her gaze swept back and forth, searching the narrow gully. Several bushes grew along the bottom. The branches were broken on the nearest one, as though something heavy—a bear?—had torn through them.

Her body tensed as she approached the bush with caution, aware there might be danger lurking there.

Anne was so intent on the broken branches that she almost stumbled over the bundle that lay on the ground. It was almost the color of the rocks that covered the bottom of the gully, yet there was a subtle difference that caught her attention. A spot of color, as tiny as a button . . . no, several buttons. And they had been sewn on the bundle, as though for decoration.

She bent to examine the bundle, realizing immediately it was made of tanned leather, soft, supple leather, except there was a stiffness about it, too, as though a board had been placed inside.

For what purpose?

Ever aware of danger, Anne picked up a stick and prodded the bundle. A weak cry sounded from within, then stopped abruptly.

Good Lord, it sounded like a kitten.

Anne knelt beside the bundle and turned it over. It was a soft-skin pouch, with a wooden frame, laced tightly from one end to another.

No. There was a hole at one end, she realized. A hole decorated with beads. But the pouch was too large for what it contained, and the lacings had been drawn so tightly there was only a narrow slit left.

The mewling sound came again. Weak, abrupt, as though whatever lay within the bundle was barely alive.

Anne's fingers trembled as she loosened the lacings to reveal a tiny head covered with coal black hair.

"Oh, my God!" she muttered. "It's a baby."

A baby with black hair and dark eyes that were scrunched up as though in pain.

"There now," Anne murmured, picking up the soft leather bundle that must surely be a cradleboard. "You're fine now, little baby. You're here with Annie, and we're going to find your mother."

It didn't take long to find her. The broken branches told their own story. The young mother lay on the other side of the bush, her eyes open in horror as they had obviously been when she died.

Propping the cradleboard against her thigh, Anne closed the woman's eyes and bowed her head in silent prayer. Her eyes misted, and a lump clogged her throat. The baby was alone now, left without a mother as she, herself, had once been.

She scooped up the cradleboard and looked at the infant inside. "Don't worry, sweetie," she said softly. "I'll take care of you."

Anne was on the verge of leaving when she noticed a difference in the woman's legs. One was much larger than the other, swollen, perhaps.

A quick examination revealed the fang marks that told her the woman had been bitten by a snake.

Venom. The young mother had died from the poison.

Was the snake hidden somewhere nearby?

Anne held the cradleboard tightly as she hurried down the gully, searching for an easier way out. She had only gone a short distance when the gully widened, the sides sloping outward, making her escape easier.

Scrambling up the slope, Ann hurried back up the path leading to the wagons.

She cuddled the baby close and caressed its silky cheek as her thoughts whirled, making and discarding plans. She would have to find Zeke Masters and tell him about the dead woman she had found. He would see she had a decent burial, and perhaps locate the child's father as well.

But first the baby needed feeding.

Anne carried the babe back to her wagon and quickly stirred together a mixture of sugar and water. Then she tried to spoon some into the infant's mouth. The sugar water dribbled from the corner without reaching the babe's throat.

"Come on, little one," Anne soothed, spooning more into the baby's mouth. "Swallow just a little for me, please."

As though understanding what Anne wanted, the tiny throat muscles worked, and some of the liquid was swallowed. But not enough, Anne knew. Not nearly enough to keep the babe alive.

Realizing she needed help quickly, Anne went searching for the doctor. But she found Zeke Masters first.

After listening to her explanation of how she had come to find the baby, he fixed his astonished gaze on the babe, then shifted it back to stare at Anne as though he suspected she had lost her mind. "Why in hell did you bring the baby with you?" he growled. "Ye gads, woman! That's the last thing you should have done!"

Anne's gaze darkened with anger. "What, exactly, should I have done with the baby, then?" she asked sharply. "Leave it there to die?"

"Better it than us," he grated.

"For God's sake, Zeke!" she exclaimed. "You don't really think this baby presents a danger, do you?"

"Not in itself," he replied gruffly. "But there's a father out there somewhere, and he's sure to come looking for the kid."

"And when he does we'll turn the child over to him," she said. "But until then, I'm going to see that it's taken care of." She shifted the baby in her arms. "Where's the doctor? I want him to examine the baby."

A movement nearby caught her attention, and she turned to see Colby approaching. Her lips tightened. He always seemed around when she least wanted to see him.

"What's going on here, Masters?" he asked suspiciously, as though he had already been told about the baby. "Where'd she get that baby?"

Although Anne wanted to tell him it was none of his business, she told herself that her tongue had already gotten her into enough trouble and managed to keep silent.

Zeke Masters explained how she had come to find the babe, and Colby exploded. "Hell's fire!" he said. "Ain't she got no better sense than to bring an Indian brat here!"

Colby stepped close enough to see the baby, and Anne tightened her arms protectively, afraid he would try to take it from her.

"Dammit!" Colby snarled. "You can't really mean to let her keep it, Zeke! I thought you had more sense than to—"

"When I want your advice, Colby, then I'll come ask for it," Masters growled. His gaze met Anne's again. "Last time I seen Doc, he was checkin' on the Turner young 'un. I 'spect he's still over there."

"What's wrong?" Colby asked sharply. "Does the brat have some kind of disease? If you brought fever on this wagon train, then you're gonna regret it, young lady."

Paying the man no heed, Anne hurried toward the Turner wagon, silently uttering a word of thanks to the man upstairs for allowing that particular family to cross the river with the first wagons.

Moments later the doc was examining the baby, who proved to be a boy. "He's dehydrated," Robert Wilson said, "and he's got a few scratches, but nothing of real consequence. There's no telling how long he's been without food and water, though, and with a babe so young, it makes his chances of survival that much slimmer." His gaze fixed on Anne again. "Are you going to take care of him?"

"I most certainly am. And that man, Colby, is having conniption fits about it. If he had his way, the baby would be left behind to die of starvation." Her lips flattened, and her blue eyes flashed darkly. "I don't know how anyone can be so mean spirited."

"Not everyone has your caring nature, Anne," he said softly. "Does Colby have a particular reason for leaving the babe behind?"

"Zeke said the father would come looking for it and there would be trouble."

"He might be right. Even so, we cannot, in all good conscience, abandon the baby to its fate."

"No. And we won't. Nothing, or no one, will hurt this baby while I'm taking care of it."

A thin, mewling sound came from the blanket, and Anne looked at the tiny infant. "I've got to find a way to feed him, though," she said. "I tried to give him sugar water, but most of it dribbled out of his mouth. I need a baby bottle, but I don't suppose there is one on the wagon train."

"You're wrong about that," he replied. "Darcy Williams brought one along with her. She didn't have enough milk to nurse her baby."

The name wasn't familiar to Anne, but that was nothing unusual. She didn't know half the people here. Driving the mules all day and cooking the meals and washing up never left time for visiting.

"Do you think she might lend me a bottle?"

"I don't see why not. She doesn't need it anymore. Her baby died two weeks after we left Missouri."

"Oh, God," Anne cried. "That must have been awful for her. I hope lending the bottle won't remind her of her own loss."

"I'm sure she'd be glad to help."

"Do you know where her wagon is?"

"Yes. She's on the other side of the river. But don't worry about it. I'll ride over and fetch the bottle for you."

Anne returned to her own wagon and sat down in the rocker to comfort the babe. She felt such an overwhelming need to protect the tiny infant from harm that she was unaware of the passing of time until the doctor arrived with the bottle.

Moments later the baby was sucking with a fierce intensity that tore at Anne's heart and made her want to weep for joy.

The babe would live; she would see to that.

Chapter Nineteen

Lucas sat astride the Lineback dun and watched the sun go down in a blaze of glory, painting the western horizon with hues of crimson, magenta and gold.

It was his favorite time of day. A time for reflection, to mull over the day's events, to shrug aside his disappointments and count his blessings.

But, today, Lucas derived no pleasure from the sunset. He was too weary. Bone weary. And he was troubled. And he was a damned fool!

The only pleasure to be had these days came in one small package wrapped in female form.

Anne.

Lucas wanted her. Desperately. His body craved her, needed her, like a thirsty man needed water.

And he could take her, Lucas knew. He had the legal right to do so. They were married. He could take her to bed, could make her want him, desperately, before filling her with his need. But he would not do so. And the reason was simple. He not only wanted Anne's body, but he also wanted her heart.

Fool! a silent voice chastised.

"Yeah. I'm a complete fool!"

Lucas nudged his horse, anxious to get back to the wagon train and the hot meal that his wife would have waiting for him.

Twilight had descended, covering the land in deep shadows, when Anne spotted the horse and rider in the distance. Her arms tightened around the sleeping babe, and she hurried to the wagon and tucked the infant into the warm nest of blankets near the tailgate.

"Sleep tight." Anne's voice was a soft whisper as she caressed the baby's plump cheek with a fingertip. "Don't make a sound, little baby. Not until I've had a chance to talk to Lucas."

Although the rider was too far away to identify, Anne was almost certain it was Lucas who approached, so she went about the business of heating his supper. By the time he had unsaddled the dun and rubbed it down, his food was waiting for him.

Her heartbeat quickened as he seated himself on a crate beside the makeshift table. "I hope you're hungry," she said, her gaze meeting his, then skittering quickly away. "Hawk killed some rabbits and brought one to me. I hope you like rabbit dumplings."

Lucas had been watching her closely. She was obviously nervous. He tried to put her at ease. "Do you mean he left some for me?"

She flushed. "Lucas . . . does it really bother you . . . Hawk coming around so much?"

"No," he said gruffly. "I was teasing you, Anne."

He took the plate she offered. "Are you going to eat with me?"

"I ate earlier," she replied. "But I'll have some coffee."

They sat together in a companionable silence that she hated to end, yet knew that she must. She had to explain about the infant before someone else told him. Someone like Colby, who would surely embellish the tale, coloring it with forecasts of doom.

Anne watched Lucas eat in silence, wondering how to break the news, and wondering, as well, how he would react to her words.

In the end she just blurted it out.

He listened quietly until she stopped talking, then asked, "Where is the child?"

Anne swallowed around the knot that had lodged in her throat. "I made a bed for him in the wagon." She gripped his forearm. "What ... what are you going to do, Lucas?"

His face was expressionless as he rose and went to the wagon with Anne only one step behind him. Her heart beat fast with trepidation. "Lucas. Please tell me. What are you going to do?"

He threw her a quick glance. "I won't hurt the babe, Anne." He pulled the blanket aside, and a smile curled his lips. "He's so small," he said softly. "Are you sure he didn't suffer any harm?"

Anne uttered a sigh of relief and leaned against her husband, feeling utterly delighted with his reaction. "I took him to the doctor, and Robert examined him. He said the baby is a newborn. Not more than a week old. And he was hungry and dehydrated, but otherwise unharmed."

Luke's gaze met hers, and she saw only concern in his eyes. "Do the others know about the babe?"

"Some of them. Zeke Masters. Colby ..."

He grimaced. "And how did Colby take it?"

She shrugged. "Not very well. He wants to leave the baby behind. The others, though ... well, Zeke *is* worried about the baby's father bringing hordes of painted savages down on us, but he eventually agreed the baby couldn't be left to die. And the doctor, well, Robert was noncommittal.''

"You did the right thing, Anne. You couldn't leave the babe to die.''

"No," she agreed softly. "I couldn't. But I was afraid you might not see that. And that you would be angry with me.''

He took her hand and rubbed his thumb over her palm. "Angry with you for caring about the babe?" His lips curved in a wry smile. "Is that the way you see me, Anne? Harsh and uncaring? Do you believe I would be so cruel as to begrudge time and food to an infant?"

The backs of Anne's eyes stung, and she knew that tears weren't far away. "No. I . . .''

"I could never do that," he went on. "When my parents died I was alone. Yet someone—my mother's people—cared enough to take me in. Without them I would never have survived.''

Lucas smiled tenderly at the woman who stood before him, her blue eyes bright with unshed tears, caused, no doubt, by her worry over the fate of a babe that was not her own. A babe that was not even of her own race. And he wanted to take her in his arms, to twirl her around and around, to laugh with delight at what he had discovered. There was no need to guard his heart. Anne was nothing like Barbara. Nothing.

And he should have known that from the beginning.

Barbara would never have fought beside him when the Indians attacked the wagon train. Nor would she have worked as Anne had done to make sure the supply wagon got through the flood.

Barbara would never have suffered as Anne had done, without a word of complaint. And Barbara would never have looked twice at an Indian baby . . . much less brought it back to care for.

"Anne," he said gruffly. "I was—"

"Do you think Zeke is right?" she asked anxiously. "Do you think the baby's father might not understand why we have him? That he might even believe we were trying to steal his son?"

Remembering what he had come across earlier in the day, Lucas replied, "Masters might be worrying needlessly about the baby's father."

"What do you mean?"

"While I was scouting the area, I ran across a dead Sioux warrior. And, judging by the sign left there, he was attacked by a small band of Utes. More'n likely a hunting party. And the dead man wasn't alone when it happened. There were several smaller prints nearby, as though he'd been traveling with a woman, or a child. I'm guessing, though, that he was traveling with his wife."

"His wife? And there was no sign of her nearby?"

"No. I think she stayed out of sight until they rode away. The bushes were trampled, as though she'd taken refuge there. And the moccasin prints led this way."

Memory of the dead woman rose in Anne's mind, and she felt again the sorrow of her death. "She *could* be the woman I found," Anne said huskily. "And if she is, then the baby has no one left to care for him . . . except us."

"I believe that is so."

Her chin firmed with determination. "He belongs to us now, Lucas."

"For how long, Anne?" he asked quietly.

"For all time," she said indignantly. "You don't take a baby to raise for a short time and then give it away to someone else. There are human emotions involved, Lucas. The baby will learn to love us, and we'll love him and . . . and . . . it would be like tearing my heart out to give him up, like losing a child I had borne myself."

"I realize that. But I wondered if you had."

Her expression was puzzled. "Of course I do."

"Then our arrangement would need rearranging." Luke's eyes devoured her. "Don't you agree?"

Anne's breath caught in her throat. "Our arrangement?"

He nodded, his gaze never leaving her. "Our bargain."

"Bargain?" Anne knew she sounded like a parrot, yet she wasn't sure what he meant.

"The bargain we made when we married," he explained gently. "Or have you forgotten so soon?"

"The bargain we made . . ." Her voice trailed away, and she stared at him with sudden realization. "You mean the one where we split up after . . ."

"Exactly," he said wryly. "That bargain." He arched a dark brow. "You do realize that a child needs two parents, don't you?"

"Of course. But I had forgotten that we'd agreed . . . forgotten that we planned . . . that we . . . Oh, shoot! Of course the baby needs two parents!" A flush stained her cheeks. "Would you mind so terribly, Lucas, if we stayed together? Just long enough to raise the child, of course. It would mean fifteen years or so, but, as you say, he needs two parents."

"No. I don't mind," he replied. "Not even a little bit. But fifteen years might not be long enough . . . since there might be other children."

Her eyes widened. "Other children?"

"Yes," he said firmly. "Other children." He gripped her shoulders and shook her gently. "You realize that more than the length of our marriage must change, don't you? We can't live together for years without some kind of closeness developing between us." Something flickered in his dark eyes, something hungry, needful. "A man has needs, Anne."

"Yes. Well . . ." She cleared her throat. "I suppose you're right."

"Then, you agree?"

She nodded, unable to look away from him. And then his head lowered until his mouth hovered only inches above her own. "Shall we seal our new bargain with a kiss?"

Before she could answer, his mouth covered hers, and Anne thought she had never before felt a kiss so sweet, so full of yearning.

Sliding her arms around his neck, she wound her hands through his dark hair and returned his kiss with such fervor that he could not mistake her feelings.

A cry broke them apart, and as one, they turned to the wagon and the babe who lay there. The infant's eyes opened, then closed again, as whatever had awakened the child had already been forgotten.

They were still watching the babe when Mary, having heard the news and made her husband bring both her and Jessie across the river on horseback, arrived to see him for herself. And while she was admiring the babe, he opened his coal black eyes and blinked up at her.

"Now, isn't that the sweetest little darling you ever did see?" Mary cooed. "How are we going to get you back to your people, little man?"

"We aren't," Anne said quickly. "He doesn't have anyone, Mary. Lucas found his father a few miles from here. He'd been killed by Ute warriors."

Mary's hand flew to her mouth, and she turned to Luke in horror. "Ute Indians? Oh, my gosh, Luke. Do you think they'll come after us?"

"No need to worry about that, Mary," Lucas said gruffly. "There were only four of them. A small band of hunters. Not nearly enough to take on a wagon train of this size."

"Thank the Lord for that," Mary replied. "We've been

plagued with enough troubles since we left Independence.
We certainly don't need any more." She leaned over the
wagon again and tickled the baby's neck. "No, we don't,
little fellow," she cooed. "We don't need no more, do
we?" She looked up at Anne and Lucas, who hovered
nearby. "What are you going to name the little fellow?"

Anne blinked in astonishment. "Name him?"

Mary laughed. "Surely you're going to name him. We
can't go around calling him boy . . . or, hey, you! He has
to have a name."

"Of course he does," Lucas agreed. "How about Little
Fox? Or Lone Wolf?"

"Good heavens! You don't want a heathenish name,"
Mary said quickly. "What this young'un needs is a good
Christian name. Something like John, maybe. Or Adam.
Or maybe Ezekiel."

"I don't think so, Mary," Lucas replied. "The boy is
from the Sioux tribe."

"But he'll be raised among whites," Mary said. "And
if he's given an Indian name, people will be more aware
of the red blood that flows through his veins."

"His blood is the same color as yours and mine, Mary!"
Anne had known about the prejudice that abounded. Even
in the twentieth century it had not been eradicated. But
she had thought Mary would be more tolerant. "I'm going
to name the baby Forrest."

"Forrest?" Mary lifted an eyebrow. "Why?"

"Because I like it." She turned to Lucas. "What do
you think?"

"Forrest?" He tested the name.

"I guess it sounds okay," Mary said musingly. "It's
certainly better than being named after an animal. Or a
bird. Or anything of that nature."

Anne's gaze never left Lucas. "Is that all right with
you?"

Lucas smiled at Anne, pleased that she wanted him to

be satisfied. "Yes, Anne. Forrest is a good name. A strong one. It is a name to make him proud."

Curling a long arm around Anne's waist, Lucas pulled her snugly against his side.

Mary went back to admiring the baby, lifting Jessie for a closer look, since the child had been so uncharacteristically patient.

Soon others began to arrive, women bringing their younger girls, wanting to see the tiny infant.

The women stayed later than Lucas would have liked. But finally they were gone, and Anne shook out their bedrolls and placed them beneath the wagon a few feet apart.

Becoming aware that Luke was watching her, she looked up and met his eyes and saw the question there. "What?" she asked.

"Together, Anne," he said quietly.

Her brow wrinkled. "Together?"

He nodded, his gaze going to the pallets, before returning to her again. "Together," he said firmly. "Like we agreed."

She could have argued that they had never mentioned bedrolls, or any kind of sleeping arrangements. Yet she remained silent, because, even though they hadn't spoken aloud the terms of their agreement, they had reached an understanding.

Carefully rearranging the blankets, she spread one down to sleep on and left the others to use as covers.

She had barely finished preparing their bed when Lucas scooped the baby into his arms, then crawled beneath the wagon.

"The babe will have to sleep with us for the time being," he said. "To share our body warmth while we're camping out."

He handed her the child, then stretched his length out

on the bedroll and, when she was beside him, covered the three of them with the blankets.

With a sigh of pleasure, Anne nestled against her husband's large frame, feeling the heat generated by his body seeping through her.

Lucas slid his arm around her waist and pulled her closer against him, reveling in the feel of her soft curves, of her silky curls that were tucked so firmly beneath his chin.

The weariness that he had felt earlier was completely gone now, drained away by the woman who nestled against him. He brushed a gentle kiss across her cheek, his breath whispering softly against her flesh. "Warm enough?" he asked huskily.

She nodded, her curls bobbed caressingly against his neck. "Yes," she replied. "Your body is like a warm stove on a cold winter's night."

And getting hotter all the time, though Lucas wouldn't speak the thought aloud. He felt he had to go slowly, and he needed time for her to adjust to their changed relationship. And it *was* going to change.

But he would wait until they reached their destination before consummating their marriage. It would not be easy, yet he was determined to be free of watching eyes when he claimed her body.

Yes, he would wait, would take it slow and easy. And he would court her. By the time they reached their destination, she would be more than willing to consummate their marriage. For her own sake, as well as the babe's. And Lucas needed that, more than he cared to admit.

Anne had shown herself to be a loving woman, and Lucas had gone a long time without love in his life. But, perhaps, if he was lucky, that time would soon come to an end. Perhaps Anne would grow to care for him, would be his wife in every sense of the word.

Anne didn't know it, but from this moment on, her heart was under siege.

Dawn was breaking in the east when Crazy Fox found that which he had been searching for. He looked down at the dead man, his expression giving no sign of the pain that was in his heart.

At his feet lay his only son . . . killed by Utes if the signs he read were to be believed. Although it was obvious a knife had dealt the fatal blow, the arrow embedded in his shoulder belonged to a Ute warrior.

He did the necessary things to assure that his son would reach the land beyond, where the Great Spirit waited; then Crazy Fox searched the ground for signs of his daughter-in-law. He saw the place where she had hidden from the attackers, then followed her footprints until they ended near a deep gully where sliding rock and shale told its own story.

After descending the slope, he found the place where Bright Water had fallen and saw the freshly dug earth that was her grave.

Dropping on his knees, he dug frantically, needing an answer to the question that had tormented him ever since he had found his son's body.

When he saw her remains, he felt a sense of relief. The babe had not died with her. It was easy to see what had caused her death, for her body was swollen from the venom of a snake.

He covered her again with the good earth, knowing she had been buried by white-eyes who had probably taken the babe.

His grandson.

Crazy Fox's mouth thinned with grim determination. He would return to his village to inform his wife of her son's death so she might grieve for him. And then he would take up the trail of the white-eyes.

His grandson would be returned to his family. To his grandparents. He vowed it. And the white-eyes who had taken him would pay with their lives.

Whatever it took, he would make them pay.

Chapter Twenty

It was two weeks before Crazy Fox took up the trail that would eventually lead to his grandson, and when he finally rode out of the village, his wife, Laughing Woman, rode beside him.

She would not listen to his arguments against going with him, refused to be swayed from her decision, which was unusual for a woman of the Sioux, who was generally obedient to her husband's wishes.

But Crazy Fox could not find it in his heart to be firm with her, to treat her harshly. She had lost her only son, and she had taken that loss hard.

Even now her face was lined with grief, and he feared that expression would not change until she held her grandson safely in her arms again.

Had he acted immediately, he could have had many warriors riding beside him now, but he had waited too long, recognizing Laughing Woman's need to mourn her loss, and in doing so had lost that opportunity.

The wagon train had moved on . . . their destination

unknown to the People. And the warriors could not be gone from the village for an unspecified time lest their enemies attack while they were away.

So much had been lost during that mourning time. Yet he could not blame his woman for mourning. Not when he also mourned.

Nevertheless, during those weeks of mourning, he had reaffirmed his vow. He would not rest until he rescued his grandson . . . and he would deal harshly with those who had stolen him away.

The days passed swiftly for Anne as the wagon train continued on its journey. Yet things were different since she had found Forrest. She was happier now, happier than she had ever been. Even the land around them appeared to reflect her feelings. The valley they traveled through was lush with long, waving grass, and there was an abundance of trees growing on the mountains that towered on both sides of the wagon train.

It was a beautiful land they traveled through, wondrous land, and she was able to share her joy in that beauty with the man who shared her dreams at night.

Lucas.

Sometimes he arrived just as the wagons were being drawn into the protective circle. At other times, it was almost dark before he returned. But return he did, without fail. And he was more at ease with her company, smiling often and teasing her as she sat in her rocker with Forrest in her arms.

As he had done before, Hawk joined them occasionally, consuming with obvious pleasure the meal she had prepared. Afterward the two men would talk quietly about what they had seen during the day. It was on one such occasion that Anne learned they were being followed.

She stopped rocking and watched the two men closely,

looking for some sign of unease, yet she found nothing in their expressions to cause her alarm. Still. . . .

"Are you both so certain the Indians are following us?" she asked.

Both men looked at her, but it was Lucas who answered her question.

"No," he replied. "They could just be going in the same direction we are."

"Then, why do you think they're following us?"

Again, it was Lucas who answered. "There's only two of them, Anne. And there's nothing ahead of us but wilderness. No villages to visit, nothing to keep them going . . . unless they are following someone."

"Only two Indians?" Her relief showed in her wide blue eyes. "Then, they won't attack us. Not when there's only two of them and there are so many of us."

"No. They won't," Lucas replied. "That's why I haven't mentioned it before." His dark eyes dropped to the infant in her arms.

Anne sucked in a quick breath and tightened her arms around the babe, feeling as though he had just been threatened. "It . . . it couldn't be anything to do with Forrest?" she said. "You said you found his father . . . that he was dead . . . killed by Utes."

"Yes. I'm certain it was the father. Don't take on so, Anne," he chided gently. "I'm sure there's nothing to worry about."

Although Anne heard his words, they didn't ring true. She was almost certain that Lucas was worried, too. More than he wanted her to know.

Lucas *was* worried, but he realized that he had already said too much. If, as he suspected, the Sioux who followed them were relatives of the baby, then he would have to be returned to his family to prevent a war. Because, even though there were only two of them at this moment, in matters of this kind, the tribe stood together. The relatives would follow, and when the travelers reached their destination, the Sioux would move their village and bring others of their tribe if there was a need.

And that must not happen. There would be enough trouble in making a home and supplying it with food without having to fight off warring Sioux.

Hawk suddenly broke the silence. "Any coffee left?"

"Yes," Anne replied. "But you'll have to help yourself to the pot. I left it warming over the coals."

He did so, then looked at her. "Want some?"

She shook her head. "I've had plenty," she replied. "Anyway, I can't drink coffee and rock the baby."

"You're going to spoil him," Hawk said. "I heard him crying today."

"Crying is healthy," she replied. "It's just his way of telling me something is wrong."

"It is not the way of the People, though, Anne. And is certainly not healthy for the village."

"What do you mean?"

"The People have many enemies. A crying baby would give away the location of the village."

"But, Hawk. It's unreasonable to expect a baby to keep quiet. It has no other way to express itself."

"And yet it must learn to keep quiet to ensure itself, and others, of continued safety."

"But how would you teach a baby not to cry?"

"A crying babe is taken into the forest and left there until it stops crying."

Anne gasped. "Alone?"

"Yes. If someone stayed with the babe, it would not be effective."

"But that's cruel!"

Hawk shrugged. "Life is cruel."

Anne turned to Lucas. "Do you approve of this practice, Lucas?"

Lucas chose his words carefully. "Would it be less

cruel to allow a whole family to die than for a baby to be left to cry for a while?''

She lowered her eyes. ''No. I suppose not. But I don't want to leave Forrest to cry.'' Her blue eyes were stormy. ''We won't do that, Lucas. A child needs love, and Forrest will have it . . . from both of us.''

As though he knew he was the subject of their conversation, Forrest opened his eyes and yawned widely. ''This child will be raised with love and kindness,'' Anne said fiercely. ''I intend to see that.''

Lucas watched her with the babe. She would make a good mother. If she had the chance. But he was still worried about the Indians who followed them. If they were the baby's relatives, then they would have no choice except to hand the child over.

And he didn't want to be taken by surprise.

Tomorrow, he vowed, he would meet with those Indians, and he would discover their intentions.

It was a vow that he was unable to keep, though, because when the new day dawned, the Indians were nowhere to be found.

Three days later Lucas topped a rise and decided his journey was at an end. He looked at the valley below, lush with grass and water, and knew why he had made the journey to Oregon.

A sense of peace washed over him. He would build his cabin beside the silvery creek that was lined with willow trees.

When informed of his decision, the wagon master frowned. ''Are you sure you want to drop off here, Lucas?'' he asked gruffly. ''We may go on for a hundred miles or more before the rest of these folks are satisfied.''

''Then, you travel without me,'' Lucas replied. ''I found my valley.''

"I reckon I'd better take a look at what you found before I go any farther, then," Zeke replied. "These folks have learned to trust your judgment, and I might save myself a few miles."

The wagon train was ordered into a circle while a group of men rode out together. It was several hours before they returned, and to a man, they were jubilant at what they had seen.

A celebration was held that night. And the next morning the wagon train changed directions, headed straight for the mountains. It was late afternoon when they reached the top of a rise. And there, spread out before them, lay a valley. A wild, magnificent place where, it appeared, no man had ever gone before.

It lay in pristine splendor, where dark conifers blended magically with the lighter green of aspens. The subtle blending of colors was repeated over and over again as grassy slopes became foothills and those same foothills became mountain peaks.

Lucas reined up beside their wagon. "This is it," he said softly. "This is where we stake our claim."

Our claim. Anne liked the sound of that. Her gaze narrowed on the valley below as she looked for the place they would build their home.

"Move along there!" came a shout from the wagon behind Anne.

She yelled at the mules to hurry them along, "Giddyup there, mules!" and snapped her whip in the air above their backs.

The mules picked up speed, the wagon gaining momentum as they eased down into the valley.

Lucas was the first to lay out his claim. And when he had done so, Henry Baker staked out the adjoining land.

"Knew the women would want to be neighbors," he told Lucas as he pounded in the last stake.

The Colbys settled north of the Bakers, and Thomas Warren and James Odelbert claimed land in the foothills.

Anne had no time to wonder about the other pioneers. She was kept busy with the baby and with providing food for the men who were building the Bakers' cabin.

Hawk had volunteered to help, as had Zeke Masters, who would soon be going back east to form another wagon train. Robert Wilson, James Odelbert and Thomas Warren had also volunteered. And with Henry Baker and Lucas, the count of working men numbered seven.

The valley that had been so silent was now filled with noise. It was a joyful time for the pioneers who had traveled so far to find the promised land. And it showed in their voices.

They laughed easily, the sound mingling with those of farm animals. Dogs barked. Cows mooed. Pigs oinked. And above all else were the sounds of building. Men chopping down trees. Saws grating against wood.

Each man worked at what he did best. Thomas Warren was especially good at making shingles, and the thin slices of wood seemed to slide off the cedar heartwood as he continually tapped the froe with his maul, working with a speed that was astonishing to watch.

Sweat poured off the men as they toiled, but they continued to work tirelessly. Each man had assigned himself a job. Lucas and Hawk chopped down the trees, and James Odelbert measured and cut the logs. Robert Wilson and Thomas Warren took over from there, bundling the logs and working with the mules that continually balked at skidding the logs to the cabin site where Zeke Masters and Henry hewed and notched them.

Amazing though it seemed, the walls were raised that morning. The men took a short break while they ate the noon meal, then went right back to work.

Anne fed Forrest, then left him with Jessie, who had a way with the baby. As the women stored the leftover food and washed the dishes, their eyes continually strayed to the cabin.

"Ain't it a sight to behold?" Mary's voice was filled with pleasure. "I never thought I'd be sleeping in my own house tonight."

"Neither did I, Mary."

Anne watched Lucas, fascinated by the muscles that rippled beneath his flesh as he hoisted another split and notched log to Hawk, who was straddling the highest log on the south wall.

After setting the log in place, Hawk turned back to Lucas, who was ready with another one. And so it went, log after log, until the roof was set in place. But the work didn't stop there. There were shingles ready to attach before the work was completed.

Several hours later, as the sun dipped low over the western horizon, the last shingle was nailed down.

Anne was bent over the fire, turning the spit where a haunch of deer was cooking, when she heard the shout.

Startled, she spun around and saw mild-mannered Henry Baker, laughing and dancing and whirling his wife around and around.

"Henry Baker!" Mary scolded. "What's got into you?"

"It's done, Mary!" Henry shouted, his face alight with joy. "Do you see it standing there, woman? We're in Oregon and our cabin is ready for us to move in! We're gonna be sleeping in our own cabin tonight!"

"Of course we'll sleep in it, you old fool! I sure ain't sleeping under the stars again when there's a perfectly good cabin over yonder, just waiting to be used!" Mary wiped at the corners of her eyes with her apron, trying to hide her tears of happiness.

Henry smiled at his wife and hugged her tightly. "You know what, Mary?"

"What?"

"I love you!"

"Henry!" Mary's voice sounded shocked, but a smile curled her lips. "What a thing to say, and with everybody listening, too."

Anne smiled at the two of them, envious of their relationship. Then her gaze sought out Lucas, who had been watching her with hungry eyes.

She shivered as she thought of the night to come. They would finally be alone, even though they would continue to sleep under the stars until their own cabin was built. Would Lucas decide to consummate their marriage tonight? And was she ready for that?

Yes. She was more than ready.

But Anne was to be disappointed. Lucas waited until she was asleep before he crawled into the bedroll. And when she wakened the next morning, it was to the sound of voices.

The work crew had already arrived.

Anne hurried to make breakfast for the seven men, but Forrest seemed determined to claim her attention. He wailed with displeasure every time she tried to leave him.

She was glad when Mary and Jessie arrived to help.

Jessie went to the baby and kept him entertained while the two women finished making breakfast, then called the men to eat.

"What's wrong with Forrest?" Lucas asked, taking the plate she handed him. "Is he sick?"

"I don't think so," she replied. "I think he's just wanting to be held."

He frowned at her. "You're spoiling him, Anne. He needs to learn not to cry."

Anne's lips thinned with displeasure. "That's nonsense!'' she snapped. "It may be the Comanche way, but it's not mine. And Forrest is my baby now."

"I thought he was our baby," he said quietly.

Shame flooded her cheeks, and she lowered her expressive eyes. "He is, Lucas. But I don't want him left to cry." She curled her fingers around his forearm. "Don't let's argue," she said softly. "This should be a happy time for us."

His gaze softened. "Yes," he replied. "And tonight, after our cabin is built . . ."

Although his voice trailed away, Anne read the promise in his eyes. Tonight was the night when he would claim her for his own.

Anne smiled up at Lucas. "Tonight," she whispered.

Lucas was smiling when he turned away from her. Soon his axe rang out as he set about chopping down trees to build their cabin.

The work went quickly, as it had with the Baker cabin, and by the end of the day the men were unloading the wagon, carrying crates and chests and barrels into the newly erected cabin.

While the women finished preparing the evening meal, Lucas built shelves inside a long wooden crate and nailed it against the wall beside the rudely constructed fireplace where most of the cooking would be done.

As they had the night before, the men ate heartily, shoveling the food in their mouths as soon as they received the plates that were heaped high with good things to eat.

And when they finished their meal, the men lingered over coffee and talked together about the cabin they would build come morning.

"You're gonna need more than one room, Doc," said Zeke Masters. "Since you're the only doctor hereabouts, you'll be needing extra room for the sick folks that are sure to come around."

"Most of my patients will be treated in their own

homes," Wilson said, "but you're right. I'm going to need an office for my medical practice. And there is sure to be an occasional traveler stopping by that will need my services." His gaze traveled between Thomas Warren and James Odelbert. "Perhaps we'd best wait until we have the other cabins built before we start on mine, since both Odelbert and Warren will require only one room."

"No way, Doc," said Odelbert. "We need yours done first in case I chop off my leg and need a place to recover."

That comment brought laughter, but everyone agreed that the doctor's cabin should be the next one to go up. It was also agreed that only one room would be built; then, when time allowed, they would add another for his patients.

It was late when Mary yawned widely, and that appeared to be the signal for everyone to leave. She helped Anne clean up before departing with her husband and daughter. Then Hawk left with James and Thomas. Wilson and Masters were the last to go.

And then Anne and Lucas and Forrest were alone.

Together, they set up the four-poster bed he had purchased at the fort, then Lucas fastened wide strips of canvas on the support boards and added the corn shuck mattress that had been stored in the bottom of the wagon.

As Anne spread sheets on the mattress, she thought of the night to come and felt her cheeks flush with color. It was followed by a prickling at her neck, and she knew that Lucas was watching her.

Slowly, she turned around to meet his eyes. Hungry eyes. Needing, wanting. Yes. He wanted her. And she was hungry for him. Her gaze went to the cradle he was holding, and she smiled with delight.

"Where did that come from?"

"Hawk made it for the baby."

"That was sweet of him."

His lips twitched. "Yes. Sweet."

Lucas placed the cradle near the bed, then straightened. "If you don't need me for a while, then I'm going to bathe in the creek."

"A bath. Oh, that would be wonderful."

He arched a dark brow. "You could come with me."

She laughed huskily. "I'd best make do with a pan of warm water tonight. Forrest was cranky today, and I don't want to take unnecessary chances with him."

A frown crossed his face. Then it disappeared as quickly as it came. It was obvious he thought she was spoiling the baby, and just as obvious that he didn't want anything to spoil their first night in their new home.

Anne filled the cooking pot with water and set it over the coals outside so it could warm. Then she lined the cradle with blankets to keep the baby warm during the night.

She had barely finished when Forrest woke and started to cry.

The water was cold against his flesh, but Lucas took his time with his bath, knowing it would take Anne even longer with hers. He would like to have watched her bathe, yet knew it would take her a while to become used to such liberties.

He could wait until then.

More than an hour had passed before he left the willows lining the creek and stopped to look at his cabin. It was a sturdy building, one that would last for hundreds of years. After he had helped with the other three cabins, he would start work on the barn. It would take a while to build since there were fields to plow and make ready for spring planting. But there was plenty of time.

Come next summer, he would add a room to the cabin. A bedroom, so he and his wife would have some privacy. And when Forrest was older, they could add another room.

He could share it with his brothers, and if sisters were born, then another room would be added.

Luke's lips curled in a smile. Life had finally become worth living. He had a family now. A son. And a beautiful wife who felt no distaste for the blood that ran through his veins.

Yes. Life was good. And it would soon be even better. No more restraining himself. No more cold baths to make his body behave. The cabin was built now, and there was privacy aplenty for him to consummate his marriage.

Tonight. And like a damned fool he stood here, admiring his new cabin, while inside that cabin his woman waited for him.

He strode forward eagerly, whistling a happy tune as he pushed open the cabin door. As he had expected, Anne was there. But she was not alone.

A Sioux warrior stood over her, his visage fierce, his stance threatening, and nearby stood a woman, her dark hair shorn short, as though she was in mourning. And she was holding out her arms, reaching to take the babe that Anne was clutching so tightly against her.

So the time is now.

Lucas had been afraid it would come.

Anne edged around the warrior and ran to her husband, who circled her waist and pulled her against his side. "Wh-what do they want, Lucas?"

There was sorrow in his eyes when he looked at her. "Don't you really know, Anne?"

Her eyes widened with horror. "No!" Her arms tightened around her precious bundle. "They don't want the baby. They came for food! Give it to them. Give them anything they want, Lucas, but make them leave." She buried her head against his chest. "Please, Lucas. Make them leave."

Sorrow darkened Luke's eyes as he stroked her soothingly. She depended on his strength to drive the Sioux out. And he had no doubt he could do so. But if they were relatives of the boy, they had every right to claim him.

He met the warrior's eyes and spoke in his tongue. "What do you want here?"

"My grandchild. The child that you stole from us."

"We did not steal him. My woman found his mother dead. If she had not taken him with her, the boy would not be living today."

"Then, she has my gratitude for saving his life."

"She loves the boy," Lucas said. "You can see that. It will cause her pain to lose the babe."

"Lucas?" Anne queried. "What is he saying? What do they want?"

Both men ignored her.

The warrior looked at his own woman, and when he spoke, his voice was edged with sorrow. "My wife mourns the loss of her only son. Do you expect her to give her grandson away?"

"Lucas?" Anne said again.

"The babe is their grandson, Anne." Lucas tried to take the baby from her, but she leapt away like a she-cat bent on defending its young.

"No!" she cried. "You can't do this! Forrest doesn't know them. He'll cry for me! Oh, God, they'll punish him for crying!" Sobs shuddered through her as she fought so desperately to retain her hold on the babe who had come to mean so much to her. "You can't take him, Lucas! I won't let you do this!"

"Anne," he chided gently. "Listen to me. He is all they have left. They are too old to have any more children. He belongs with them."

"If you take him away, Lucas, I'll never forgive you! Do you hear me?" she shrieked. "If you take away my baby, I'll despise you until the day I die!"

Sorrow dimmed his eyes, yet he would not be swayed.

He eased the baby away from her and handed him to his grandmother. He saw the sadness in her eyes as she looked at Anne, who was slumped beside the bed, her body shuddering with sobs that would not be contained. But when the grandmother looked at the baby again, her sadness dimmed, and the love in her eyes burned bright.

She looked at Lucas and spoke in the Sioux tongue. "You are a good man. You can give her many children to take the place of my grandson."

Lucas knew she was right, yet realized as well that because of what he had done this night, Anne might never allow him to touch her again, let alone do what was necessary to ensure children.

But Lucas knew, in his heart, that he had only done what was necessary. The Sioux could be allies or they could be enemies.

The need for allies was great, for they already had too many enemies. Yes. He had only done what was necessary.

But would Anne ever forgive him?

He suspected she would not.

Chapter Twenty-One

Anne grieved for the babe. And, although she realized she was being unreasonable, she continued to blame Lucas for the part he had played in that loss.

She refused to speak to him. Instead, she went about her daily chores in silence, ignoring his presence when he entered the house.

At first, Luke tried to console her, to make her realize that he'd had no choice, but Anne would not be consoled. If he persisted, she simply walked out of the house and away from him.

In time, he stopped trying.

Anne continued to cook his meals, to wash his clothing and clean his house. But the dreams she'd had for the future were gone. She no longer looked on the house as theirs. When she had lost Forrest, she had lost everything. Now her dreams of a family were gone, swept away like dry leaves in a windstorm.

Each day was harder to face than the one before. Lucas was grim-faced, his body tense, whenever she was near.

It would have been easier if she didn't have to face him every day. But they had made a bargain. And she would abide by their agreement, would help him prove out his land; then she would select the parcel she wanted and have her own house built there.

But she would be alone.

So damned alone.

Anne knew she was wallowing in self-pity, but worry over Forrest kept her awake at night. Her emotions were fragile, and she cried too easily and hated herself for doing so.

It had been ten days since the baby had been taken from her, and she hadn't spoken a word aloud since that time. Lucas had stopped talking to her five days ago.

They had reached an impasse, where each one avoided the company of the other. She slept in the house, and Lucas slept in the shed that he had built beside the house to hold his tools and equipment.

How much longer could they go on this way?

It was on the eleventh day of Anne's self-imposed silence that Mary and Henry Baker came calling. Henry stayed outside with Lucas to allow the two women some privacy.

Mary took one look into Anne's tormented eyes and realized something drastic would have to be done if her friend was to retain her sanity.

She had occasion to know what Anne was feeling. She had lost her first babe, only days after it was born. But, unlike Anne, she had found comfort in her husband's arms.

"You look like you haven't slept in weeks," Mary said bluntly. "And Lucas looks no better."

Anne swallowed hard, trying to blink away the tears that were never far from the surface these days. "Do you want some coffee, Mary?" she asked.

"If it's already made."

"It is." Anne removed cups from the shelf. "Lucas doesn't linger over morning coffee anymore. In fact, he doesn't stay around much at all these days."

"Can you really blame him?" Mary asked gruffly. "Just look at yourself!"

"I don't have to look." Anne felt hurt by the other woman's words. "I know what I look like, Mary." She poured coffee and set the steaming cups on the table before seating herself across from Mary. "I keep thinking about Forrest, and wondering if they're taking care of him." She blinked as weak tears filled her eyes. "I loved him so much, Mary."

"And you think Lucas didn't?"

"Apparently not enough." Tears trickled down her cheeks, and Anne wiped them away with the back of her hand. "I have nightmares about him. That's why I can't sleep at night. Every time I close my eyes I think I hear him crying."

Mary covered Anne's hand with her own. "Does Lucas have nightmares, too?"

Anne's lips trembled, and she lowered her eyes. "I don't know," she whispered. "We don't talk about it."

"I see." Mary saw more than her friend knew. "What do you talk about?"

"Nothing."

Mary raised an eyebrow. "You don't talk at all?"

Anne shook her head. "Not anymore." She uttered a long sigh and looked out the window where she could see Lucas and Henry Baker in deep conversation near the corral.

"How long do you plan on punishing him?" Mary asked sharply.

Anne's head jerked back as though she had been slapped. "I'm not punishing him!"

"Then, what do you call it?"

"I-I-he . . ." Anne clenched her hands, her nails digging

into her palms. "You weren't here, Mary! I begged him! I pleaded with him, and he wouldn't listen. I told him I'd never speak to him again if he made me give up the baby."

"So you're bent on making him pay. Is that it?"

Anne scraped back her chair and leapt to her feet. Her face was chalk white. "Don't you understand?" she cried. "He was all I had!"

"He wasn't yours to keep, Anne. He had a family and they came after him. It's as simple as that. Lucas couldn't have done anything else. It isn't right for you to blame him for what happened."

Tears streamed down Anne's cheeks as she faced the other woman across the table. "You weren't here, Mary. Lucas wouldn't listen to my pleas. He tore Forrest away from me, and gave my baby to those Indians." Her face was pale, her eyes stricken with remembered horror. "Do you know how they treat babies that cry? They take them into the forest and leave them there . . . alone."

"Being alone for a while won't do any permanent harm, Anne," Mary said sternly. "And from all I've heard about the Sioux, they love their children. That baby will be cared for. You need have no worry on that account."

Anne refused to listen. "He didn't know them!"

"He didn't know you before either, yet he sensed something that caused him to trust you . . . and make you his wife."

Anne clenched her fists against her mouth, trying to stop her sobs. Yet she could not. They shuddered through her, shaking her body with each breath she took.

"Wh-what am I g-going to do, Mary?" Anne cried. "Forrest was my reason for going on. I lost everything I had when that tornado swept me into the past. I have no parents, no family, nothing."

"You have Lucas."

"Lucas doesn't care for me! Forrest did!"

"What nonsense is this?" Mary asked. "Anyone with eyes in their head can see how much Lucas cares."

"No, he doesn't. He took—"

"Now, you stop that!" Mary ordered. "Lucas did what he had to for the sake of the settlement. Would you rather have had a war party coming here and taking our scalps, murdering our children and raping the women?"

"Of course not."

"Then, pull yourself together and be a wife to Lucas. Stop blaming that man for something he couldn't help. He returned their grandchild just as he returned my Jessie to me. And for the Lord's sake, break the silence between the two of you. Tell Lucas what you're feeling. Let him comfort you and take comfort from you."

Anne sat down again, her head bowed low. "I'm not so sure he would listen to me now."

"And why not?"

"Because I-I've been such a bitch."

Mary's lips twitched. "You said it, Anne. And I certainly won't disagree. But at least you're willing to admit it now. That's an improvement."

Anne breathed a shuddering sigh. "Lucas won't speak to me anymore. I know he won't. I can't really blame him either. But it's been so hard. I miss the baby so much, and I—" Her voice broke, and her eyes misted again.

"Anne McCord! Stop feeling so sorry for yourself and think of the folks that have a real reason to complain." She swallowed her coffee and pushed the cup toward Anne. "I need another cup," she said. "And yours needs heating. And we need to discuss a way of helping out one of the less fortunate families that settled here and are too proud to ask for help."

Anne wiped her eyes and poured coffee into Mary's cup, then added more to her own. "Who are you talking about, Mary?"

"Sarah Jane and Elijah Smith. He's been doing poorly

ever since we got here, and I just found out they're still living in their wagon. With winter coming on, they're going to be needing some kind of shelter, pro'bly food, too, since he's not been well enough to hunt. Right now, though, we've run into a stump. Elijah is a proud man, and he won't look kindly on charity. And none of us know how to get around that, but I thought if you set your mind to it, you might think of a way to help.''

''Short of just building the cabin anyway and dumping food there, I don't know what we could do.''

Mary scowled. ''Now, Anne McCord! You oughtta be able to come up with a better solution than that.''

Anne sighed deeply. ''Tell me something about them,'' Anne said. ''What did Elijah do before joining the wagon train?''

''He was a boot maker. Done quite well from all accounts. Don't know why he decided to pull up stakes and come along to Oregon.''

Anne looked at the toe of her boot which was scuffed and worn. ''I need a pair of shoes,'' she said slowly. ''Maybe he would consider a trade. Boots for everybody who donates their work.''

''Now, that's a splendid idea.'' Both Henry and Lucas had already put forth that suggestion, but Anne didn't have to know that. ''Now all we need is someone to organize things.''

Lifting her cup, Anne sipped at her coffee. It was strong, reviving. Just what she needed to make her think clearly. ''What about Zeke Masters?'' she asked. ''He's used to organizing things. He ought to make a convincing spokesman.''

''Yes, he would,'' Mary replied. ''But Zeke's already gone. He left two days ago to go back to Missouri.''

''I didn't know that. He might have said good-bye.'' Anne felt hurt that he had left without her knowing. ''What about your husband, Mary? Would Henry do it?''

"Uh-uh." Mary shook her head. "He has the tact of a raging bull. No. He won't do."

"Luke. . . ?"

"Not him either. He's worse than Henry." She held Anne's gaze. "The truth is, Anne, you're the one that should do it. You and Luke together. Luke can organize the men, and you can handle the women."

"I don't know if Lucas—"

"Of course he would. Lucas is the best man for the job."

"What job?"

Anne turned to see Lucas and Henry Baker entering the cabin. She couldn't quite meet Luke's eyes, knowing how unfairly she had been treating him. Instead, she looked at a point just beyond his right shoulder. "I-I—" Anne cleared her throat and tried again. "Mary came to tell us about the Smith family, Lucas. It seems they are in need of help."

She threw him a quick glance and then couldn't look away. There was no word to describe the expression that spread across his face. It was a mixture of relief, anxiety, and an easement of the tension that he had carried for so long.

"What kind of help?" he asked.

"Uh, Mary will explain." She shoved back her chair. "Would you like some coffee?"

"Coffee sounds good."

"Henry?" Anne inquired.

"Sure enough," he said, seating himself on a crate.

Lucas took the chair Anne had so recently vacated and listened to Mary explain. When Anne returned with coffee, he reached out a long arm and pulled her down onto his lap. "You can share my chair," he said, snugging her close against him.

For a moment Anne held herself stiffly while they talked together, but since Lucas seemed perfectly at ease, and unaware of the hand that was stroking her arm, she slowly relaxed in the crook of his arm.

"It sounds like a damned good idea to me, Mary," he said. "And I'd be glad to do anything I can to help." He looked down at Anne. "Is that the answer you gave, too, Anne?"

She nodded. "But I only answered for myself. I didn't know if you'd have time to help."

"I'll take the time. And, I warrant, so will the other men."

It seemed only moments later when Mary and Henry took their leave. Anne slid off Luke's lap and went to see them off. As she waved good-bye to them, she wondered if Lucas had been acting a part for Mary's benefit when he cuddled her against him.

She hoped not.

She hadn't liked being at odds with him. Not even a little bit.

That night, as Anne was on the verge of going to bed, it began to rain. Moments later, the door opened, and Lucas entered the cabin, his bedroll slung over his shoulder.

"Brrrr," he shuddered. "I hope you don't mind me sleeping here, Anne. It's cold out there. That shed leaks like a sieve when it's raining."

"Of course I don't mind," she replied. "It's your house. And there's plenty of room on the floor."

"No," he said gruffly, meeting her eyes with a long look. "It's *our* house."

"But we had an agreement . . ."

He dropped his bedroll beside the fireplace and gripped her shoulders. "We amended the agreement, Anne. Don't you remember?"

"Yes." Her lips quivered. "But it was because of Forrest."

"Not entirely." Something flickered in his dark eyes. "We need to talk about what happened."

"I know." Moisture dimmed her vision. "But I don't think I can right now."

"Yes." He shook her lightly. "You can. Don't you know that it helps when you share a sorrow? I need to share mine, Anne. I need it badly."

"Yours?"

He nodded. "I loved him, too."

Anne burst into tears. "I'm sorry," she sobbed, throwing her arms around his neck and burying her head against his chest. "Oh, God, Lucas, I'm so sorry. I had forgotten that you cared, too."

They held each other in their grief, and somehow, they wound up on the bed. "It's all right, honey. It's all right." His fingers tangled in her silky curls, and he spread kisses across her face. "Don't cry now, you're not alone anymore."

Anne shuddered beneath his touch. It felt so good to be in his arms again, to trust in his strength. "Lucas." Her voice was hesitant, uncertain.

"What is it, Anne?"

"Would you . . . I don't want to be alone tonight. It's been a nightmare, trying to sleep in here with you outside."

"Shhhh," he whispered, kissing away her tears. "Everything is all right now, love. You're not alone anymore. I'm here with you."

Love. She swallowed hard. He used the word as an endearment, and she needed to remember that. "Lucas, are you going to sleep on the floor?"

He laughed huskily. "Not unless you make me."

She nestled closer against him, taking comfort in his strength. "Would you mind terribly if I slept in your arms tonight?"

His embrace tightened convulsively. As did his body.

Down, boy, he silently commanded. *She just needs comforting.* "No, love," he said gently. "I wouldn't mind at all."

Uttering a deep sigh of satisfaction, she whispered, "Then stay, Lucas. Let me have one night of peace."

Peace. It was little enough to ask. Yet Lucas knew that in granting her that peace, he would suffer through the fires of hell this night.

Chapter Twenty-Two

Anne's heart raced swiftly as she stumbled through the forest, trying to avoid the branches that reached out, snatching, pulling at her clothing like great claws bent on keeping her from him.

Her breath puffed in and out, keeping time with her heartbeat, and there was a tight knot of pain lodged somewhere in the vicinity of her heart.

But, no matter how much that ache persisted, Anne knew she couldn't stop, that she had to go on, had to reach the babe who depended on her for his very life.

And all the time she ran, Anne could hear him, crying . . . somewhere in the distance ahead, heart-wrenching sobs that contained fear, as her baby, her only son, cried desperately for help.

Anne stumbled and fell to the ground, then pushed herself upright again and went on. But no matter how fast she ran, the babe remained just out of her reach.

Oh, God, help me!

It was a silent cry, a scream that came from deep inside.

She could hear the terror that emanated from his cries. Oh, God, how could one tiny being hold so much terror?

She had to reach him. Had to hold him in her arms, needed to quiet his fears. Anne knew exactly where the baby would be. She had seen the place before, so many times since he had been taken from her. She had tried to reach him, yet the forest always held her back.

And all the time she was aware of imminent danger. Knew a sense of desperation that was completely over-powering.

Flailing her arms wildly, Anne tried to push aside the branches that seemed determined to hold her back. Her heart pounded swiftly within her breast, sounding like a jackhammer trying to dig through several layers of con-crete, and she was afraid it would explode before she could reach the babe.

And then she saw him. There, just a short distance ahead of her, hanging from the limb where they always left him.

He was screaming louder now, his mouth open, his cries piercing, his dark eyes round in his fear. Forrest knew about the danger, had always known. He was aware of hungry wolves that slunk toward him, ready to spring, to pull him down and rip apart his tiny limbs.

And he was calling out to her.

"Anne! Anne!"

Sweat beaded her forehead, and she struggled desper-ately to break through the limbs that fought just as hard to restrain her.

"Anne! Wake up! Wake up, Anne! You're having a nightmare!"

Jerking upright, Anne's eyes flew open, and she stared at Lucas with wide-eyed horror. "Oh, God," she cried, shuddering with remembered terror. "Oh, God, Lucas! It was horrible! It was so damned horrible."

Her heart was racing as though she had been running,

yet she was in bed, inside the cabin with Lucas, who was staring down at her with sympathetic eyes.

"You were dreaming," he said gently, wiping her tears away with a corner of the sheet. "It was only a nightmare, Anne. Only a bad dream that's over now."

She threw her arms around his neck and buried her head against his chest. "I know," she sobbed. "But it was so real. So damned real. I thought I was really there."

His arms tightened around her. "I know, honey," he soothed. "Nightmares are like that. They can scare the living daylights out of you. But they're not real, Anne. You have to remember that. Nightmares are just your fears coming to life in your dreams."

Lucas kissed the top of her head. It was obvious Anne had been dreaming about the baby, that she was worried about his safety. But how long could she endure such dreams without losing her sanity?

He had never felt so helpless in his life as he did right now. It tore him apart to see her this way, to know that he was unable to ease her pain.

Knowing that, he could only hold her, stroking her back gently, soothing her as he would a child until the vividness of her nightmare faded enough to ease her mind.

He continued to hold her, stroking her tenderly until, finally, after what seemed like eons, her sobs ceased and she relaxed against him.

"Anne," he said huskily, tilting her head and forcing her to meet his eyes. "We need to talk about this."

She swallowed around the lump in her throat.

"I think it would help if you told me about your nightmare." A tear dropped from her wet lashes, and he caught it with his fingertip.

Lucas was so good to her, offering her comfort when she had treated him so abominably. He was a kind man. A decent man. And, even though it hurt to talk about her loss, she needed desperately for Lucas to understand what she was going through.

"I dream about him so much, Lucas," she said shakily. "And the dream is always the same."

He kissed her cheek, found it wet, and wiped away the tears with the back of his hand. Then he kissed her again. "Go on," he urged. "Tell me." He turned her head slightly, found her other cheek damp and licked away her tears.

Heat coiled through the pit of her stomach as Anne felt his tongue on her flesh. She sighed deeply, her fingers curling against his chest. "It's always the same," she said again. "Forrest was alone in the woods. And there were wolves all around him. He was in danger, and he was crying for me. But I couldn't get to him, no matter how hard I tried to reach him."

"It was a foolish dream," he said, his lips moving lightly over hers, touching, tantalizing, making her want him even more. "A very foolish dream."

"But he's not used to their ways," she protested. "And he might cry. He doesn't know any better, Lucas, and they'll leave him alone in the forest, and—"

"Hush, Anne," he soothed, silently damning Hawk for telling her about that particular custom. "The babe is all right. If they have to leave him for even a moment, there will always be someone nearby. His grandparents love him. They would never endanger his life. Anyway, he never cried much. You're worrying needlessly."

He smoothed her hair back gently and kissed her forehead. "I know you're afraid for him. But he's all right. I promise you that. He is well loved by his grandparents. He's all they have left of their own son." He brushed his mouth over hers again. "You need a child of your own," he said softly. "A babe to hold in your arms, to suckle at your breast."

As though to demonstrate, his head dipped lower and

his mouth closed over one soft nipple, moistening the thin fabric that covered her breast and causing it to cling to the nub that hardened instantly at his touch.

Anne groaned with pleasure, and her fingers twined through his hair to tug him closer. "Then, give me one," she whispered huskily. "Please, Lucas. Give me a child of my own."

His dark eyes were intent when he lifted his head and met her gaze. "Are you sure, Anne? Are you very sure that's what you want?"

"Oh, yes, Lucas." Her voice was a husky sigh. "I'm very sure."

It was all he needed. Luke's mouth covered hers, molding itself to her lips, and his tongue probed gently, tracing the seam of her lips.

Anne gave no thought to resistance. She opened her mouth to allow him entrance. He was quick to take advantage and entered that moist cavern to taste the sweetness he found waiting there.

A moan of pure pleasure erupted from Anne's throat as Lucas stroked her tongue, then swept the roof of her mouth, as though intent on searching out every inch of that moist cavity.

Feeling shivery with the pleasure he was creating, Anne moved her tongue against his, tentatively at first, then quickly, thrusting forward eagerly, tasting, then retreating as though they were dueling with swords.

With a low growl, Lucas twisted suddenly, pushing Anne down against the mattress in an action so sudden that her eyelids flashed open and she stared up into his passion-glazed eyes.

"What. . . ?"

Before she could utter another word, Lucas' mouth was covering her breast. The fabric of her nightgown drew taut as his lips closed over her nipple, and he sucked hard, as though he meant to draw fluid from deep within.

"Lucas!" she gasped, clutching the back of his head to pull him closer.

She felt as though she were being consumed by a blaze that began deep within her body. She needed to be closer, needed to be joined with him. He had started a fire deep inside that was going to burn her alive if he didn't do something to quench the flames.

"Please, Lucas," she begged.

He dragged his mouth away from her breast and looked down at her, his eyes flickering darkly in the moonlight that streamed through the window. "Please what, Anne?" he asked hoarsely. "What do you want from me?"

"You!" she cried desperately. "I want you!"

As though her words were a catalyst, Lucas quickly removed his clothes, then covered the soft mound between her legs. Anne cried out with the pleasure his touch brought.

He slid her nightgown higher, bunching the hem around her waist until there was nothing between his flesh and hers. And then he slipped a finger between the soft folds of skin and felt the heat there. Woman heat. Just waiting for him.

That thought sent a jolt of pleasure through him that was almost his undoing. He struggled to control himself. He had to make sure she was ready or that first thrust of his body would be painful for her.

He moved his finger through that moistness, working it gently as she cried out her pleasure over and over again, begging him to stop the torment, to take the last step that would join the two of them together.

For all time, he told himself. She would be his, for all time.

As her sweet cries continued, her pleadings becoming more urgent, he positioned himself above her. Her nipples swelled eagerly as he cupped her breasts in his palms. And then he entered her, covering her mouth at the same time and driving his tongue into that sweet moistness that awaited him. He captured the small cry of pain that quickly turned into moans of pleasure.

Her body was his, fed by the fires of passion that he fueled. And the flames leapt higher and higher with each movement as he plunged faster and faster, leading her along unexplored highways.

Lucas kept his emotions under tight control as he made love to Anne, unwilling to reach that final plateau before she was ready. He continued to move in that age-old rhythm as he stoked the fires of passion that were burning out of control.

Anne's body lifted with each thrust of his, matching his movements as she climbed toward that distant plateau that remained just out of reach. She could feel the sweat on her body, the incredible heat of his as he took them higher and higher, until finally, they catapulted through eternity together, shuddering with ripples of ecstasy that went on and on, and on.

And when it was over, they lay entwined, completely exhausted, yet joined together in body as well as mind.

Chapter Twenty-Three

Anne woke to bright sunlight.

"So you're finally awake," a deep voice rumbled close beside her.

Lucas. She arched her back to stretch sore muscles and became aware that she was held fast in his arms.

A slow, sensual smile crossed her lips as she tilted her head to meet his eyes. "Good morning," she said. "Is it as late as I think it is?"

"Depends on how late you think it is," he replied.

"Late enough that we should be out of bed."

"I guess that all depends on who decides when we should be up."

"I guess it does."

His lips lowered, and he kissed her softly. She returned the kiss fervently. The sudden intrusion of his tongue was welcomed by her own burning desire. His sensual expertise sent wildfire coursing through her veins.

She felt his body harden against hers as his rough hands slid down her body to caress the firmness of her breasts, and her own hands were eager as her fingers circled his flat male nipples. She could feel his heart beating in a rhythm that exactly matched her own, could feel the rigid strength of him, rising to the need.

Oh, God, I love him so!

The thought had Anne melting against him, her body arching into the lean hardness of his, and as his tongue began to stroke hers, she slid her hands up and twined them through the thick darkness of his hair.

This was her man, of that she felt certain. They were made for each other, and no matter that she was from a time far distant from his, she believed fate had always intended them to be together.

That knowledge stayed with her as they began the incredible journey that led them on the path they had taken the night before, toward a distant sun that was coming apart, and when that bright orb splintered, the universe trembled with the force of their passion.

The sun was well above the eastern horizon when Lucas finished breakfast and, after stealing another kiss from his blushing bride, left the house to begin his chores.

He fed the stock, made sure they had enough water, then returned to the house. "Guess we'd better ride over to see Sarah Jane and Elijah before we do anything else," he told Anne.

"Do you think he'll agree to our plans?"

Anne had only a vague memory of Elijah. In her mind's eye she saw a grim-faced man who rarely smiled. How had he won the heart of Sarah Jane, who was so lovely that she was bound to have attracted many a male eye?

But, then, perhaps theirs had been an arranged marriage, and Sarah Jane had no choice in the matter. Anne was still puzzling the matter over in her mind when they reached the place where the Smith family had set up their camp.

Although Elijah had already been ailing when they staked out their claim, he had taken pains to choose the site where they would build their cabin. At the moment there was only a tarp stretched between trees to shelter them from rain.

The children gathered around their mother as Lucas dismounted and turned to help Anne down.

"Hello, Sarah Jane," Anne greeted. "I hope you don't mind us dropping in like this. You know my husband, Lucas, don't you?"

Sarah Jane nodded. "We've met a time or two." She bent to pick up her youngest child, a boy who looked to be about two years old and had been clinging to her skirt. "Could I offer you breakfast?" she asked. "We were just about to eat."

Anne refused the invitation, then helped Sarah Jane feed her children while Lucas went to talk with Elijah, who was too sick to leave his bed. It was obvious the woman was curious, so Anne explained their reason for coming.

Tears of relief moistened Sarah Jane's eyes, and she quickly wiped them away. "I don't know how to thank you," she whispered.

"What's wrong, Ma?" asked the oldest boy, who looked to be anywhere between eight and ten years old.

"Nothing, Frank."

"Then, why are you crying?"

"Because I'm happy," she replied.

"Oh." He took another biscuit and shoved it into his mouth, obviously wondering about the peculiarities of women.

Moments later, Lucas joined them.

"What did he say?" Sarah Jane asked.

Lucas' smile was really all that was needed.

* * *

The wagons arrived in the first light of day. And, as before, the men worked at building the cabin while the women cooked the food they had brought with them. By noon the walls had all been raised, and by dusk the roof was in place.

Then they were standing together, laughing, admiring the cabin they had worked so hard to build for the family who needed it so badly.

Tears flowed down Sarah Jane's cheeks as she thanked them for what they had done.

"Hush," Anne chided. "We were glad to do it."

As the others began to drift away, Anne squeezed Sarah Jane's hand. "I know you must be worn out from taking care of your husband as well as your children."

"I do what must be done."

"I just wanted you to know that I'm here for you if you need me, Sarah Jane. You can call on me anytime. Day or night."

"Thank you," Sarah Jane replied. "I need a friend."

"As we all do," Anne said softly.

Soon afterward they took their leave.

Anne's mind was still on the young woman and her family when they entered their own cabin, so it came as a complete surprise when Lucas swept her into his arms and carried her to the bed.

"What are you doing?" she gasped.

"Just loving my woman," he growled, burying his face against her neck. "Any objections?"

"Not a one," she replied. "Not a single one."

It was late the next morning when Lucas saddled up the buckskin mare that he was planning to breed with the Lineback dun.

He would rather have returned to the homestead and spent the day making love to Anne, but he realized there was too much to be done to waste daylight in that manner. Especially since he had already lost a good three hours that morning doing exactly that.

After casting one last, hungry look toward the cabin, Lucas urged the buckskin mare toward the mountains that loomed above them.

A few of the cattle he had left in the blind canyon had strayed into the brush where there was no water and a greater chance of being trapped by wolves or a bear, and it was midafternoon by the time he'd rounded all of them up and driven them back to the rest of the herd.

Without fences, he knew, it was likely to be an endless chore. And, although there was plenty of brush around to make a fence, Lucas didn't like the idea of penning the cattle completely until he knew how many predators might be around to deal them misery.

A head count told him that his stock was all there, so he reined the mare toward the Smith farm. He needed to see Elijah, to make sure the man was recovering as he should. And Lucas intended to ask his opinion about a pair of boots for Anne. He wanted them to be something special, and already had an idea for the design.

He found Elijah much better; in fact, the man was seated at his table drinking coffee. The two men discussed Luke's idea and the boot maker asked his wife for paper and quickly sketched the design.

"Do you need these right away?" he asked.

"I don't suppose I do," Lucas replied.

"That's good. Hawk just left here. Wanted some moccasins done in a hurry."

"Hawk?" Lucas said. "I thought he'd gone back to Texas."

"Seems he changed his mind. I'm surprised you didn't see him since he was headed for your place."

"Mine?"

"Yeah. Said he had some unfinished business there." Elijah grinned. "Maybe he's missing those biscuits your wife used to supply him with. He danged sure brags about 'em enough."

"Yeah, he does do that." Luke's eyes were thoughtful as he gazed toward the hill that separated his place from the Smith homestead. "What time was he here?"

Elijah's thoughts had already turned to his work again, and the question caught him by surprise. "Who?" he asked.

"Hawk." The word was gritted through Luke's teeth. "What time did he leave here?"

"I don't know," Elijah muttered, frowning down at the paper that he had been sketching on.

Lucas cursed inwardly. "Was it morning, or this afternoon, Elijah?"

The man looked up at him, and his frown deepened. "It was before Sarah Jane called me for the noon meal. At least I think it was. If it's important, you could go ask her."

"It's not important," Lucas replied.

But it was. He didn't like the thought of Hawk spending time with Anne. He knew he was being unreasonable, but the man had spent way too much time with her during the journey. And it was time he backed off. Better yet, it was time for him to find his own woman, one who would supply him with biscuits so he wouldn't be hanging around Anne so much.

Luke was leaving the copse of pines that grew near the cabin when he saw a rider headed south. He knew it was Hawk, who was only now leaving the cabin, and he cursed softly, his jaw clenched.

What in hell had Hawk been doing there so long? He

must have known that Lucas would be gone most of the day.

Lucas didn't like it. Didn't like it one bit.

Anne was crimping the edges of a dried apple pie when Lucas entered the cabin. She spun around quickly and stared at him in surprise.

"Lucas!" she exclaimed, throwing her arms around his neck. "I didn't expect you so soon."

"Apparently not," he said dryly.

She smiled at him, her cheeks flushed. With shame, or pleasure? He pushed the thought aside. Nothing shameful had been going on here. He trusted Anne, and he trusted Hawk. Most of the time.

He hugged Anne to him, covering her lips with his own in a kiss so passionate that it left both of them breathless.

"What are you doing back so soon?" she asked.

"I wanted to see you," he replied.

"I'm glad."

He waited for her to mention Hawk, but she didn't say a word about him.

Finally, he could stand it no longer.

"What was Hawk doing here?"

"Looking for you."

"I guess when he didn't find me he decided to wait?"

"No. He said he'd come another time." She kissed his nose, then his lips. "What did you really come home for?"

"You don't believe it was to see you?"

"I'd like to. But I know how much work you have to do."

"I decided to take the rest of the day off. We're going to go swimming."

Her smile widened, and her eyes shone like stars. "Really?"

He kissed the end of her nose. "Really."

A short time later they were cavorting in the water, laughing and splashing each other like children at play.

She flung water at him, then turned to flee, but he caught her in a hard embrace, pulling her against the length of him.

Anne breathed in the fresh scent of his flesh, nuzzled the hair that curled tightly on his chest and ran her hands along his muscular shoulders and then down the hard flesh of his back.

There was a hard sensuality about him that took her breath away.

Anne tilted her head back, her gaze locked on Luke's. His eyes were deep, burning with emotion, blazing hotly and threatening to consume her.

"Luke," she said softly, yearningly.

Lucas tried to break the spell she held over him. He had never wanted to feel this way again about any woman. Not ever. Yet Anne had woven her web so well that he was unable to escape from the silken bonds that held them together.

As Barbara Fairchild had.

That thought took his breath. But he quickly denied it. She couldn't be like Barbara!

There was no way such sweetness could be false. But, it was, then he was truly lost, for he was held fast by invisible bonds that could never be broken.

"Make love to me, Lucas," Anne whispered sweetly. "We need to make a baby. I need someone to love, and to be loved by. Someone of my own."

"I know." He sighed deeply, wondering if that was the only reason she needed him. Did she have no need for Lucas, the man?

He narrowed his eyes against the pain of wanting her.

How could he resist what she was offering so sweetly, when his body was rigid with his need. God, he had hungered for her for so long. And now, even though he had already claimed her, his desire had not lessened.

How could he resist her when she was the air he breathed, the blood that flowed through his veins. And he hungered. Oh, Lord, how he hungered for her.

Anne kissed his chest, touching his fiery skin with the tip of her tongue, and her touch was like flames licking at him.

"Anne, sweetheart."

"Give me a child, Lucas," she whispered. "Please, give me a child."

He remained motionless, every muscle taut with his need. She held his gaze as she reached for him, raising a trembling hand and stroking his cheek, and he shuddered at the gentle touch of her fingers, feeling as though he had been stroked by lightning.

Anne felt a muscle twitch in his jaw, knew that he was losing control of the restraint that he had placed on his passion.

"I won't hold you to the marriage if you don't want it," she said softly. "But I need a child." Her eyes stung with tears that overflowed and spilled down her cheeks. "Give me that one thing, Lucas. Please. Don't make me go through life without knowing love."

I love you, his heart cried, but he remained silent, unwilling to utter the words that would make him so vulnerable.

"You ask so little for yourself, Anne," he said gruffly. "And offer so much."

She placed a hand on the hard ridge that centered his body and caressed it gently. He shuddered beneath her touch as her fingertips traced his hardness, and she leaned forward to trace the shape of his mouth with her tongue.

Luke sucked in a sharp breath, and a raw sound escaped his throat. As though encouraged by the sound, Anne probed the corner of his mouth, seeking entrance. Of their own accord, his lips moved just slightly, enough so that she could enter the welcoming darkness.

She trembled as her knees weakened, sliding her arms around his neck while she continued to probe his inner warmth with her tongue. Her nipples had become taut with desire, and they pressed hard against his chest.

With a muttered groan, he swept her into his arms and carried her to the creek bank where a bed of grass awaited them. His tongue dueled with hers, stroking her softness with rough movements that had her heart racing as though she had been running a marathon.

Soon he was positioned over her, and she shifted her legs, welcoming the hardness that probed for entrance. Soon they moved together in a rhythm as old as time as they stoked each other's passions and climbed that distant peak where they would each find release.

Chapter Twenty-Four

It was several days later when Henry Baker stopped by to invite them to a celebration dance. Lucas was away, looking for a stray calf.

"We're going to slaughter that ornery black goat of ours, and the spotted one, too." Henry looked almost mournful as he sat atop his mount, extending the invitation. "I always knew this was gonna happen one day."

Anne frowned up at the man. "There's no need to slaughter the goats if it bothers you, Henry. I'm sure Hawk could supply enough venison to feed an army."

"He prob'ly could," Henry agreed. "But Mary ain't gonna be satisfied unless she sees that old black goat roasting on a spit. She told me that, just this morning, when she served up them burnt flapjacks."

Anne's lips twitched. "Oh, I see." And she did. Mary was a good cook who never burned anything . . . unless it was on purpose. "What did the goat do?"

Henry sighed heavily. "He went and et Mary's good petticoat. Right off the clothesline."

She covered her mouth to stop a giggle from escaping. "Not the pink silk?"

"Yep. It was the pink one, all right. And Mary's mad enough to eat nails. She ain't never gonna cook a decent meal while that goat's alive." He looked toward the rise that separated the homesteads. "Guess I better get along now. Gotta keep that goat outta trouble until he's slaughtered, else Mary won't be fit to live with for a long while. You want me to tell her to expect you?"

"I wouldn't miss it," Anne replied. "And we'll come early to help."

"Ain't no need," Henry said. "Mary's gonna have fun cooking up that ornery goat. She said to tell the women they could bring a covered dish if they was of a mind."

"I'd be more than happy to do so."

Anne was delighted at the thought of a celebration and immediately began to make plans. She could make a potato salad and some oatmeal cookies. And a pot of beans. And she would wear the blue gown. No, she couldn't wear that one. The last time she wore it she had caught her toe in the hem and ripped the skirt.

Remembering the bolt of cloth Lucas had bought at Fort Laramie, Anne opened the trunk and took it out. There was enough material on the bolt for several gowns, and a couple of shirts for Lucas as well. She would make the skirt full and sew a wide ruffle at the hem, and when Lucas twirled her around, it would flare out around her legs.

She unwound several yards of material on the bed, recalling the hours of instruction her grandmother had given her, and using the pattern she had bought along with the bolt of fabric, she cut out the bodice of the new gown.

As she sat in her rocker, stitching up the shoulder seams, the thought of dancing to fiddle music with Lucas again gave her so much pleasure that it bubbled forth in the form of an exuberant laugh.

Lucas, having just entered through the open door, studied her smiling face and wondered at the cause of her happiness.

Barbara had looked that way when she had been double-dealing with another man. The thought sent pain stabbing through him.

He would be damned if he would allow himself to be cuckolded twice in as many years.

"What's so funny?" he growled.

"Lucas!" Anne put aside her sewing and sprang to her feet, wrapping her arms around her husband's neck. Her face glowed with pleasure as she planted a kiss on his mouth, then drew back to smile at him. "Guess what, Lucas?"

She was hard to resist when she looked so angelic, with her eyes glowing and her tousled nutmeg curls framing her piquant face. He was a damned fool! he silently chided himself as he closed his arms around her. Anne was not a conniving bitch like Barbara Fairchild. Nobody could fake the adoration he saw in her eyes.

Slowly, his lips curved into a smile. "What?" he asked softly, his head lowering toward hers.

"We've been invited to a party, Lucas!"

His body tensed as he realized it wasn't the sight of him that caused her so much pleasure. It was the thought of going to a party.

"Mary and Henry are the ones giving it. They're slaughtering two of their goats to feed their guests." Anne's eyes sparkled like blue diamonds. "You know that old black goat that's always giving Mary so much trouble? Well, he won't be doing it anymore. Henry said Mary's determined to see that goat roasting on a spit since he ate her good petticoat." She giggled. "You should have seen Henry. He looked so pitiful when he talked about the burnt flapjacks he had for breakfast and—''

''No!''

She blinked at him in surprise. ''What?''

''I said no, Anne!''

''I don't understand.''

''What part don't you understand?''

''Are you saying you're not going?''

''I'm saying *we* are not going.''

She pulled away from him and stepped back, her expression puzzled as she watched him. ''But why, Lucas?''

''Because I said so!''

His voice was harsh, determined, not to be questioned.

''That's not a good reason, Lucas.''

''It's reason enough.'' He turned away from her and looked pointedly at the stove. ''I don't see any sign of a meal, Anne. Have you been working on that damned dress all day long?''

''No,'' she said tartly. ''I have not!'' She stomped to the stove and took the lid off a pot of stew. ''There's your meal, sire.'' She spread her skirt in a mock curtsy. ''But I'm afraid you'll have to serve yourself. It's the usual thing for a cook and housekeeper to have some time off. And, by golly, I'm taking mine right now.''

Anne stomped across the room and went outside, slamming the door behind her. She needed some space, some time away from him to stop the tears of hurt that had suddenly filled her eyes and even now were raining down her cheeks.

She heard the door open behind her, then Luke's voice, harsh, demanding. ''Anne! Come back here, Anne!''

Ignoring him, Anne walked faster. She kept going, heading toward the thick growth of pines that would allow her to come to terms with the pain Lucas had inflicted with his harshness.

She hated herself for her weakness. She was a fool for

allowing him to make her feel this way. Yet she couldn't just turn off her feelings. She loved Lucas. And she had begun to hope that he loved her, too.

But he had never said the words she needed so badly to hear. He had never told her he cared.

The tears fell faster, and she began to run, pushing aside branches that scraped her delicate skin, unaware of anything except the pain in her heart.

Suddenly, she was brought up short by a long arm that snaked around her waist and pulled her against a hard male chest.

Lucas.

"Anne," he said hoarsely. "I'm sorry. I didn't mean to hurt you. Please don't cry."

She knuckled her eyes, trying to stop the tears that continued to flow; but the hurt had gone deep, and they would not be denied so easily.

Lucas cursed himself for a fool. He had judged Anne too harshly. Why couldn't he stop likening her to Barbara Fairchild? How long would it take to forget that woman and what she had done to him?

"I'm sorry," he said again. He wiped her tears away and kissed her damp eyelids. "Don't cry, sweetheart." He spread kisses across her face. "Please, Anne, don't cry anymore. I'm so sorry."

"I don't understand," she said, her voice quivering with hurt. "What made you so angry, Lucas? What did I do that was so wrong?"

"Nothing," he said gently. "I should have explained why we couldn't go."

"Explain it to me now."

"There's simply too much work that needs doing, Anne. The barn needs building yet, and the stock has to be fed and ... well, hell, we just don't have time for useless pursuits."

Her mouth tightened, and her gaze narrowed. "Are you going to build your barn during the celebration?"

"Of course not." His lips firmed. "But we need our rest." He kissed her hard then, as though to seal a bargain. Then, taking her hand, he led her back toward the cabin. "Let's go back now and eat our supper, Anne."

It was a silent meal. When it was over, Anne poured Lucas a second cup of coffee and refilled her own. She had been thinking the situation over and knew, without a doubt, that something was going on in his mind that she didn't know about. Something was interfering in their relationship, and whatever it was, she needed to know about it, before it destroyed the both of them.

"Lucas," she said, watching him over the rim of her cup, "we need to talk about what happened."

"There's nothing to talk about," he said gruffly.

"Yes, there is." She set her cup down and eyed him severely. "We need to get it out in the open, Lucas. Whatever is bothering you—"

"Dammit, Anne," he snarled. "Leave it alone!"

"No!" she snapped. "I'm tired of walking on eggshells around you, mister. If you want to end this relationship, then you can damn well tell me so!"

"This is not a relationship," he said evenly. "It's a marriage, Anne. And you might keep that in mind."

"What do you mean by that?"

"Anne . . ." He splayed his fingers through his dark hair. "Do we have to argue like this? It was a hard day, and tomorrow prob'ly won't be any better."

"Did you find the calf?"

"No. The wolves may have got it. But I intend to look again tomorrow. The calf is a heifer."

A heifer. If it lived, it would provide several calves in the years to come. "I'm sorry, Lucas. I know how much you want to build up your herd."

"Yeah."

"I know you're tired," she said gently. "But we still need to talk, Lucas."

"All right, Anne. If you say so. But pour me another cup of coffee first."

She did so, then took her seat at the table again. "Tell me something about your younger years, Lucas."

He shrugged his shoulders. "There's nothing much to tell."

"What about your family?"

"They're dead."

"Yes. I know. But I'd like to know about them anyway."

"I don't remember much about them. My mother was Comanche. My father a white trapper. Our cabin caught on fire, and my father got me out, then went back for my mother. I never saw either one of them again."

"How old were you?"

"Six or seven. I don't really know. And neither did anyone else. We had no neighbors. My mother's people hadn't seen her for several years, so they didn't know either."

"No near neighbors? Then you were alone?"

"Yes. For a while. Most of the summer."

"My God!" she exclaimed. "How did you survive?"

"By my wits." His thumb traced the rim of his cup. "I knew how to trap rabbits."

"How did you cook them?"

"I didn't."

"My God!" she said again. "It must have been awful." It explained a lot, Anne realized. She had sensed a savagery about Lucas that at times seemed barely held in check.

"I don't think about it now."

"How did the Comanche find you?"

"My mother's brother came to visit. And since I'd stayed close to the burned-out cabin, he found me. He took me back to the village, and I stayed there for several years until my father's brother ransomed me.''

"Ransomed you? From your mother's people?''

"Yes,'' he said dryly. ''My mother's parents were failing in health, and the inducement of gold was too much to resist. When my uncle heard what had happened to my parents, he considered it his Christian duty to put me through school.'' He smiled grimly. ''He wasn't too happy when I refused to go with him unless he allowed Hawk to go with me.'' His mouth turned down at the edges. ''I'm thinking now I should have left him where he was.''

"Hawk? Your uncle put Hawk through school, too?''

"Yes. Hawk has as much education as I do. And like me, he chose to return to his old hunting grounds.'' His voice became harsher. ''He appears to want everything I have.''

"What do you mean?''

"That's enough about me,'' he said shortly. ''Suppose you answer a few questions.''

"What do you want to know?''

"You don't talk about your family either. What does your father do?''

"He owns a chain of computer companies.'' She smiled. ''He's a wealthy man, Lucas. And at first, I kept expecting him to come after me. That's why I was forever watching the skies.''

"You expected your father to come out of the skies? Does he have wings?''

"I figured he'd hire a helicopter . . . or several. And search planes. There's several bases in Wyoming. And he has many friends with enough power to organize a search for one lost daughter.''

"Helicopters? Planes?'' He studied her. ''I've never heard of either of them.''

"That's because Orville and Wilbur Wright haven't

invented airplanes yet. And it was even later before helicopters were ever thought of.''

"And what are airplanes and helicopters, Anne?''

"They are flying machines that carry people inside like
carriages.''

He threw back his head and laughed. "Are you saying
they learned to put wings on carriages?''

"Not wings exactly. Not like a bird anyway. But true,
Lucas. In my time we have flying machines.''

"And do ducks fly backward?''

"I'm telling you the truth. We travel in machines. Man
has even walked on the moon.''

She could see he didn't believe her, yet perhaps, some-
day, he would.

Soon afterward they went to bed, and although he didn't
make love to her, she slept with his arms wrapped around
her.

Lucas cursed softly as he watched Hawk swing Anne
around amidst a swirl of skirts. The two were laughing
together as though they were the only two people in the
world.

He had been wrong to relent and bring Anne to the
dance. He should have stuck to his guns and kept her at
home. But she had been so insistent that Mary would be
hurt if they didn't come that he had finally agreed. Now
there she was, in Hawk's arms as he had imagined she
would be. And there was little he could do about it unless
he was willing to appear a fool in front of the others.

"I'm surprised that you allow it.''

Lucas swung around to face the man who had spoken
so harshly. Colby. He should have known.

"Allow what?'' Luke asked mildly.

"Them.'' Colby nodded at the dancing couple. "If it

was my wife being danced around the fire by a redskin, I'd shoot him dead where he stood.''

Lucas thought about telling Colby nobody would think of waltzing his wife around a fire or any other place, then decided it would be unkind to the man's wife and held his silence on that matter.

''Seeing as how you're part Indian yourself, though,'' the man continued, ''I guess it don't matter so much who takes a shine to her.''

Luke's hands fisted, and he fixed the other man with a hard glare. ''If you say another word, you're going to find yourself flat on your back, Colby.''

The man backed quickly away. ''I was just passing the time of day,'' he said hastily. ''Wasn't meaning no harm.'' He negated the apology—if that's what it was—by adding, ''It don't matter none to me who romances your wife.''

Then, as though he realized he had already said too much, he strode quickly away, putting distance between himself and the man who looked as though he was about to tear him limb from limb.

Lucas watched Hawk and Anne with a narrowed gaze as the music came to an end and the fiddler laid aside his instrument, obviously intent on quenching his thirst before the next dance.

Anne was laughing up at Hawk as they drew near Lucas, and he waited until they were beside him before reaching out and snagging her wrist. Drawing her against him, he curled his arm around her waist and pulled her close.

His lips stretched into a wide smile that closely resembled a snarl. ''It's past time we were leaving, Anne,'' he growled. ''Way past time.''

''But, Lucas, the dance has hardly begun.''

''We've got work to do tomorrow.''

Hawk studied his friend and saw the rage that was

barely held in check. "Maybe we should talk before you leave," he suggested mildly.

"I don't think we have anything to talk about," Lucas said grimly.

Anne was aware that people were watching them, and a red flush crept up her neck. "You're being unreasonable, Lucas," she hissed.

"No," he said firmly. "I'm being a husband. And I say it's time to go home."

"Me Jane. You Tarzan? Is that the way it is, Lucas?"

"I don't know what you mean."

"You're being hateful."

"And you're creating a scene."

"Lucas," Hawk said mildly. "I really think—"

"I don't give a damn what you think, Hawk!" Luke was grim, determined to leave, and his wife was damned well going with him.

Hawk held up a hand and backed off. "Hold it, Lucas. I'm not looking for a fight."

"Then you'd damn well better leave my wife alone!" Lucas snarled. He pulled Anne toward the corral where they had left the horses. "Come on," he said gruffly. "We're going home."

But Anne was having none of it. Lucas was being unreasonable. "Stop it," she muttered, twisting her arm, trying to free it from his iron grasp. "I'm not going anywhere until I thank Mary for inviting us."

"It's not expected."

"I don't give a damn if it is or not!" she snapped. "I'm going to thank her anyway!"

Realizing she wouldn't be swayed, he went with her to find Mary. And he managed a smile as Anne made up an excuse for their early departure, claiming an unsettled stomach was the reason.

But it wasn't just a claim, he realized on the way home, because they had only gone a short distance when Anne pulled her pony up short and slid off the mare and made a dash for the bushes where she lost the contents of her stomach.

Luke unfastened the canteen from his saddle and moistened his neckcloth and offered it to her. He felt like a clod for upsetting her so much that she had thrown up. But when he tried to apologize, Anne stared right through him, refusing his help even to mount her horse.

The ride home was made in silence.

When they entered the house, Anne gathered up the extra quilts and spread them on the floor, obviously unwilling to share the bed with him.

With a muttered curse, he gathered up the quilts and headed for the lean-to. He would be damned if he would apologize again. Just let her stew in her own juice for a while.

Chapter Twenty-Five

Lucas tossed and turned on the bedroll, trying to find a way to ease the aches and pains that plagued his body, since his mind refused to rest.

He remembered the way Anne had looked when he had spoken so harshly to her and cursed himself roundly for ruining her pleasure. He was a damned fool! He deserved to sleep out in the cold. But, dammit! He couldn't stop comparing her to Barbara Fairchild!

Anne was not Barbara. She would never betray him like the other woman had done. And he had to remember that or put his marriage in serious jeopardy. Hell! His marriage was already in serious trouble!

He should be taken to the nearest tree and hung.

How had this happened anyway? He had sworn never to love again, and yet, here he was, tied up in knots because his wife—his wife, dammit!—was so angry she refused to sleep with him.

He shifted to another position, but it was just as hard as the one before.

Why was he out here anyway, sleeping on the ground, when he had a soft bed inside the cabin. His cabin. His cabin and his wife!

Luke jerked upright, gathering up the quilts and stomping toward the cabin. He would be damned if he would sleep on the ground when he had a perfectly good bed to sleep in, and a perfectly good wife to snuggle up with.

He entered the cabin, prepared to demand his rights, and found his wife curled up on her side sound asleep.

Sighing heavily, Lucas shed his clothes, climbed into the bed and pulled her against him. She sighed deeply and snuggled close, murmuring softly in her sleep.

But even though Lucas had claimed what was rightfully his, he knew the day would come when they would have a showdown. And he prayed that when that day came, he would be prepared to accept what fate decreed. Even if that fate was to lose what was most precious in the world to him.

Anne.

Early morning sunlight streamed through the window and tickled Anne's eyelids. She sighed and opened her eyes, feeling disappointment sweep through her as she realized she was alone in the bed. She had dreamed Lucas came to her in the night and pulled her into his embrace.

But it had only been a dream.

The fire was burning in the stove, which meant that Lucas had come and gone; but he would be expecting breakfast soon, so she rose quickly and dressed herself, then hurried to put the coffee on to boil.

After slicing the salt pork, Anne spread the pieces in the iron skillet. And when the meat was finally sizzling in the pan and the biscuits were in the Dutch oven, she poured herself a cup of coffee and sat down to gather her thoughts.

She usually enjoyed this time of morning, but at the moment, she was too worried about the state of her marriage to enjoy anything.

Hoping to remedy that, she lifted her coffee cup and breathed in the aroma . . . and felt her stomach turn upside-down.

"Oh, God," she cried, clapping a hand over her mouth, and racing quickly outside.

She barely made it to the woodpile before her stomach turned inside out. Anne retched until her stomach muscles were sore and her legs were trembling with weakness.

Then, unwilling for Lucas to know, she covered the foul stuff with dirt to hide the evidence of her upset stomach and entered the house again to rescue the pork that was in danger of burning.

After she had done so, she ate a dry biscuit that had been left over from the day before, hoping it would settle her stomach enough to finish cooking breakfast. Then she sat down at the table and put her head in her hands.

Any other time she would be elated at what she suspected. But not now. Not with Lucas feeling toward her as he did.

Anne was almost certain she was pregnant. And what should have been a happy time in her life was not.

How would Lucas react if she told him? she wondered. Would he be happy, or would he feel trapped? She couldn't stand that thought, so she decided to keep the news to herself. At least for a while.

Footsteps outside the door told her Lucas was coming, so she hurried to put his breakfast on the table. She knew the moment he entered the cabin, was aware of his eyes on her as she poured his coffee in silence, then scooped eggs and salt pork onto a plate, turned the biscuits onto a platter and set them before him.

"Aren't you going to eat?" he asked quietly, noticing she had only set one place.

"No. I'm not hungry."

"Anne." He reached out to her, but she quickly moved away.

"Don't, please."

"Don't what?" he asked harshly.

"Touch me." She turned away. "I don't want you touching me."

"Damn it, Anne. You're my wife."

"Only for the moment."

"What do you mean by that?"

"We had an agreement."

"Which we broke. By mutual consent, if you care to remember."

"I changed my mind." She met his eyes with a long look. "I know we can't get an annulment now. Not after what happened between us. But we could get a divorce."

"There'll be no divorce."

"I believe I have something to say about that." *Please, Lucas,* her heart cried. *Tell me you love me. Hold me in your arms and kiss me.* "I refuse to stay with a man who cares so little about my feelings, Lucas." *Tell me you care,* she silently begged. *Please, Lucas, say the words even if you don't mean them.*

"I'm the same man I always was," Lucas growled. "The one you begged to give you a baby."

"I was wrong."

He splayed his fingers through his hair. "Did you ever think there might already be a child?"

She looked away so he wouldn't read the guilt in her eyes. "Yes. I thought of that."

"And if there is one?"

"What are you asking me?"

"Do you intend to raise our child alone?"

Her face paled, and she lowered her dark lashes. "This conversation is useless."

"No," he denied. "I won't let you go, Anne, so put

it out of your mind." He couldn't let her go. It would be too painful.

"I-I don't want to—" She broke off, turning away from him, fighting against the rising nausea that would surely give her away. "I have to get some fresh air," she said quickly, moving toward the door.

He scraped back his chair as though to stop her, and she held out a staying hand. "No, Lucas! I need to be alone. I need time to think."

Lucas watched her leave the room, hurrying away from him as quickly as she could. His shoulders slumped as he stared down at the meal she had prepared. He couldn't eat a single bite. His appetite had fled along with his wife.

"What in God's name happened?" he muttered.

They had been so happy together, for a short while; then everything had fallen apart. Just as it had with Barbara.

But Anne wasn't Barbara, he reminded himself. His heart told him so. And if he lost her, then he might just as well lie down and die because life wouldn't be worth living anymore.

"Hello, the house!"

Anne smiled as she set aside her mending. She would know that voice anywhere. She went to the door and found Hawk on the verge of dismounting from his horse.

"What a pleasant surprise, Hawk," she said by way of greeting. "I didn't expect to see you here today."

"I didn't expect to be here," he replied. "Is Lucas around?"

"No. He went to the box canyon where he's keeping those wild mustangs he rounded up. You could ride over there if you need to see him."

"No. It was you I came to see."

"Why?"

"Sarah Jane Smith has come down with something or

other. I'm not sure what it is, but the baby's caught it, too. Elijah is well enough now, but he's no hand with babies. That little one is screaming its head off, and we don't know what to do with it. I went for the doc, then I decided to come on by here, hoping you'd be willing to lend them a hand.''

''Of course. Just let me get a shawl.''

Moments later the two of them rode away from the cabin.

Lucas was headed home when he saw the two riders leaving his cabin. Hawk was easily recognizable by his build, but the other one was smaller . . . possibly a woman.

His heart began to thud with dread as he urged his horse onward, denying the possibility that Anne would have gone with Hawk. But when he reached the house, he knew he had been wrong.

His hands clenched into fists, and he fought the urge to ride after them. Surely there was a good reason she had gone with him. He had to trust her or their marriage was only a sham. Over before it had even begun.

He waited and waited. The hours passed, and Anne did not return. And still he waited. The sun went down and twilight covered the land. And still he waited.

It was past nine, and the sun had long since gone down, when he finally heard the sound of hooves and knew she was returning. The rage within him was so terrible, it was almost a tangible thing.

He tried to control his feelings, tried to hold his rage in check until she could offer some kind of explanation. Any kind would be acceptable. And then he realized she was not alone. Anne entered through the open door with Hawk trailing close behind her.

The cabin was dark, lit only by the moonlight streaming through the windows and doorway, and Lucas was only a dark silhouette, seated at the table, his hands wrapped around a coffee cup that had long since gone cold.

"Lucas?" Anne's voice shivered down his spine. "Why are you sitting alone in the dark?"

"Where have you been?" His expression was ferocious, his voice quiet and deadly.

"Why . . . don't you know?"

"How the hell should I know?"

"Colby was supposed to—"

"Where have you been?" he asked again.

"Now, wait a minute, Lucas," Hawk said quietly.

As though struck with a hot iron, Lucas erupted from the table and leapt toward Hawk with every intention of tearing him limb from limb.

"Lucas!" Anne shrieked. "Stop it!"

Lucas waded into Hawk with both fists, prepared to do his worst. Hawk sidestepped the first blow, but the second one landed on his jaw. Hawk went over, taking a chair with him.

"Stop it, Lucas!" Anne cried, trying to get between the two men. But Lucas was determined. He shoved her aside and went after Hawk again.

Hawk refused to stand there and take a beating, no matter if Lucas was his friend. And at the moment, that relationship seemed doubtful.

The two men were evenly matched, equal in size and strength, and their boxing skills had been taught by the same hand during their years at university. A fight between them could go either way.

Lucas realized that, but he didn't care. His urge to beat Hawk against the floor was too strong, too savage. He dodged a blow, then swung toward Hawk, who quickly danced away from him.

Hawk had never seen Lucas so enraged, and amazing though it seemed, that anger was directed toward him. It would have been better if they could have talked it out, whatever Lucas had stuck in his craw, but it was more than obvious that his best friend was not in a mood to listen to reason. He sent another blow toward Lucas, a lucky one that landed on his chin before Lucas could avoid it.

With a bellow of rage, Lucas threw himself on Hawk, knocking him to the floor and pounding away at him.

The two men continued to fight, rolling on the floor, each striking blow after blow on the other's flesh until blood was flowing freely from each of them.

Anne realized she had to do something before they killed each other, yet she didn't know what she could do. She looked around for something, anything to stop the fight, and her gaze landed on the bucket of water on the washstand. She grabbed it up and flung the cold water over both men.

The douse of cold water drenching them from head to foot shocked the two into realization. They looked at each other, taking in the swelling eyes that were already beginning to darken, the bloody noses and scraped and bruised flesh.

Then Hawk did something completely unexpected. He threw back his head and laughed. "You sure as hell haven't lost your fighting skills, brother."

Lucas stared at him for a long moment, then sighed ruefully and rubbed his sore chin that would surely sport a purple bruise by morning. "Neither have you."

"I haven't had so much fun since the night we took on the whole tavern on that waterfront in New Orleans."

Lucas laughed then. "I'm surprised you still remember."

"Why in hell wouldn't I remember?" Hawk asked. "With all those fists flying and chairs crashing around us. I remember the fight all right, but I don't remember what it was all about."

"I think it was over a woman."

"Is this one over a woman, too?"

Lucas frowned at him. "You're damned right it is. Where in hell did you take my wife?"

"Is that what this is about?" Hawk asked. "You should have just asked me instead of throwing your fists around. Sarah Jane Smith was sick. We were taking care of her kids while Doc took care of her." His eyes narrowed. "I would have rode back to tell you, but Colby stopped by and said he was riding this way and he would tell you what was going on." He sighed ruefully. "I guess he didn't."

"No," Lucas groaned. "He did not."

Knowing he owed his wife an apology, he looked for her among the shadows, but she was nowhere to be found. "Damn!" he said. "I guess I've really done it now."

"I'd say you have, old son," Hawk agreed. "Indeed you have."

Chapter Twenty-Six

The moment the two men started laughing, Anne ran out into the night. For some reason, the laughter and camaraderie they shared—leaving her somehow excluded—was even worse than the fight had been.

And what in the world was the matter with Lucas anyway? she wondered. He had made it clear enough that he didn't care for her, that they had no future together, yet he was ready to beat his best friend's brains out for simply being with her.

It was a dog in the manger attitude, and she wasn't going to put up with it.

"Oh, God," she cried. "Help me! I don't know what to do anymore!"

If she was back home, she would simply move out. Get herself an apartment in another city, find a new job and put herself as far away from the source of her pain as possible ... even though it would be more painful to leave him behind. But at least there wouldn't be this constant friction, the day-to-day battle of being with him and knowing he didn't love her.

And there was the baby.

If there was a baby.

The *if* was really not to be considered, though, as far as Anne was concerned. She was almost certain of the pregnancy, because her emotions had always been kept under her firm control. Even after she had been mugged in that dark alley in Dallas, she had taken it in stride. Although she had felt an icy rage that she had been so violated, she hadn't given in to that emotion. Hadn't let it control her. Instead, she had gone out and enrolled in a self-defense class, had learned how to protect herself in case she was ever confronted with a situation like that again.

But this time she hadn't been mugged. This time she had been hurt by someone she loved, and the pain of his betrayal was a hundred times worse than anything she had ever known.

Though Lucas had never lied to her, never said he loved her, but she had hoped he would, that in time he would feel more than passion for her, that he would eventually come to care for her as she cared for him.

But what happened tonight wasn't love. It wasn't about caring. It was about possessing, about owning, and Anne was determined to be owned by no man. No matter what century she lived in and no matter that she was wildly in love with that man.

"Oh, God, help me," she whispered. "I want to go home. Just let me go home."

She needed her mother, needed Gram, needed someone to hold her, someone who cared enough to soothe away the hurt. But her grandmother was gone, her mother was gone, and her father, all that was left of her family, would not even be born for another century.

"Anne!"

Anne jerked around. From her place beneath the pines, she could see Lucas standing in the doorway of the cabin, his large frame silhouetted by the lamplight that reached out into the darkness.

"Anne," he shouted. "Where are you?"

Anne didn't answer. Instead, she moved farther into the pine thicket. She wasn't ready to return to the cabin yet, didn't want to face Lucas, knowing how little he cared for her.

A rustling in the trees ahead caught her attention, and she froze. "Who's there?" she asked sharply.

A soft chuckle was her only answer.

"I said, who's there?"

A branch snapped beneath heavy feet; then a man stepped from behind a tree to face her.

"Colby!" she exclaimed. "What are you doing here?"

"Just looking," he replied, the corner of his mouth curling in a malicious smile.

"More like watching the results of your meddling," she spat.

He laughed again. "It ain't my fault if you married a man that don't trust you," he said. "He's so mad that he's likely to give you a good beating when he catches up to you, and that'll be no better than you deserve."

"Why?" she asked. "Why do you hate me so much? What did I ever do to you?"

"Ever since the breed brought you to the wagons, you was there flaunting yourself, teasing and going on until a man couldn't hardly think of anything else," he said, easing purposely toward her.

"That's not true," she said, backing away from him. "I never teased you, nor anyone else."

He grinned widely. "Nobody will believe that now. Not even your man. Else he wouldn't have been trying to beat that Injun's head bloody."

"It was because of you." Anne's nails dug into her

palms to keep from lashing out at him. "That fight was all your fault. You told Hawk you were passing by here, that you would give Lucas a message, telling him we were at Sarah Jane's cabin, taking care of her children. But you lied, didn't you? You deliberately lied so this would happen."

"Yeah." He smirked. "I did exactly that. And I'm gonna do even more, and nobody's gonna listen when you tell 'em either."

"I will."

Anne spun around and saw Lucas standing behind her.

"Go to the house, Anne," he said grimly. "I'll take care of this."

Without a word Anne headed for the house, perfectly willing to let Lucas handle the man who had done everything he could to make her life a misery. On the way there she met Hawk, who was just entering the forest.

"Anne," he exclaimed, taking her hands in his. "We were worried about you. Where have you been?"

She explained about Colby and said, "I know Lucas can handle him, but Colby won't be fighting clean."

"Don't worry about Lucas, Anne. He could handle a dozen men like that one." He walked her back to the cabin and made her sit down in her rocker. "When is the babe due?" he asked gently.

"I'm not sure there is one."

"There is," he replied. "Pregnant women have a look about them. And you have that look. When are you going to tell Lucas?"

"I don't know." She studied her hands. "Do you think he will be angry?"

"Lucas wants a family, Anne. Didn't you know?"

"No. We never really talked about it."

"Then, do so now." He sighed heavily and looked out into the darkness, toward the mountain peaks rising in the distance. "I guess it's time for me to move on."

She wanted to protest, yet knew she would not ask him to stay. "Where will you go?"

"Texas. Or maybe even New Orleans."

"Where you fought Lucas over a woman."

He laughed abruptly. "We fought the whole damn tavern over that woman."

Jealousy streaked through her at the thought of Lucas and another woman. "Must have been some woman."

"Yeah. She was."

Anne studied him for a long moment. "I wish I could go somewhere, too."

"You don't mean that," he said gently. "You don't want to leave Lucas."

"Lucas doesn't want me, Hawk. He married me to get more land. We had an agreement. I broke that agreement. And now he wants out."

"You're wrong."

Anne turned to see Lucas watching her.

Hawk cleared his throat. "Well, I guess it's time for me to be off," he said gruffly.

"Now?" Anne asked.

"Yeah," he replied. "It's for the best."

"You won't come back before you leave?"

He smiled at her tenderly. "No. I'll be saying my good-byes now." He looked over at Lucas, then bent and whispered in her ear. "Tell him how you feel," he said gently. "You might be surprised." His lips touched her forehead and then he moved away from her and looked at Lucas again. "If you ever need your back watched, Lucas, just send for me."

"Where?"

"Guess I'm headed for New Orleans."

"New Orleans is a big place," Lucas replied.

"I'll keep in touch with Maisie," Hawk said. "She'll know where to find me."

The two men left the cabin together, and a short time

later Lucas returned alone. Anne heard the sound of hooves and felt saddened to know it was Hawk riding away.

Lucas lifted her chin and wiped away her tears. "Are you crying for Hawk?" he asked gruffly.

"I'm crying because my best friend is leaving and I might never see him again."

Something flickered in his dark gaze. "I'd like to be your best friend, Anne."

"You're my husband, Lucas.. For the time being, anyway."

"There will be no divorce, Anne." The words were not harsh, as they had been when he had said them before. Instead, he spoke with a gentle determination. "I want you to live here with me, but if you won't, then I'll build you a cabin nearby."

"No. I want the cabin away from here."

"No. You can have your cabin. But it has to be close enough so I can know you're all right." He gripped her upper arms and pulled her upright. "This is a harsh land, Anne. There's no law here, except for what we make ourselves. Men like Colby will always try to take advantage of women like you. And if you're alone, you'll have no protection." His expression was hard. "I couldn't live with myself if anything happened to you."

"Nobody would blame you."

"I'd blame myself."

He appeared to be struggling to control some deep emotion. Then, "I wish we could start over again, that we could go back in time to the place where you asked me to give you a baby."

She swallowed hard. "Why?"

"Because I would do everything differently. I would show you how much I care about you, that I—"

"You care for me?"

"Yes." He shook her gently. "I care about you. I love

you, Anne. So damn much that it hurts to know that I've driven you away from me. Right now I want to hold you close to me, to kiss you until you're breathless, to be inside you and make you cry out like you did before.''

"Then, why don't you?'' she asked.

"Why don't—?'' His voice broke off and he jerked her into his arms. His mouth covered hers in a hard kiss that left her breathless. Then he began working on her buttons with fingers that trembled.

Suddenly he stopped and swallowed hard. "Anne, I can't do this if it's merely passion, if you're only doing your wifely duty.'' He looked at her expectantly, fear of rejection deep within his dark gaze.

"Oh, Lucas. I have loved you for so long, but have been afraid of your reaction. After all, we did have an agreement.'' She grinned mischievously.

Lucas's heart soared, but he had to explain his abominable behavior, to break down the last barriers between them. "I guess there's some things we need to get straight first.''

"What things?'' She worked at the lacings at the neck of his shirt, determined to rid him of that covering.

"About why I was so pigheaded stubborn, always comparing you with a woman that was best forgotten. A woman that wasn't worth beans in the first place.''

Finished with the laces, she tugged the shirt over his head and threw it aside. "Is that what you were doing?'' she asked sweetly. Her hands caressed his muscular chest before they dropped to the laces on his britches.

"Yes,'' he said, frowning at her as she stooped to push the buckskins down his legs. "That's exactly what I was doing.''

Realizing she couldn't take his britches off as long as he wore the moccasins, Anne knelt at his feet to remove them. "Who was she, Lucas?''

"What?" She looked so adorable kneeling there that he couldn't remember what he had been saying.

"The woman," she prompted, tossing the moccasins aside.

"The woman," he repeated.

"Yes." She finished removing his buckskins, and they joined the moccasins on the floor. Then she leaned back on her heels and smiled up at him. "The woman who isn't worth beans."

"Oh! That woman. Her name is Barbara—" He broke off, sucking in a sharp breath as Anne reached out and stroked the hardness between his legs.

"Who?" she asked again.

Her fingers surrounded him, stroking gently, and his staff rose swiftly, hard and throbbing. His eyes were dark with need, yet glazed, almost stupefied. "Anne," he groaned.

"Who was she?" Anne asked sweetly.

"Dammit, Anne!" Lucas growled. "Will you stop that?"

"Stop what?"

"You know damn well what." He reached for her then and yanked her upright and worked at the buttons on her gown again. "What's the matter with these things anyway?" he muttered.

She laughed huskily and shoved his fingers aside. Her eyes admired him, standing there in the altogether, while she removed her gown and laid it aside. She knew she was behaving abominably, that they would have to talk later about the woman who had dealt him so much pain.

And when they did, she felt certain that she could convince him of the reality of her "past," as well as share with him the bundle of joy that would be their future together. Yet right now, Anne had other things in mind. She needed to feel his arms around her again, needed his mouth on hers.

And she wasn't going to wait any longer.

Lucas was apparently of the same mind, because, unable to wait a second longer, he took matters into his own hands and ripped away the camisole that covered her creamy mounds. The pantaloons were dealt with in the same manner.

Then they were on the bed, and he was entering her as they began traveling along that familiar pathway that would lead them to the stars.

Put a Little Romance in Your Life With
Fern Michaels

__Dear Emily	0-8217-5676-1	$6.99US/$8.50CAN
__Sara's Song	0-8217-5856-X	$6.99US/$8.50CAN
__Wish List	0-8217-5228-6	$6.99US/$7.99CAN
__Vegas Rich	0-8217-5594-3	$6.99US/$8.50CAN
__Vegas Heat	0-8217-5758-X	$6.99US/$8.50CAN
__Vegas Sunrise	1-55817-5983-3	$6.99US/$8.50CAN
__Whitefire	0-8217-5638-9	$6.99US/$8.50CAN